Angel Discovered

By Kelly Harrel

Michelle—
Always remember,
dreams do come true!
(Proverbs 16:3)
♡, Kelly

Copyright © 2011 Kelly Harrel
All rights reserved.

ISBN: 1460969448
ISBN-13: 9781460969441

This book is dedicated to my parents

for teaching me to believe in myself

and

Mrs. Betty Bacon for believing in me as a writer.

Acknowledgements

I would like to thank the following people who made this book a reality:

My fellow writers at critique group – I appreciate your encouragement and constructive criticism; especially the men for putting up with my love story and even saying they enjoyed it.

Ashley Ludwig – Thank you for being the mentor I needed. I appreciate your time and advice.

Denise Harmer – Thanks for your editing expertise. Coffee doesn't seem like payment enough.

My readers – Thank you for the time you put into reading it, especially in the beginning stages when it was really rough, and encouraging me that it was a story worth telling.

All my brothers and sisters in Christ – Your prayer support means the world to me.

Michele Blischke – Thank you for being my spiritual mentor and encouraging me on as I run this race.

Tammy Sanchez – Reader, advisor, encourager, photographer and prayer partner –and you thought I wore many hats! Thanks for being my best friend.

My children Noah and Rebecca – Thank you for being supportive of my writing and never being jealous of my laptop.

My husband Jeff – Now you have made all my dreams come true. I love you.

And most of all, my Heavenly Father – Thank you for making me who I am and loving me in spite of my downfalls. To You be the glory.

Chapter 1

3:30 p.m. The radio switched on.

"That was 'Only for You', one of my favorite love songs from Adam Riley. Here's Bob with a news update."

"Thanks, Kathy. There has been mayhem at the mall the past two nights as thousands of screaming fans gathered hoping to catch a glimpse of Tyler Stevens. He's shooting Hard Target, his new action adventure movie, on location. Filming is expected to continue through this week and part of next."

"Tyler Stevens is so gorgeous. Oh, I would love to meet him."

"You and half the women in America. They say this may be the one to earn him a nomination for best actor this year."

"Yes it will." Tyler pounded the off button on his radio alarm. The night had been eight hours of filming chaos. He could still hear the screaming of the director ringing in his ear over his co-stars forgetting their entrances and the numerous technical difficulties the sound crew experienced. Yawning, he pulled on a robe and made his way downstairs.

That annoying construction. By the time he fell asleep the cement trucks arrived. With ten acres in his backyard, he needed a swimming pool. Phase one of the backyard construction was completed last spring. The stamped concrete patio included full-size wet bar and built-in barbeques. For entertainment there was a sand volleyball court, an outdoor pool table and darts. The pool would complete the party atmosphere.

The cool kitchen tile soothed his sore, bare feet. Temperatures already hit triple digits and it was only May. Another reason for a pool, a way to cool off during the sweltering LA summers. Scratching his bare chest, he opened the refrigerator. Three Diet Cokes, a brick of cheddar cheese, and week old Chinese take-out. Tomorrow must be the maid's shopping day. His stomach growled, yet he felt nauseas from lack of sleep.

Tyler grabbed a soda and the cheese. Settling at the kitchen table with a knife, he began to carve out his snack. He observed the construction workers in the backyard through the sliding glass door. His skin crawled at having them on his property. Even requiring background checks didn't put his paranoid mind at ease. The world was filled with whackos and he wanted nothing to do with them.

Mitch's name flashed on Tyler's caller id, his trusted, but somewhat annoying manager.

"What?" Tyler believed in keeping phone conversations to the point.

"Mr. Drake requests permission for his daughter to come on the premises."

"Who?" Tyler spotted Mitch outside standing beside an older man, staring at the ground, nervously shuffling his feet.

"Richard Drake, the pool contractor." Mitch turned and looked towards the kitchen windows, trying to spot Tyler. "His car is in the shop so his daughter is coming to get him."

"He can walk to the gate."

"C'mon, Tyler. It's over a mile."

Tyler walked to the window to be seen by Mitch. "The old man probably needs exercise. Besides, his six week bid is going on eight. Tell him he's working on borrowed time."

Tyler started to hang up when he saw Drake grab Mitch's cell phone.

"Mr. Stevens?" Richard's voice shook as he spoke.

"What?"

"I'm sorry Mr. Stevens, but it will only be this one time." Tyler watched him nervously scratch his head as he paced. "I was in a bind and my daughter graciously agreed to take off work and drive a half hour out of her way to pick me up. She doesn't even know whose house she's coming to."

Tyler loved making others sweat. "You know, Drake, I'm paying you good money, and a lot of it. I don't appreciate problems. The pool will be done next week and crap like this won't happen again." Tyler cursed, hanging up his phone. "Give a man some money and he thinks the world owes him."

Tyler admired himself in the mirror. Likened in looks to James Dean and Tom Cruise with his brown hair slicked back and five o'clock shadow, he flashed his million dollar smile, exposing those dimples every woman loved. He prided himself as being hailed one of Hollywood's greatest actors at the age of twenty six. He visualized himself accepting the Actor of the Year award, thousands giving him a standing ovation.

"Bring it!" He clapped his hands, heading toward the kitchen.

Mitch interrupted thirty minutes later as he checked his email on his phone. "Mr. Drake's daughter is here."

Tyler checked the clock. "Don't they work until five?"

"Maybe her clock is fast."

"Let her in." Tyler hit the off button. The king of his world, Tyler held all the controls and thus hated surprises. Nothing good came of them. They were inconvenient and at times embarrassing.

A small economy car came into view. Typical for a college chick. Drake probably bought it after her high school graduation. Middle-class families were completely predictable.

The cloud of dust settled as she parked among the workers' trucks. The door swung opened and slender legs appeared. He had no idea what he expected, but it wasn't this blonde beauty. As she walked, she ran her hands over her slender hips, straightening her blue flowered sundress. Nervously she fidgeted with her bangs and smoothed the back of her shoulder-length blonde hair which was pulled back to reveal her face.

Walking up beside Drake, she greeted him with a kiss on the cheek as he continued on reviewing plans with other workers. The men flocked, greeting her with hugs and smiles. Tyler was captivated by her interaction with the men, laughing, patting their backs or hugging them. He wanted to meet her.

Turning to face the window, Mitch answered his phone. "Yeah, Tyler?"

"I want to meet her."

"Who?"

"Drake's daughter, you moron. Bring up her and Drake."

Surprise covered her face as Mitch spoke. Drake frowned as she hopped up and down, pulling on his arm like a child in a candy store. Drake wrapped up with his men and then they followed Mitch. Tyler checked his perfect reflection in the microwave.

The grand doorbell announced their arrival. Confidently he opened the door as Mitch conducted the introductions. "Tyler Stevens. Lauren Drake. And you know her father, Richard."

"It's a pleasure." Tyler slowly brought her hand to his lips. Lauren blushed as he kissed it. "Please come in."

Richard and Lauren followed him to the living room. Sitting in the leather chair Tyler motioned for them to sit on the couch. Mitch stood by the door, eyes fixated on Tyler.

"I've been pleased with your work, Mr. Drake." Tyler brushed lint off his pants. "You came so highly recommended. I wanted to take the opportunity to let you know that and meet your daughter. I like to get to know people that work for me on a personal level."

Richard showed no response, but Lauren smiled from ear to ear.

"I love your movies. You're one of my favorite actors." She leaned forward, shaking her foot nervously.

"Thank you." Tyler humbly bowed his head. "I'm filming a new movie right now, to be released next spring." A dramatic pause came before his great revelation. "If you're interested in attending tonight, I could make arrangements. We're on location at the mall from nine until five in the morning."

Shock covered Lauren and Richard's faces. Mitch even raised an eyebrow.

Lauren grabbed her father's hand. "I'd love to..." Richard cleared his throat, causing Lauren to turn toward him. The somber look on Richard's face and shake of his head made her sigh.

Lauren turned toward Tyler. "I have to work tomorrow. It would be difficult to keep up with all those fourth graders without sleep."

"Oh." Tyler's eyes widened. "You're a teacher?"

"Actually, I'm a student teacher, a teacher in training. Two more weeks until I finish." Her voice was laced with such sweetness, innocence. Reality hit him. A schoolteacher?

Tyler caught Mitch's eye. "Congratulations." He flashed a smile at Lauren and then her father. "You must be very proud."

"I am."

"Well." Mitch stepped forward. "Tyler needs to get ready."

"It was nice to meet you, Mr. Stevens." Richard helped her to her feet.

"Please, call me Tyler. The pleasure was truly mine." He kissed her hand again, this time staring into her eyes. "Perhaps we will meet again."

Before she could respond, Tyler turned toward her father. "Thank you for stopping by." He shook Richard's hand. Mitch held the door open for Richard and Lauren to walk out. She glanced back as her father led her away.

"What was that?" Mitch started in once the door was shut.

Tyler leaned back down in the chair thoughtfully. "She was cute, pretty. Intelligent. Can't get that in models."

"School teacher, Tyler." Mitch reminded him. "Fourth grade schoolteacher. The press will bury you."

Tyler smiled slyly. "I've had gorgeous and beautiful. I need something new, vibrant. It's time for a change." Tyler stood, making his demand known before he left. "I want her number."

∽

"Oh, my gosh, Dad." She gasped, "That was Tyler Stevens. THE Tyler Stevens."

"Don't be so impressed, honey." He led her to the car. "He's not that great of a guy."

"He is so gorgeous." Lauren smiled at the thought of him.

"He knows it, trust me."

"Are you listening to anything I'm saying?" Her father's lecture about the downfalls and evils of actors lasted for twenty minutes on the way home. She listened, a grin on her face the entire time.

"Of course. Actors are not to be trusted. They only have one thing on their mind. Or was it two things? Sex and money. Right?"

He sighed. "This guy is nothing but trouble. He's just a charmer."

"Of course," she said. "It's part of his job."

"He manipulates people."

Lauren paused. "It's probably more give and take, don't you think?"

"He has no morals."

She laughed. "Most of America has no morals."

He placed his hand on her shoulder. "Honey, I need you to take me seriously."

"Dad, I am serious." She gently patted his knee. "I'll probably never see him again. But he happens to be gorgeous, my favorite actor, and I met him today. I have an awesome story to tell my friends. I still can't believe I was at Tyler Stevens' house."

"It's an impressive house. Amazing property."

Lauren turned to look at him. "I'm sure his pool will be beautiful."

"His pool is paying for your last semester of student teaching and two months of car payments."

"I'll send him a thank you card." She turned her attention back to the traffic. The music played on her Christian radio station for several minutes before she spoke again. "If your car wouldn't have broken down, would you have told me you put in his pool?"

Richard inhaled deeply and sighed. "You know I believe in respecting people's privacy. Even though you are my daughter, I have a reputation to uphold."

"I appreciate that about you. You're a great businessman."

"But I know he's your favorite." Richard placed his hand on her shoulder. "I've been dying to tell you. I guess God worked everything out."

"Funny how that happens."

Lauren ran to her room to call her best friend as soon as she arrived home from dropping her dad off to pick up his car.

"Abrams, Robles and Wright. This is Shelly. How may I help you on this beautiful day?"

Lauren chuckled. "Are you a little bored?"

"Out of my mind," Shelly answered cheerfully. "How are you?"

"Feeling out of my mind. You'll never guess who I met today."

"Mickey Mouse?" The clicking of Shelly's computer keys continued as she guessed.

"Smaller ears, no tail. Just as famous. Totally gorgeous." Lauren took her dirty clothes hamper out of the closet.

"Do I know him?" Shelly sounded curious.

"In a way." Lauren tossed her jeans and shirt from her hope chest to the green basket.

"Have I met him?"

"Maybe in your dreams." She began carrying her laundry downstairs.

"You are driving me crazy! Who is it?"

"Are you sitting down?" Lauren's phone beeped as she opened the garage door. "Hold on. I have another call." She clicked over before her friend could protest.

"Hello?"

"Hi. It's Tyler."

She stopped mid-step as her heart skipped a beat. Was she dreaming? "Hi."

"Listen." The wind whistled in the background. "I was thinking you might like to come watch me tomorrow night, Friday. Teachers don't have to work on Saturdays, do they?"

"No, I don't work Saturdays." Slowly she continued down the steps.

"So?"

His charming voice made her weak in the knees. Lauren dropped her laundry basket and bit her lip out of excitement. "I'd love to."

"Perfect. I'll pick you up at eight?"

"That would be great." He was picking her up, like a date. It was a date!

"I'll have Mitch get your info."

"Sure." She thought her heart would explode it was beating so fast.

"Good-bye, Lauren." His sweet, sexy voice caused her palms to sweat. "I look forward to seeing you tomorrow."

Her hand shook as she clicked back to Shelly.

"Oh, my gosh." Lauren sat on the bottom step in the garage to keep her knees from buckling.

"Who was it?" Shelly practically screamed.

Lauren took a deep breath. "Tyler Stevens."

"Tyler Stevens?" Shelly's laughter surprised her. "Yeah, right. In your wildest dreams."

"I met him today. My father is building his pool."

Silence.

"Shel, he asked me on a date tomorrow night."

Lauren hadn't prepared for the scream that followed. By the time she moved the phone her ears were ringing.

"Tyler Stevens?"

"What time do you get off?" Lauren returned to her laundry. "Come over. I'll give you all the details."

"Honey, I'll be there in ten minutes."

Lauren chuckled. "Take your time. I need to break the news to my dad."

"Okay. Tyler Stevens. You're the woman."

Lauren's head was spinning in disbelief. Inhaling, she closed her eyes. Exhaling, she turned to the door. "Lord, help my father not flip."

She removed pots and pans from the cupboard when she entered the kitchen. "How about spaghetti?"

"Sounds great." He sat at the kitchen bar, scribbled notes on the pad in front of him.

Deep breath. She busied herself by heating up water. "Tyler Stevens called. He invited me to attend his shooting tomorrow night."

Her dad shook his head. "I warned you. He's a sweet talker with one thing on his mind. You would just be another conquest."

Lauren glared at him. "I understand your concern, but this is an opportunity of a lifetime I'm not going to pass it up. As for being his conquest, not even a movie star will change my values."

He frowned, standing and walking to her. "I'm sorry, honey. I don't mean to imply you can't make right choices. Please think about what you would do if he pressures you."

Lauren grinned. "I'll slap him and have the limo take me home."

Her father wrapped his arms around her. "I just worry. You're all I've got."

"I know, Dad." She squeezed him harder.

"Start from the beginning." Shelly set a brown grocery bag on the kitchen counter as she walked in. "Don't leave anything out."

Lauren turned from doing dishes. "Leftovers are on the bar. Help yourself."

"Don't mind if I do." Shelly pulled Lauren's favorite chocolate brownie ice cream from the bag.

"What's this for?" Lauren laughed.

"To celebrate." Shelly rubbed Lauren's back. "It's not everyday my best friend meets Tyler Stevens. I would have bought cheesecake or something fancy, but I'm still waiting for my raise." Shelly piled spaghetti on her plate. "So?"

"Well, I went to Tyler's house to pick up my father…"

Shelly's eyes bulged, her jaw dropped. "You were at his house?"

Lauren shared every detail, pausing only when Shelly choked on her food out of disbelief.

"I can't believe you're going out with him." Shelly carried her empty plate to the sink an hour later. "What are you wearing?"

Lauren finished off her ice cream. "No idea. I have to worry about next week's lesson plans tonight."

"Lauren, have you lost it?" Shelly knocked on her head. "Hello! You're going out with Tyler Stevens tomorrow. You don't have time to worry about lesson plans. Every woman dreams of such an opportunity."

"It's my dream to be a teacher. To do that, I need to finish my student teaching." Lauren placed her bowl in the sink. "So, if you will excuse me, I have lesson plans to finish."

"What time are we meeting tomorrow?"

"He's picking me up at eight."

"Great. I'll be here."

She shook her head. "I don't know, Shel. It would look bad to have screaming fans at my house when he picks me up."

"Well, maybe I'll happen to drop by to return something."

"You don't have anything of mine." Lauren rinsed the dishes.

"Can I borrow your leather jacket?"

"Sure."

Shelly beamed, heading for the closet. "See you tomorrow."

"Oh, Lord," Lauren prayed in bed that night, "Tyler Stevens. I am amazed and excited. Please help me stay focused on you. Help me not be swayed by worldly things and desires." Tyler's flawless face and handsome smile came to mind. "He is so gorgeous, God. Please help me resist temptation."

Her father's words of warning came to her. Maybe this was a test. Should she run, learn from her mistakes? But then the Word of God came to her.

All things are possible.

"God, I need Your strength to resist temptation. Fill me with Your spirit. May I be Your light. Even movie stars like Tyler Stevens need You."

Her heart raced from the excitement of the evening, but as her prayers focused on others, she quieted her heart and soul before the Lord. Peace came over her as she drifted off to sleep.

Chapter 2

"Hello!" Mitch shouted into the phone.

"Good morning, Mitch." Tyler glanced at the clock. 6:05 a.m. "Hope I didn't wake you."

"No, been up for hours." Tyler heard the grogginess in Mitch's voice.

"Tonight's the night, lots to prepare."

Mitch was quiet for so long Tyler thought he had fallen back asleep. "Oh, yes. The schoolteacher," he finally responded.

"I need fresh flowers and an amazing breakfast waiting for us at six thirty tomorrow morning." Tyler barked out the orders. "I need the Ferrari cleaned today. Spotless, inside and out. And don't forget the champagne."

"How romantic." Mitch yawned. "And if she doesn't come home with you?"

"Oh, Mitch, life is too short to worry about what-ifs. By the end of the week she'll be mine."

༄

Lauren raced through the door of the preschool just as her shift began. Wiping bottoms and noses, cleaning toilets and floors weren't the most glamorous jobs, but it fit well with her class schedule since her freshman year in college and paid enough for her car and gas. Since she began student teaching, she could only work three hours a day. When she wasn't disinfecting surfaces and toys that afternoon, she was pacing. Her co-worker Beth noticed after an hour.

"Got a hot date tonight?"

Lauren stopped mid-pace.

"Are you going out tonight?" Beth raised an eyebrow.

"Kind of." Lauren leaned over to pick up a toy on the floor to appear busy.

"Oh, my gosh." Beth sat on a preschool table. "With who?"

After five years of working together, Lauren trusted Beth completely, but she couldn't handle the drama she received from Shelly. "This guy I met a few days ago."

"Did you meet him at school? Is it the father of one of your students?" Beth lifted a two-year-old in her lap to tie his shoe.

"No way." Lauren dropped the car in the correct bin. "I met him through my dad."

"What's his name?"

Knowing there was no avoiding her questions, Lauren sat by Beth. "Tyler."

"Where are you going?" Beth set the boy loose again.

"He mentioned something about the mall." Lauren hated only telling Beth half-truths, but she knew if Beth found out later, she wouldn't hold it against her.

"Tell me about him." Beth leaned forward. "Is he tall, dark, handsome?"

"Pretty much so." Lauren smiled at the thought of him. "Definitely the most gorgeous guy I have ever dated. He has an amazing smile and cute dimples. He seems sweet, but according to my dad, he's just a smooth talker."

Beth stopped a three-year-old from eating his crayon. "That's a dad's job, shoot down every guy that isn't perfect for his princess. Some days I wish I listened to mine when he warned me about Greg."

"You don't mean that." Lauren heard about the arguments and the make ups during their first year of marriage. She was the voice of reason, reminding Beth the stress and struggles were worth it.

"No, I don't." She re-directed the little girl to playing with cars. "So, what else do you know about Mr. Wonderful?"

"He is not a Christian." Lauren sighed.

"Honey, don't worry about it." She squeezed Lauren's shoulder. "Your sweetness can save anyone."

◎

"Hair up or down?" An hour and three phone calls later with Shelly she finally figured out what to wear. White Capri pants, white camisole under her floral print sleeveless shirt and her cute white sandals. Semi-causal, somewhat mature, but slightly whimsical according to Shelly. Now she suffered from a hair crisis.

"Definitely down. You don't want to look too much like a teacher."

Yes, hair down was better. She fidgeted with her hair when she got nervous and didn't want to end up pulling it down.

Her dad walked up behind her as she applied her eye makeup. He gently ran his hand down the back of her hair.

"You look beautiful."

"Thanks." She turned to him as she finished. "You okay?"

He nodded. "Be careful tonight. Don't put yourself in any compromising positions."

"I won't." She hugged him. "If I need anything, I'll call."

"God will always leave a way out. Make sure to take it."

The doorbell rang. They checked the clock. 7:55 p.m. "He's early." Lauren nervously straightened her hair.

"I'll get the door." He started out of the room.

"Be nice." Lauren grabbed her father's arm.

"Don't worry." He winked as he walked downstairs.

Lauren closed her eyes, took a deep breath. She gently held the cross that hung from her necklace between her fingers as she prayed. "Please Lord, be with me tonight. Calm my nerves, keep me safe, and may my actions glorify You."

"Lauren," her dad called from downstairs.

"I love your house." Her heart raced at the sound of his voice. Tyler Stevens was in her house. So unbelievable. "The Victorian design is so unique."

"It is the result of my wife's dreams and hard work."

Lauren entered through the formal Victorian living room to find Tyler and her dad in the family room, staring out the large picture windows at the backyard. Blue jeans and a white shirt had never looked so good.

"Is Mrs. Drake home? I would love to meet her."

"Mrs. Drake passed away about four years ago." Richard turned his attention out the window.

"Oh, umm, sorry." Tyler set his gaze outside.

"I'm ready." Lauren broke the silence.

Tyler turned with a smile that melted Lauren's heart.

"Yes, you are." He approached her, gently taking her hand and kissing it. "You look great."

"Thank you." She felt her cheeks blush as the blood rushed through her body. "I guess we should be on our way." Turning to her father she kissed his cheek. "Bye Dad. I'll see you tomorrow."

"Okay, honey. Be safe."

"Nice to see you again." Tyler shook Richard's hand, and then offered his arm to Lauren. "Shall we?"

They were in the living room when the doorbell rang.

"Oh." Lauren acted surprised. "I wonder who that could be."

"Knock, knock." Shelly let herself in as she always did, finding herself face to face with Tyler. Her eyes widened and jaw dropped.

"Shelly." Lauren raised her voice to bring Shelly out of her trance. "Meet Tyler Stevens. Tyler, this is Shelly."

"It's a pleasure." Tyler extended his hand.

Shelly shook it, closing her mouth.

"What are you doing here?" Lauren gazed at the jacket over Shelly's arm.

Shelly shifted her attention to Lauren with a smile. "I wanted to return your jacket. Thanks for letting me borrow it."

"No problem. Would you mind putting it in my room? We're on our way out."

"Sure." Shelly stepped aside. "Have fun."

"Nice to meet you." Tyler acknowledged Shelly.

"My pleasure."

Walking out the door she glanced over her shoulder to see Shelly mouth the words "He's so hot." Lauren bit her bottom lip, containing her laughter.

Tyler's shiny red Ferrari awaited them. Nervousness arose again as Tyler opened the door for her.

"Nice car." Lauren tried not to sound too impressed.

"Thanks. It's one of my favorites."

A scream followed by hysterical laughter came from inside the house as she climbed into the car.

"What was that?" Tyler turned towards the house.

Lauren laughed. "Shelly loves my father's jokes."

He slammed her door. Lauren relaxed into the seat, slowing her breathing.

He's just a guy, and we're just hanging out...

When he hit 60 mph before leaving her street, she stopped trying to convince herself anything about the situation was normal.

"How was your day?" Tyler glanced her direction.

"A little hectic, but not too bad for a Friday." Lauren didn't know what to do with her sweaty palms. She couldn't wipe them on the leather interior. "Language arts and math went well." She tried to ignore her racing heart. "Art was messy. Thank goodness we had free play for PE." She hoped folding her hands in her lap would keep them from fidgeting.

"Friday free play." Tyler nodded. "You give a spelling test today?"

"Of course. Every Friday."

"Sounds like school when I was a kid. Not much has changed."

"You'd be surprised. Half of my fourth graders read at a second grade level. Many have siblings or parents involved in gangs. They're up until midnight because of all the commotion in their house and streets."

"Are you teaching in the hood?"

"Not really. There are a few schools in the district that are worse than mine."

"Still, that must be scary."

Was he concerned for her? How sweet. "I feel like the students and parents appreciate me more than some affluent families might. When I connect with students and help them, I feel successful. That's what teaching should be about."

"Are you going to teach at this school when you are done with, - what's it called?"

"Student teaching. Probably not. I'll apply to different districts. The district hires you and then places you at a school."

"Do you have a say where you end up?"

"A job is a job. I'll go where they send me."

"Good point." Tyler stopped at the light. "My first film was not a script I was excited about, but it was the break I needed." He checked her out from head to toe. "I would have liked school if my teachers were as good looking as you." He gently brushed her hair away from her eyes. "You're beautiful."

His sweet, sexy voice saying those words melted her. She knew it was a line, but it sounded sincere.

"Thank you." Lauren shyly lowered her head.

Tyler chuckled, speeding off as it turned green. "Usually the response is 'I know'. It's refreshing to meet someone so humble."

Lauren knew she should take it as a compliment. Tyler accelerated to eighty as they entered the freeway, impressing Lauren with the performance of his car, but causing her to turn away from the speedometer. She took a deep breath and reminded herself to relax.

"So, what's this film about?"

"I play a drug dealer turned cop." Tyler smiled. "See, there's hope for your students."

Lauren raised an eyebrow. "That they could be arrogant actors when they grow up?"

"Ouch." Tyler laughed. "I guess I deserve that." They drove in silence for a few minutes. "You really think I'm arrogant? I've been on my best behavior."

"I think you're fine. My dad is convinced actors are Satan's spawn."

"As well he should. That's a father's job, right? To hate every man that comes after his daughter and protect her."

"He's a little overprotective. Especially since my mother died."

Tyler focused on the road. "I didn't mean to upset him by bringing up your mom."

Lauren shook her head. "He tends to talk about her as if she is still alive, which makes people ask questions. It's been a hard road, but he has come along way in the past several years. She passed away about four years ago from breast cancer. She fought hard." She stared out the window, her voice becoming quieter. "We both feel peace that she's in heaven now free from that pain and suffering."

The silence told Lauren the conversation turned too heavy for him.

"You were telling me about your movie."

He seemed very relieved at the change of subject. "We're shooting a scene between me and the criminals through the mall. Make-up and costumes take about an hour. We start around ten p.m. and wrap about six a.m."

"Cool." Her nervousness turned to excitement.

"By the way, I told them you were my cousin. It's the easiest way of getting you in without causing a lot of commotion."

"That's fine."

Tyler chuckled. "And your father doesn't have to worry about me hitting on you during the shoot."

The words lingered in her head as the music suddenly faded to ringing and Mitch's name appeared on the radio display. Tyler hit a button on the dashboard. "Yeah?"

"All the arrangements are made. The food, flowers…"

"Mitch," Tyler interrupted. "Say hi to Lauren."

"Hello Lauren."

"Hi, Mitch."

"You two have a great time tonight."

"Don't worry." Tyler smiled. "We will."

Lauren was enthralled by make-up artists who made bullet wounds, cuts, and bruises appear on Tyler's flawless skin. While he was off meeting with the director and writers, she dozed in the comfy swivel chair in his trailer until someone woke her and led her inside the mall. From a distance she could hear fans screaming.

Burley men carrying equipment and lights hurried in every direction. She didn't move from the chair she was put on out of fear of being in someone's way. The director yelled, cueing lights and actor, until there was sudden silence when the filming began. Tyler had so much energy and talent. Seldom was a scene redone because of him.

Tyler glanced her way throughout the night, always with smile or wink, sending her pulse racing. Around midnight he showed up with a Diet Coke and sandwich.

"How are you doing?" He handed her the plate.

"Good." She opened the mustard pack to apply to her turkey sandwich. "There is so much to watch."

"That's not true. There's only one person worth watching." With a wink he was off. Lauren shook her head. He was so hot and he knew it.

"So," Tyler causally stretched, placing his arm around her once they returned to his Ferrari at six a.m. "how about breakfast at my place?"

Lauren covered her mouth as she yawned. "I would love to, but to tell you the truth, I'm exhausted. I haven't slept for twenty-four hours. I would hate to fall asleep in my scrambled eggs."

"Sure. Maybe another time." He moved his hand back to the steering wheel and started the car.

No sooner had she settled back in her seat and closed her eyes than she felt herself drifting off to sleep.

"Good morning, sunshine." Lauren heard his voice, felt him caressing her cheek with the back of his hand.

Smiling sleepily, she opened her eyes to Tyler's beautiful brown eyes staring at her. "Sorry I fell asleep."

"Don't be sorry. I enjoyed watching you."

Lauren rubbed her eyes, turning towards the kitchen window. Her father sat drinking coffee and reading the paper at the kitchen bar.

"I have to go." She covered her yawn.

Tyler leaned over and kissed her cheek. "Thank you for joining me tonight."

"It was my pleasure." Tyler caught her arm when Lauren opened the door.

"I would like to have you over for dinner next week, if that's okay."

Lauren turned with a smile. "I'd like that."

Tyler reclined on the couch, staring at a blank plasma screen with a bowl of strawberries in his lap and a bottle of champagne in his hand. His plan failed. He glanced at her occasionally as he drove her home wondering what was so appealing about her. Pretty in a schoolgirl kind of way, she had a good personality. But since when did he care about that? Her smile, genuine and untarnished made her seem so pure, simple. If only life was like that. Tyler couldn't remember a time his life was simple. And he had never been pure.

A knock on the door came around eleven a.m.

"Come in, Mitch." He hung his head back and yelled.

The door squeaked as it opened.

"Hello, Mitch. Good to see you." Tyler took a swig from his bottle.

"I expected to find you lounging in your robe smoking. What's wrong?" Mitch sat in the armchair. "Did she turn you down?"

"These things take time." Tyler ate a strawberry and washed it down with his champagne. "Especially with a virgin."

"Did she admit that to you?" Mitch seemed shocked.

" Doesn't need to. She's your typical 'Daddy's Girl.' And Drake knows I'm out to corrupt her. What he doesn't realize is I'm doing him a favor..."

Mitch leaned forward. "Tyler, I don't want to ruin the fun of your conquest, but I need to warn you this needs to stay away from the press."

"Have you ever slept with a virgin, Mitch?" Tyler continued staring at the TV. "There is a rush of power..."

Mitch moved in front of him. "If this story gets out, you'll be made out to be a sex-crazed pervert. That would do serious damage to your career."

Tyler's eyes locked on Mitch's. "Mark my words, this will be over next week. The press won't have time to know anything about it."

"That's all I wanted to hear." Mitch pulled out a script, throwing it at Tyler. "Here's some light reading. Next week you meet the producers. Have a nice day."

Chapter 3

"I'm dying to know." Shelly blurted out. "Did he kiss you?"

"Shelly. I was sleeping." Lauren rubbed her burning eyes.

"Answer my question and you can go back to sleep."

"Kind of." Lauren reached for her glass of water to sooth her dry mouth.

"What do you mean 'kind of'?" Annoyance filled Shelly's voice. "Did he or didn't he?"

"On the cheek."

Lauren didn't move the phone fast enough to escape Shelly's scream, which was followed by hysterical laughter.

"If you do that again, I will hang up." Lauren sipped her water and replaced it on her nightstand.

"Sorry. Don't be so testy."

Lauren closed her eyes and settled into her pillow. "Shel, you don't understand. I've had no sleep."

"Just one more question. Did he ask you out again?"

"He invited me to dinner next week."

Lauren heard the scream as she hung up the phone.

Lauren pulled herself out of bed at one p.m. After a shower she felt refreshed and headed up to the church.

Brookside Baptist Church. The sign showed its age, as did the small building. The sanctuary was rarely filled half way on Sunday mornings, but most of the families had been there for as long as Lauren could remember.

She stopped at the door to Pastor Jim's office. He was staring at his computer screen in such deep thought he didn't see her.

"Knock, knock."

Pastor Jim smiled. "Lauren, come in. I'm putting the final touches on my ending for tomorrow. What's up?"

Lauren walked in, stopping in front of his desk. "I came in to get the materials ready for Children's Ministry tomorrow."

Pastor Jim leaned back in his chair. "I put Mrs. Irving's snack for Children's Church in the kitchen. How's student teaching?"

Lauren smiled. "One more week and I'll be done."

Jim shook his head. "Seems like yesterday you were in elementary school yourself. I'm very proud of you, Lauren. You have grown up to be a responsible, caring young woman. Children's Ministry has run so smoothly the past two years with you leading it. You are a wonderful teacher."

"Thank you, Pastor Jim. I appreciate that."

"Thank you for blessing us with your talents."

Lauren went to her room to finish laundry after getting home. She had left her phone at home so she checked her messages as she hung up clothes. "Sorry I keep screaming. I can't believe my best friend is dating Tyler Stevens. This is like an awesome dream. Call me tonight. I'm dying to know the details." Lauren laughed at Shelly's pleading voice.

"Lauren. This is Tyler." Lauren froze with her pants on a hanger mid air. "I was wondering if we could get together for dinner tomorrow. I enjoyed getting to know you last night. I'll give you a call back around five."

Lord, I can't believe it, Lauren thought, sitting on the edge of her bed. She took a deep breath as her phone rang.

"Hello?"

"Hi Lauren." His sexy voice caught her off guard. "Did you get my message?"

"I did. I just walked in from church- work- I mean, working at church." Her heart began to race.

"Oh. Did you get enough sleep today?"

She couldn't believe he called, let alone so soon. "I slept until about one."

"Good. How about dinner tomorrow?"

"I would love to, but I'm in charge of the children's choir practice on Sunday nights."

"Oh." Obviously not the response Tyler was hoping for, he paused for a moment. "What about a picnic tomorrow afternoon?"

"I have church until 12:30."

" I'll pick you up at one?"

Lauren's palms moistened with anxiety. "Sure. That would be great."

Lauren walked down to dinner ten minutes later with a smile from ear to ear.

"Still on cloud nine, I see." Richard set the chicken and rice on the table.

"Actually, Tyler just called to invite me on a picnic tomorrow afternoon."

"What about church?" Richard raised one eyebrow as he sat.

"After church, Dad." Lauren took Richard's hand as she prayed.

"Lord, thank you for this food and the wonderful man that prepared it. I pray you will help him to relax and trust his daughter's judgment and Your shield of protection. In Jesus' name, amen."

"Amen." Richard echoed. "So, tell me about last night."

Lauren scooped rice on her plate. "He was a gentleman, Daddy. He asked me about myself and teaching. All night he checked up on me. He's an amazing actor, with so much energy and talent."

Richard passed the chicken. "Is he as arrogant as I thought?"

"Not really." Lauren stabbed a piece and plopped it beside the rice.

"Hmmm." Richard moaned doubtfully. "Where are you going tomorrow?"

"He didn't say. He's picking me up at one."

"Don't forget about choir."

Lauren cut her chicken. "I won't, Dad. I have my priorities straight."

"That's what I'm counting on, sweetheart."

"Oh, Lord," Lauren prayed that night, "I'm still amazed. Thank you for an awesome day. I don't understand why Tyler Stevens is calling me, but thank you for the opportunity to share my faith with him." She drifted off thinking of Tyler's handsome face.

◈

"Tell me about church." Tyler asked as they pulled away from her house in his speedy red car the next afternoon.

Lauren was surprised he asked, but was happy to reply. "Our attendance is up in Sunday School, which it usually is this time of year. In children's church we studied my favorite story, David and Goliath."

"I've heard that one." Tyler turned to Lauren. "The little boy and the giant, right?"

Lauren raised an eyebrow in surprise. "Very good."

"Why is that your favorite?"

"I like the message it has. No problem is too big for God to handle."

"Hmm. I thought the point was little guys can come out on top."

"With God's help." *Oh Lord, help me be a witness for you. Somehow this is possible with You.*

"How long have you been going to church?"

"Since I was five."

"Don't you know all the stories by now? Why keep going every week?"

Lord, I can't believe he cares. "I go to worship God by singing, teaching others and learning more about Him. Church gives me the opportunity to hang out with other Christians. They support me in what I'm going through and help to hold me accountable. "

Tyler laughed. "That's why actors stick together. We understand the problems, the stress and pressure; and we don't ask each other for autographs."

Lauren grinned, shaking her head.

"What?" Tyler turned to her.

"Tyler Stevens. It's hard to believe."

"I have to admit it's impressive that you haven't asked for my autograph yet."

Lauren laughed. "I have better than that. Do you know how much a phone message from Tyler Stevens goes for?"

"You're kidding, right?" The stern look on Tyler's face surprised Lauren.

"Don't worry, I respect your privacy. I think the magazines that intrude on people's lives are worthless. The only person that knows I met you is Shelly."

"That's probably best." The tone of Tyler's voice told Lauren it was more than a request.

Lauren nodded, changing the subject. "How was your day?"

Contracts, producers, readings- didn't make much sense to Lauren, but his voice mesmerized her.

Once off the freeway, Tyler opened the sunroof. In no time at all, Lauren could smell the salty sea air. She closed her eyes, inhaling the cool, sweet breeze. The sound of crashing waves made her grin. When Tyler mentioned picnic, she thought park. She never imagined the cliffs. How romantic…

Tyler pulled into the driveway of a house. "We're here."

They entered through the kitchen. It looked like a model home with the beautiful wood floor, sandalwood cupboards, a picture perfect walk-in pantry, shiny appliances, sea foam green walls and kitchen towels that coordinated with the pictures on the walls.

"Is it your place?" she tried not to sound too impressed. Mansion in the hills, beach house, what kind of life was that?

"Yeah, bought it a few years back. Lived here for a while. It's great for parties and hanging out. Go ahead and check out the view from the patio while I get the food together."

The French doors opened wide to a covered wooden deck larger than the entertainment room she walked through. The mosaic table made of shells and sea glass caught her attention first. Then there was the Jacuzzi, big enough to seat eight. Finally she made her way to the railing, overlooked the rocks and water below. Waves crashed against the rocks as seagulls called to each other. The scene was so picturesque it took her breath away.

"It's gorgeous."

Tyler placed his hands on the railing on either side of her. "That's why I wanted to share it with you. I knew you would appreciate it."

Lauren turned to find him inches away from her face. "Thank you for thinking of me."

Tyler instigated the kiss. Lauren gently pulled away.

"I don't mean to be rude." Lauren placed her hand on his chest. "But I'm really hungry."

"Good, because I have lots of food. I wasn't quite sure what you liked."

A platter with a dozen different sandwiches lay on the island, surrounded by a huge bowl of fruit, chips, potato salad, pasta salad, a green salad, and chocolate dipped strawberries for dessert.

Lauren smiled at his thoughtfulness. "This looks great." Lauren accepted the crystal plate Tyler offered her and began to fill it.

"What to drink—beer, wine, or if you want harder stuff…"

"Soda? I have to work tonight."

"That's right." Tyler sighed. "Diet or regular?"

"Regular is great." Lauren filled her plate by the time Tyler poured their drinks.

"Let's eat on the patio. I ordered a beautiful day just for you."

"You have connections, huh?" Lauren joked, following him outside.

"You'd be surprised what money can do." Tyler placed their drinks on the table and pulled out Lauren's chair. "Go ahead and start. I'll be right back."

Lord, thank you for this food. Please be with me and help me to glorify You.

"So, when you say you work at the church, is it a paying job?" Tyler joined her a few minutes later.

"My official title is Director of Children's Ministries. It's a big name for a lot of organizing and little pay." Lauren shrugged. "I guess its called ministry because you do it for the kids, not the money."

"It's important to enjoy what you do." Tyler set down his sandwich. "The projects I hated weren't worth the money I made."

"I've found God always provides what I need." Lauren stared at her folded napkin in her lap. "As long as I'm doing His work."

The conversation continued all during lunch, sharing stories about growing up, favorite activities, family vacations.

"Worse burn I ever had in my life I was fifteen and fell asleep on the deck face down on the houseboat we rented." Tyler remembered. "It hurt to wear a shirt for two weeks."

"Is that when you got into the habit of taking off your shirt?" Lauren teased. "It seems like you take it off at least twice in every movie."

Tyler winked. "Whatever sells, babe." He finished off his soda in one swig. The ice clinked in the empty glass as he set it on the table. "I guess that means you've seen my chest?"

Lauren's face grew warm. "A few times."

"In which movie did it look the best?"

Her heart was racing as her palms began to sweat. "I think my favorite was *A Kiss Good Night*. Was that scar real?"

"The on my left side?" Tyler's voice grew sexier. "Let's see." Quickly he pulled off his shirt.

Lauren instinctively moved closer. She traced the perfect skin above his rib cage where the scar had been in the movie. "It looked so real."

"Amazing the power of make-up." Tyler gently touched Lauren's hair. "Does my face look the same as in the movies?"

Lauren shifted her face to his. She smiled, caressing his cheek. "Better."

Tyler slowly leaned forward. His lips were so soft, so smooth. As he placed his hand around her back, she melted in his arms.

Put to death, therefore, whatever belongs to your earthly nature.

"Let's go inside." He moved his hands over the goose bumps on Lauren's arms. "It's getting a little chilly out here. I don't believe I've given you the tour."

"This is the entertainment room." Two high-back comfortable sofas and matching chairs faced a huge plasma TV that hung on the wall. Stereo equipment and surround sound speakers completed the room. "Just the necessities."

Tyler pointed out a full-size bathroom decorated in earth tones as they passed, across the hall from the guestroom, furnished with sandalwood furniture and paintings of the ocean. One window had a partial view of the cliffs.

"Here's my room." Tyler pushed the doors open to reveal a king-size bed with a black comforter, tan and green throw pillows. There was a smaller plasma television, DVD player, and stereo system. With the push of a button, romantic music began to play.

Sexual immorality, impurity, lust…

I'm in Tyler Stevens' bedroom. Lauren followed Tyler. *I can't believe it.*

Tyler ran his hand down the curves of her body. He kissed her neck gently. "I feel lucky to have met you."

Lauren's heart leapt as he kissed her lips passionately. Soon they stumbled to his bed. It felt so good…

…evil desires and greed, which is idolatry…

"Whoa." She pushed Tyler's hand away as he pulled at her shirt. "I need you to slow down. I don't want to go that far."

Tyler smiled mischievously. "How far do you want to go?"

Lauren scooted away from Tyler, sitting up at the head of the bed. "I want to get to know you. I'm still in awe that you're a movie star and I'm here with you."

Tyler sighed, rolled to face her. "What would you like to know?"

Lauren smoothed her tussled hair. "Are you close to your parents?"

"Not really. They say the fame has gone to my head. They don't visit, but enjoy the expensive gifts I send them." Tyler began to crawl up the bed toward her.

"Do you like acting?"

"Can't imagine doing anything else." He slowly leaned in.

"But do you like it?" Lauren pushed him back from kissing her.

"It's hard when you hate the director or the co-stars. But I enjoy becoming the character and leaving myself for a while."

With that his lips quieted hers. Lauren closed her eyes, letting the excitement over take her.

It's okay. Everything is under control.

Because of these, the wrath of God is coming

"I need to leave." She couldn't believe the words came out of her mouth.

"No, you need to stay," Tyler stated.

Lauren turned to the clock. "Jeez, it's five fifteen."

"Are you going to turn into a pumpkin?" She pushed a shocked Tyler off her and ran into the master bathroom.

"I have practice at six. Can I use your brush?" Lauren grabbed his brush and ran it through her hair.

"Sorry to run off," she entered the room pulling on her shoes, "but I need to be at rehearsal."

"And if I don't want to take you?" Tyler grinned.

"I call a cab and announce to the whole world where Tyler Stevens' beach house is."

"Point taken." Tyler followed her out the door.

"Do you have a busy week?" Tyler exited the freeway and headed toward the church.

"Not really. It's my last week, so the regular teacher is starting to take the class back."

"Last week?" Tyler raised an eyebrow. "Then you'll be a real teacher?"

Lauren smiled. "A credentialed teacher. Substitute for hire."

"Come to my house Friday night." Tyler pulled into the driveway. "I'll make you dinner to celebrate."

Lauren stared into his brown eyes. He was so sweet, seemingly sincere. "I'd like that."

Tyler leaned over to kiss Lauren, but she quickly escaped from the car.

"Thanks for lunch. I had a great time." She smiled.

"Good." Tyler returned the smile. "I'm looking forward to Friday."

"Me too. Thanks for the ride." Lauren shut the door and watched Tyler speed out of sight.

"I don't know, Shel. It would be easy to fall for him." After rehearsal Lauren lounged on the top step of the stage talking to Shelly. "He is gorgeous, but I need to slow down."

Shelly sat in the pew opposite her. "I can't believe he kissed you!"

"I know." Lauren shook her head. "He didn't want to stop. I don't get it. He could have anyone. Why me?"

"God works in mysterious ways."

"I need to slow down. We both know my track record. I don't want to repeat mistakes I should have learned from." Lauren sighed. "Please remind me not to do anything I would regret."

Shelly raised an eyebrow. "Would you really regret anything with Tyler Stevens?"

Lauren stared down at the carpet.

You used to walk in these ways, in the life you once lived. But now you must rid yourselves of all such things

"Sin is sin. I regret what I did in the past and I would regret it with Tyler."

Shelly met her on the step and wrapped her arm around Lauren. "Forgive yourself and move on. God has."

Lauren nodded, wiping the tears from her eyes. "I need to wait until marriage. Please keep me accountable."

"That's what friends are for." Shelly stood up. "Let's go get ice cream to celebrate one week until you're finished with student teaching."

"Sounds good." Lauren turned off the stage lights. "Hard to believe I'll finally have my credential."

Shelly followed her out the door. "Dreams do come true."

Chapter 4

He appeared in her dreams. Wild and crazy dreams, she woke up sweating, pulse racing. One morning she woke at three a.m. not able to go back to sleep.

She ran on pure adrenalin all week. Everyday her master teacher took over a subject so she had less teaching to do. She filled out applications for subbing, stayed up late watching TV in an effort to occupy her mind. By Friday she was so exhausted and excited she could hardly stand it.

"Are you seeing him again tonight?" Beth asked when Lauren came in Friday afternoon. All week they talked about him. She told Beth what an amazing time she had at the mall and about their picnic at the beach.

"He's cooking dinner for me at his house."

"Impressive. Does he have any brothers?"

Lauren laughed. "You're married, remember?"

"Oh, yeah. My husband does take-out well. Sometimes he can make a grilled cheese without burning it."

Lauren smiled. "I didn't ask him what's for dinner. Maybe it's grilled cheese."

She straightened her black skirt as she walked to his front door. The clicking of her heels matched the beating of her heart. Her father had frowned at her short black skirt and V-neck purple shirt, but she knew she could have a good time with no sex or physical temptations.

The grand doorbell made her feel small as it announced her presence. Her deep breath cleared her head but failed to settle her stomach.

"Hello." He greeted her at the door, immediately scanning her from head to toe. A smile spread across his face. "You look amazing, Teach."

Tyler rested his hand on her hip. Lauren quickly took it in hers, blushed as she thanked him and moved it off. Her heart continued to race, her palms sweat.

He is so gorgeous.

Tyler led her into the house. "Sorry it took me so long." He shut the door behind her. "I'm out back barbecuing."

Lauren followed him through the house. The rooms were bathed with sunlight. Fresh flowers scattered about in grand vases filled the air with a sweet smell. She concentrated on slow, deep breaths to calm herself.

"Your father did a great job." They ended up on the back patio overlooking the new pool. "I didn't think they would have it done this week. Tell him again how much I appreciate his work." It was two levels, the top being a spa and the bottom for swimming. There were seats and jets around the spa which was big enough to fit thirty people. A waterfall with rocks and greenery along the sides fell into the water below.

"It's gorgeous," Lauren agreed. "Probably one of his best."

"It doesn't compare to your beauty."

Lauren turned to Tyler inches away from her. His lips found their way to hers.

Slowly she broke from his kiss. She walked over to the patio table set with a tablecloth, china, and candles.

"It's all for you, Teach." Tyler handed her a red long-stemmed rose from the vase. "Congratulations."

"Thank you. It's good to be done." Lauren inhaled its sweet fragrance. "So, what is Chef Stevens preparing tonight?" She turned her attention to the barbecue.

"Nothing much, just some fish." He lifted the lid, revealing two shark steaks and potatoes on the grill.

Lauren smiled to see her favorite fish. "Just fish, huh?"

"I heard a rumor you liked it." Tyler returned to the table and pulled out a chair for Lauren. "Sit, tell me about your day."

Lauren shared all the details of her day. As she spoke, Tyler finished cooking and brought out a green salad, rice, vegetables and bread.

"I'm really impressed." The delicious smelling food spiked her hunger.

"Didn't think I could cook, did you?" Tyler teased as he opened wine.

"No offense, but most men can't."

"Some can't, some choose not to." Tyler filled their glasses. "Most of the time I choose not to. It's not worth my time."

"So I should feel special?" Lauren grinned.

"Definitely." Tyler started to fill her glass with wine and stopped. "You do drink?"

Lauren nodded. "I drink, just not to get drunk."

He finished filling her glass and sat across from Lauren, raising his glass. "Cheers, to your new career."

"Cheers."

"You actually fell asleep at a dinner party?" Lauren leaned back into her chair. Dinner was delicious and the conversation had turned to worse dates.

"I'm lucky I didn't do a face plant in my soup! They used words so big a dictionary wouldn't have helped. I blamed it on a late night and excused myself."

They sat, taking each other in. Tyler raised an eyebrow. "What about your best date?"

"Let's see." Lauren stared as orange, red, and yellow painted across the sky. "This guy took me to his beach house. There was a spectacular view off the balcony…"

"Sounds like a romancer." Tyler sipped his wine.

"Besides that, I would say my prom night. I went with a good friend. After the prom we went bowling in our formals."

Tyler laughed. "I bet that was a sight."

"We were the only two sober at one a.m. All the people stumbling next to us were convinced we just got married, despite the fact I was wearing red." She swished her wine in her glass. "After that, we changed and went for a motorcycle ride through the hills."

"And your father let you stay out all night?"

Lauren smiled. "My date was the assistant youth pastor. No romantic interest."

Tyler finished off his drink. "More interesting than my prom. Friends rented a hotel room and got smashed. Don't remember much of anything."

Lauren took a drink of water. "What was your best date?"

"Tonight. Without a doubt."

"C'mon." She playfully pushed his leg with her foot.

Tyler reached across the table to hold Lauren's hand. "It's fun being with you. Very relaxing."

How could she be Tyler Stevens' best date? She thought about the dreams she had during the week and giggled.

"What's so funny?"

"Nothing." Lauren covered her face in embarrassment.

"Come on." Tyler nudged her elbow.

Lauren's face grew hot. "I've been having these dreams all week…"

"Oh yeah?" Tyler perked up. "About me?"

Lauren nodded.

"What rating are we talking?" Tyler teased. "My agent told me no X-rated."

"By today's standards, probably PG-13."

As the colors gave way to the darkened sky, a cool breeze from the valley gave her chills.

"Let's go for a swim." Tyler stood. "We can be the first to test your father's work."

"I didn't bring a suit." Lauren was half afraid of Tyler's response.

He raised an eyebrow and looked her over, a smile slowly spreading. "You can borrow a shirt."

Lauren walked below to the pool as Tyler went to the house. The night so peaceful, yet her mind raced as she gazed at the reflection of the moon on the pool.

If you think you are standing firm, be careful that you don't fall!

Really, it's no big deal. Just a swim. I'll wear a shirt and he won't see anything.

No temptation has seized you except what is common to man.

Why would he want me? I'm not a movie star. There's no way I can compete with that beauty. We're just hanging out, having a good time. There's nothing wrong with that.

God is faithful; he will not let you be tempted beyond what you can bear.

Lauren dipped her toe in the pool, as warm as bathwater. Sitting at the side, she dangled her feet in the water, gazing up at the stars.

"Oh, Father, I want to make the right choice. Please help me stay true to You."

Peace overcame her as she beheld the beauty of the night sky. Hundreds of stars twinkling in the vast dark blue sky. God not only made them, He knows each by name.

When you are tempted, he will also provide a way out so that you can stand up under it.

She heard her favorite Christian song and hurried to her purse on the nearby lounge chair. She was surprised to see her dad's number on her phone.

"Hi Dad. What's going on?" Lauren glanced up to see Tyler dressed in his swimsuit heading out the back door.

"Hi sweetie." His voice seemed upset, almost shaking. "I was just reading, praying and, well, are you okay, honey? I got this feeling you were in trouble." Chills ran up her arms and spine. "I love you. I'm not trying to ruin your fun or control you, but God put it on my heart to call."

Tears filled her eyes. She turned away as Tyler approached the table.

"I'm leaving. Thanks, Dad."

She rubbed her eyes before turning towards Tyler.

"Here's your shirt." He handed it to her with a smile.

"I'm sorry." She grabbed her purse. "I need to go. It was my Dad and he's feeling bad. I need to go."

Tyler frowned as she began up the hill.

"Thanks for everything. I had a great time."

"Are you sure you can't stay?" Tyler started to follow her. "Just for a while?"

Lauren shook her head and quickened her pace.

"I'll come by tomorrow night," he yelled after her. "We'll go out."

"Sure." Lauren waved as she ran through the door.

Her father was asleep when she returned home. She called after leaving Tyler's house to let him know she was safe and on her way home. Quietly, she pulled his door shut. That was their sign. If he woke in the middle of the night, he would know she was home.

Comfy in her pajamas, she crawled into bed. She stared at the ceiling as the reality of what she had almost done rushed over her.

"God, forgive me," she whispered as tears began. "You warned me and I chose not to listen. I'm sorry. I was more focused on him than You. Thank You for protecting me, for having Dad call me. Calm the feelings I have for Tyler and help me to hold strong to You. I don't want to go down that road of disobedience again. I know the pain isn't worth it. Lead me, Lord."

Lauren rolled over, grabbing her teddy bear from the floor. Squeezing it tight, she dried her eyes on the top of its head. She began praying for family and friends. She prayed for each by name and situation to keep her thoughts focused. Within minutes she drifted off to sleep.

Chapter 5

Lauren slowly got out of bed. Her instinct was to stay in bed all day, but she knew that wouldn't help. Putting on her workout clothes, she headed downstairs. Her father left a note that her pancakes were in the microwave. Lauren smiled as she took them out. Two chocolate chip pancakes. He took good care of her.

About noon, Lauren returned to her room freshly showered. Walking out her frustrations at the gym relaxed her, until she listened to the message on her phone.

"Hey, Lauren. Tyler. I'll come by about six tonight. We could go to dinner, maybe hang at my beach house and watch the waves. See you then."

Lauren sat on her bed with her Bible. She needed direction and knew she would find it there.

"You forgot these last night." Tyler offered her the vase of roses from the night before when she opened her front door.

Disappointment came over his face as he examined her. "I thought we were going out?" She chose not to do her hair or make-up, knowing the temptation to go out was too much.

"Come in." Lauren opened the door, stepping aside. "We need to talk."

Tyler followed her into the family room. Placing the roses on the coffee table, he sat facing her on the couch.

"What's up?" his voice sounded chipper.

Lauren inhaled to calm her nerves. The smell of his cologne persuaded her to leave her values behind. His gorgeous face encouraged her to give in to the feelings she had for him. She closed her eyes to focus. "About last night."

"I've been thinking about that, too." Tyler gently rested his hand on her shoulder. "I'm sorry you had to leave. Maybe we could…"

Lauren opened her eyes and put up her hand. "Tyler, I will not have sex with you."

"Lauren, look." He suddenly caressed her hand. "I know you're scared because it's your first time. But we can take it slow."

Lauren pulled her hand away and shook her head. "I've made mistakes in my past and I will not repeat them."

"What?"

"I will not have sex again until I get married." With firmness she looked into his eyes. "I have made a commitment to God. I intend on waiting for marriage."

"What do you mean 'again'? You're not a virgin?"

"I don't see why that matters."

Tyler raised an eyebrow. "If you're not a virgin, what's the big deal?"

Lauren crossed her arms. "The Bible says sex outside of marriage is wrong. I'm attracted to you and flattered you want to be with me. But I can't be in a relationship like that."

"Let me ask you this." Tyler played devil's advocate. "What if your prospective husband hasn't waited? What if he is out sleeping with half the nation? How would that make you feel, knowing the opportunity you passed up?"

"That doesn't matter. I need to be true to God." After a deep breath, she continued. "I know sex is an important part of your relationships. I enjoy spending time with you, but I can't handle constant pressure to be physical with you. I hope you will understand and respect me for it."

Tyler gently caressed her cheek, staring deeply into her eyes. Without a word, he headed for the door.

"Want to see that new love movie tonight? I'm in the mood for a good cry." Lauren called Shelly twenty minutes later.

"Oh no, what happened?"

"I laid it out very clearly."

"And?"

Lauren squeezed her eyes shut. "He walked out without looking back."

Shelly sighed. "Oh Lauren, I'm so sorry."

Lauren took a deep breath. "Pick me up in fifteen?"

"What happened last night?" Shelly brought up the subject once they slid down in the theater seats. Lauren's eyes were red and puffy when she got in the car. They rode to the theater in silence.

Lauren sipped her Coke and grabbed a handful of popcorn from the bucket Shelly held.

"He made shark for dinner. The patio table was set with china, candles, and roses. We had wine with dinner and shared stories. Afterwards he wanted to go for a swim." Lauren stared at the movie screen. "God reminded me the danger in staying, so I left."

Shelly sighed.

"If he was worth it, he would understand," Lauren almost whispered. Then she turned to Shelly. "Besides, now is not the time to start a relationship. I have a career to focus on."

Shelly washed down her popcorn with soda. "You might not have been looking for Mr. Right, but weren't you hoping? I mean, c'mon. Tyler Stevens. It doesn't get much better than that."

"He's just a person. Without the make-up and cameras, he's just a guy that talks smooth and drives fast."

"You enjoyed it." Shelly offered her some M&Ms.

Lauren threw a handful in her mouth. "Of course I did. I'm made of flesh and blood. But, praise God, He brought me to my senses."

Shelly broke the silence a few minutes later. "It was good to see you happy again."

"No guy, not even a superstar, is worth the pain of sin."

Shelly squeezed Lauren's hand. "I'm proud of you. You did the right thing."

Lauren knew one day it would feel right. At the moment it just hurt.

The movie helped her escape reality for a while, but when she got home she slipped into bed in her pajamas, notebook and pen in hand. She flipped past the written pages, filled with joy, sorrow, excitement, and anger. With a heavy heart and tired eyes she took a deep breath as she opened to a clean page and began writing.

Dear God,

Here I am again, hurt and disappointed. I know I did the right thing, but why do I feel so terrible? I allowed myself to care and here I am once again with a tattered heart.

Lord, I don't understand why You brought Tyler Stevens into my life. Thank you for helping me not get wrapped up in him and his materialism. I pray that You might give him perspective in life. May he come to know You as Lord and Savior.

Give me peace as You prepare the perfect man for me. I pray that he will be a holy man, desiring to follow You in all he does.

A smile appeared on Lauren's face as she remembered God's promise.

Thank you God that You desire good and not evil for me, that You have a plan for success and not failure. I rest in the promise of Your peace and in Your grace.

Closing her notebook, Lauren switched off the light and snuggled down into her bed. As she closed her eyes, she focused on God and all He had done for her. Though her heart was heavy, she knew she was not alone.

Tyler awoke at three a.m. Who was next to him? It took a while for his eyes to focus. Denise, was that her name? Maybe Heather? No difference. A bit eager, maybe just a bad actress. But then again, what did he want–a stubborn schoolgirl like that Lauren? A tease that refused to put out?

Stepping out of bed he headed toward the kitchen. He couldn't stop replaying the conversation with Lauren earlier that night. What was that wait until marriage crap? Tyler had slept with "Christians." Didn't they just confess after? He didn't see the point of religion. Guilt trips and taking your money was all they were good for.

Moonlight streamed from the kitchen window as he ripped open the refrigerator door. It was packed with food from their dates. Grabbing an apple and a beer, he slammed the door. Never had he tried so hard and not received a return. He was pissed she made him look like a fool to Mitch. No one rejected Tyler Stevens.

But he did the honorable thing. Walked away and found someone else the same night. He would never beg or stay without the benefits. No woman was worth sacrificing your self-respect. He called Mitch after leaving Lauren's to make arrangements for his pool party. The women would come in droves.

"Does she realize what she gave up?" Tyler admired his reflection in the window. "Not only would I have given her the best sex of her life, I would have treated her like a queen. She'll end up marrying a pool digger like her father. She should have jumped at the chance to experience luxury. It won't come again in her lifetime."

Tyler threw the apple core in the trash and chugged the remainder of his beer as he returned to the guest room and what's-her-name.

Chapter 6

"So, Zeus, tell me of the latest occurrences in your life?" Tyler had no sooner walked through the door than Adam called.

"Signed for a medieval fantasy. Easy money with hot chicks."

"Are you engaging in independent studying with any of these fine females?"

Tyler dropped his keys on the kitchen counter and grabbed a glass for water. "No, but I had an interesting interlude with a teacher-to-be a few weeks ago."

"Continue." Tyler could hear Adam playing chords on his keyboard.

"Her father installed my pool, she came to pick him up one day…"

"Did you unveil her, too, at your pool unveiling? Sorry I missed that. Out of town yet again."

Tyler walked to the entertainment room as he spoke. "It was wild. There's still sand in the pool from the volleyball game. But that's another story." Tyler reclined on his sofa. "I took Little Miss Teacher out a couple of times, romanced her. She gave me all the signs, then laid some line on me about waiting for marriage. I don't get it. Who does she think she is?"

Adam laughed. "Someone who has you hook, line and sinker."

"What are you talking about?"

"What has you so enthralled?"

"She's confident and independent, uninterested in money and fame. She seemed to enjoy me, not just the glamour."

"So, what's the problem?"

"She won't put out." Tyler took a drink of water.

51

"Zeus, have I not taught you anything? What's rule three?" Adam stopped his music, giving Tyler his full attention.

"Don't confuse physical attraction for love."

"Believe it or not, a man can have a relationship with a woman without having sex."

"Really?" Tyler's voice rose.

"Sure. Remember your mother?"

Tyler laughed as Adam continued. "A good one comes along once in a blue moon, dear Zeus. Don't let this one go quite yet."

"Which one of your songs is that piece of wisdom from?"

"Don't forget number four. 'Know when to swallow your pride.' I'm having my annual charity event Friday. I expect both of you to be in attendance, front and center."

"Okay. I'll give her a shot on the platonic level."

"Good boy." Adam began jamming again. "Who knows? You might thank me for this someday."

∽

She blinked her burning eyes and massaged her cramped fingers. Filling out on-line applications was tedious and pain staking work. One district accepted her as a substitute, but there were several more to go.

"Knock, knock." Her dad pushed open her door. "How are you?"

"Tired." Lauren rubbed her eyes.

Walking behind her, he began massaging her shoulders. "You're really tense. Let's go to a movie tonight."

Lauren rolled back her head, cracking her neck with a sigh of relief. "I would love to Dad, but I still have a page full of questions to answer and two more applications after that."

"Sweetie, you've been working too hard on this. You need a break."

"I need to finish if I want to get a job."

"It's only been a few weeks, Lauren. Give it time. Start anew tomorrow. God is in control." Richard squeezed her shoulders and kissed the top of her head. "You have fifteen minutes to get ready."

"Yes sir." Lauren breathed a sigh of relief as she closed her laptop.

"Did you get the latest bid?" They stared at the slides projected on the screen of business ads and movie trivia.

"Hopkin's counter offered." He handed Lauren the box of Junior Mints. "I told them I would knock mine down three percent, but not lower. I can't take a loss on it."

"Good for you." Lauren took a handful and placed the candy in the cup holder between them. "You need to stand up for yourself more often."

"I think you should work for me. I need a financial secretary to keep me on the right track."

"You forget. I'm good at spending money, not saving it."

Tyler's picture flashed on the screen on a still shot of his latest movie.

"Well, our favorite movie star." Richard chomped on popcorn.

Lauren sunk lower in her seat and sighed.

"You never did tell me the end result."

"You were right." Lauren picked up her soda. "All he wanted was sex."

"I'd say I'm sorry, but I'm not. That man represents everything in the world I'm against- greed, lust, immorality." He gently squeezed Lauren's hand. "God has the perfect man for you. All you need to do is wait for God's plan to unfold."

Lauren smiled weakly. "I know that in my heart. It's just hard being patient."

"I'm very proud of the beautiful, sensible Christian woman you have turned out to be. Your mother would be proud, too."

Lauren laid her head on her father's shoulder as the lights dimmed. "Thanks, Dad."

Her cell phone started ringing as they walked through the door. She answered it on her way upstairs.

"Hello, Lauren?"

"Yes." Lauren shut her bedroom door behind her.

"It's Tyler Stevens." His voice was so matter-of-fact at first Lauren thought it was a prank call. "I've been doing some thinking."

"Really?" It sounded out of character for him, but Lauren sat on her bed to listen.

"You're not like most people I know. I really enjoyed being with you and getting to know you. I'm wondering if you can forgive my shallowness of thinking every relationship needs to be sexual and give me a second chance."

Wow. Tyler Stevens asked for forgiveness. It's flattering, but, Lord, why?

"I forgive you, but I'm not sure about the second chance."

"Why not?"

Do not conform any longer to the pattern of this world.

She took a deep breath and closed her eyes. "I won't change my mind about having sex with you. I will feel the same a week, a month, a year from now. I'm waiting for marriage."

"I don't really understand, but I will respect your decision."

Be transformed by the renewing of your mind

"That means not pushing me." Lauren spoke with boldness. "I don't want to be pushed or put into awkward situations. No kissing or trying to seduce me."

Tyler chuckled. "Don't ask for much do you?"

She sighed, shaking her head. "The right man will understand."

"I may joke about it because that's my nature, but I'll take no for an answer. I promise."

That gave her the peace she needed. "I'd be happy to be friends."

"Friends," he agreed, "with potential."

Lauren shook her head. *Did he get it?*

"Are you busy Friday night?"

"Let me check my calendar." Lauren's empty calendar lay open on her desk. "It appears I'm free."

"A friend is hosting a charity dinner. Will you accompany me?"

"Sure." Lauren bit her lip in excitement. She had only seen such events on TV.

" I'll pick you up at seven. You have an evening dress?"

"Yeah." Lauren didn't mean to lie. It just slipped out.

"See you on Friday."

A black tie affair? Lauren had nothing close to formal. What was she thinking? Lauren fell back on her bed and sighed.

"Hey, Shel." Lauren started her message after the beep. "You will never believe who called with an apology and inviting me to a charity dinner Friday night. I need to go shopping tomorrow. Call me if you want to go."

Lauren regretted leaving the message after she hung up. She needed someone to bring her back to reality, not encourage her to live a fantasy.

Somberly she walked downstairs. Her father reclined on the couch in the family room, engrossed in his nature program. Lauren curled up next to him, resting her head on his shoulder.

"Tyler called." Lauren spoke quietly. "He apologized, asked if we could try again. I told him no pressure and only as friends. He agreed and invited me to a banquet Friday night." Lauren continued speaking before Richard could protest. "I'm going to call him back tomorrow and tell him no. You're right. Nothing good would come from it."

Silence lingered in the room.

"I don't want you to get hurt." He kissed the top of her head gently. "I do want you to be happy. If you really think you can just be friends, pray about it. That's all I ask."

"You're kidding me!" Shelly's scream awakened Lauren at midnight.

"I haven't decided if I am going." Lauren rubbed her eyes. She didn't remember answering the phone.

"How could you not go? Lauren, wake up and smell the roses. Tyler Stevens wants to see you after you rejected him. This is what you were hoping for. This is so amazing. It is so God!"

"Shel, I need a formal. I have no job and bills to pay. I can't do it."

"You're subbing. And working at the preschool."

Lauren chuckled. "A formal dress would cost several weeks pay. What would I say the next time?"

"C'mon," Shelly encouraged. "I'll be over tomorrow after work to go shopping. Just put it on a credit card."

"I've prayed and realize I need to be honest. I'll call him tomorrow and tell him the truth."

"You are so stubborn." Shelly sighed. "Call me after you talk to him."

Lauren yawned. "Did you go out tonight?"

"Yeah. That guy from work, the legal assistant, took me out."

"Did you hit it off?"

Shelly laughed. "He's no Tyler Stevens, that's for sure. I'll tell you the gory details tomorrow."

At morning recess, she returned to the empty classroom after walking the kids to the playground. Her hand shook as she dialed his number. She paced as the phone rang.

I can't go. I can't afford a dress...

"Hello." Tyler practically screamed into the phone.

"Hi, it's Lauren."

"How are you?" Tyler switched on his sexy voice.

Lauren took a deep breath. "I need to be honest with you. I don't have a formal or the money to purchase one, so I can't go to the charity event."

"You just need to go shopping."

Tyler stated it so bluntly Lauren felt stupid repeating herself. "I don't have the money..."

"There's a strip of shops downtown. *An Evening Affair* is a little boutique next door to a French café. Gretchen will take care of everything."

"No, Tyler, I don't expect..."

"I promised my friend you would attend. I hate to cut you off, but I'm on my way to a reading. Anything else?"

"No." Lauren hung her head.

"Great. See you Friday."

Could she let him buy the dress for her? Would he expect something in return?

The next call she made was to the preschool.

"Can you close for me tonight?" Lauren asked Beth when she answered the phone.

"Why? You got another hot date?"

"Kind of. Tyler asked me to a dinner party on Friday and..."

"You have nothing to wear." Beth finished her sentence. "I suppose I can help you out this time."

"Thanks." Lauren was silent.

"Go ahead," Beth teased, "ask me to work for you Friday."

"You're the best. I'll make it up to you this summer."

"Deal. Knock Mr. Wonderful's socks off."

A group of ladies chattered and laughed while they enjoyed lunch on the patio of the French café beside the boutique. Lauren fidgeted with her bangs after observing their seeming natural highlights. Their lavish make-up reminded her she didn't even put on eye shadow today. She rubbed her cross necklace between her fingers, as one woman bragged about the diamonds her husband bought her. Behind her the window mannequins in their gorgeous gowns seemed to mock Lauren, standing on the sidewalk in her flowered sundress and beat-up sandals.

Lord, what am I doing here?

"What's up?" Shelly linked arms with Lauren. "I thought you'd be inside trying stuff on by now."

"I don't know about this." Lauren planted her feet firmly. "I think it's a mistake."

"Don't be silly. This way, Mrs. Stevens." Shelly dragged her to the door. "Your shopping spree awaits."

"It's not a spree, only one dress. I seriously feel sick."

"This is a once-in-a-lifetime opportunity. You're going to a banquet with Tyler Stevens and the sky's the limit." Shelly held the door open and pushed Lauren in.

"Conservative, not crazy. Do you think they have a restroom? I really feel nauseous."

A few customers shopped in the back as Shelly and Lauren approached the first rack. No sooner had they made it past the cocktail dresses than a gray-haired, petite woman wearing a tailored suit approached them.

"Hello." The petite woman extended her hand. "You must be Lauren. I'm Gretchen.

Lauren wearily shook her hand.

"Mr. Stevens' assistant phoned. He explained the event and I took the liberty of pulling a few dresses." She eyed Lauren from foot to bust. "Four, right?"

Lauren nodded.

"Follow me." Gretchen blazed a trail to the back of the store.

"Talk about service." Shelly whispered.

"Oh Shel. What have I gotten myself into?"

"Allow yourself to be pampered. You deserve it."

Lauren glanced at a slinky black number as they walked past.

"There are no price tags," she whispered to Shelly. "That can't be good."

Shelly pushed her toward the back of the store. Gretchen motioned for them to sit in plush chairs.

"First we have an elegant black silk." Lauren raised an eyebrow at the sleeveless, scoop neck and low V-back floor-length dress Gretchen held up.

"And, of course, our deep red, passionate creation. Off the shoulder sleeves compliment the full skirt." Her eyes immediately jumped to the side slit that stopped at the thigh.

"Here's a beautiful royal blue satin." A smile crept across Lauren's face. High cut front, low scoop back. It had spaghetti straps and a straight skirt with a modest slit up the back.

"They're all beautiful." *And probably extremely expensive.*

Gretchen motioned to the dressing room. "They'll look better on you than the hanger."

Lauren modeled the dresses for Shelly while Gretchen attended to her every need, pointing out the highlights of each and accessorizing with the perfect shoes, hair clip and purse to match each one.

"Do you need jewelry?" Gretchen stared at Lauren in the mirror.

"I have pearls at home. Do you think…"

"Single strand?" Gretchen dashed off.

"Yes," Lauren called.

Gretchen returned with three pearl necklaces. "Which are closest to yours?"

Lauren pointed to the medium-sized ones. After Gretchen attached them around her neck, she held up several styles of earrings. Lauren picked the three dangling pearls and put them on.

Gretchen paraded Lauren around like a superstar. "Always stand straight, shoulders back and head high. Flash those pearly whites, but keep walking. Don't look directly at the cameras, focus on Tyler. Laugh, whisper sweet nothings in his ear. Remember, you're having fun!"

"She was so sweet and helpful." Shelly held the door open for Lauren, arms full of packages. "And that dress is amazing on you."

Lauren frowned. "I still feel sick."

Shelly patted her back. "Let's grab something to eat."

"Shel, what am I going to do?" Shelly attacked the hot tortilla chips as soon as the waiter set them down. Lauren held her soda between her hands, her stomach still unsettled from the shopping trip.

"You're going to be beautiful, make Tyler Stevens fall in love with you and live happily ever after." Salsa slid off Shelly's chip back into the bowl.

"Very funny."

Shelly leaned toward Lauren. "He is pursuing you. Even after you told him you won't have a physical relationship, he wants to go out with you. That says a lot. He wants to get to know you. Be yourself and keep praying, because obviously God is watching over you."

"You're right, but the whole press thing freaks me out."

"It'll be fine." Shelly patted Lauren's arm. "Just bring home one of Tyler's cute movie star friends for me."

"Tyler Stevens." Lauren sighed, shaking her head. "You read in the Bible about God testing people. I thought my days of testing were over."

"You practically got straight As in college. No worries." Shelly turned her attention back to the chips.

"But this is life. The consequences for failing are harsher."

"What were the two of you up to tonight?" Richard glanced up from reading the paper when Lauren arrived home.

"We went shopping for my dress and then out to eat." She sat beside her father, pulling off her shoes.

"Dress for what?"

"That charity dinner with Tyler."

A disapproving look came across Richard's face. "How much did it cost?"

Lauren settled back into the couch. "I explained the truth to Tyler that I couldn't afford a dress. He sent me to a shop and everything was taken care of."

Richard shook his head. "With people like that, everything has its cost."

"He understands." Lauren's irritation increased. "He agreed to be respectful of my decision."

"I hope he does, but…"

"Dad," Lauren interrupted him.

Richard put his hand up, stopping her. "If you find yourself in an uncomfortable position, call me. No lectures or questions, I promise."

"Thank you." She hugged her father and kissed his cheek. "Good night."

"Good night, sweetheart."

"Lord, thank you for today." She closed her eyes as she relaxed in her bed. "Thank You for being in control and working everything out. I know there is a purpose for all this. Guard me from temptation. Help me to be a witness for You and bring You glory in all I say and do."

Chapter 7

The grandfather clock chimed seven p.m. as Lauren finished her mascara and began her lipstick.

"You are so beautiful." Shelly stood behind her, peering at her in the mirror. "Blue is definitely your color."

"You sure it's not too much make-up?"

"No way." Shelly fidgeted with Lauren's French twist. "You look like a movie star, or at least someone dating one."

Lauren ran her fingers over her pearls, thinking of the last time she saw her mother wear them, Lauren's high school graduation party. Her father had given her the pearls and had matching earrings made when she completed college.

I miss you Mom. I wish you were here…

Shelly ran to the window at the sound of a car pulling up. "It's a limo! A huge black limo!"

Deep breath. Lauren closed her eyes and inhaled slowly. *Lord, help me to glorify You tonight.*

"He's wearing a tux! He is so gorgeous." Shelly sighed. "You know God would forgive you."

She punched Shelly in the arm as the doorbell rang. "Not funny. We are just friends. Please stay up here until we leave."

Lauren's eyes locked with Tyler's as she descended down the staircase. He offered her his hand as she reached the bottom step.

"You look amazing." He kissed her hand.

"Thank you." Lauren returned the smile. "You're pretty handsome yourself."

Her father cleared his throat and kissed Lauren's cheek. "Have fun and be safe."

"Thanks, Dad." Lauren took Tyler's arm in hers. "Shall we?"

"Definitely." As Tyler helped her in the limo, Lauren peered at Shelly, watching from the bathroom window. She beamed with the excitement Lauren felt.

An action movie was playing on the plasma screen when Lauren slid into the limo. Stereo, frig, all the comforts of home. She settled back into the leather seat as Tyler climbed in beside her.

Why do tuxes make guys look so incredibly hot? Her heart raced and palms began to sweat. *Lord, help me. It's not as easy as I thought.*

"What?" His voice broke her trance.

Lauren raised an eyebrow. "You resemble that movie star, Tyler Stevens. I didn't realize clothes could change your appearance so much."

Tyler smiled. "You almost look like a star yourself."

"Almost?"

"You're missing that bit of arrogance we all have." Tyler removed a bottle of wine from the refrigerator. "White?"

Lauren nodded, took the glass he offered her.

"How have you been?" Tyler poured her wine.

Lauren smiled. "I'm officially a substitute."

"The dreaded substitute." Tyler settling back with his drink. "Have the kids thrown stuff at you yet?"

"No." Lauren chuckled. "I don't think they do that in elementary school."

"We did. Of course, maybe that was only to subs that had huge warts on their nose."

Lauren narrowed her eyes at him. "You were a trouble maker in school, weren't you?"

"All the teachers hated me, all the girls loved me."

"Somehow that's not hard to believe." *His eyes are so blue. I could stare into them forever…*

Lauren shook herself from the trance. "What have you been up to?"

She settled back as Tyler recapped the wrap of his last film. Peace overcame her with each word he spoke.

He's just a guy, a very rich, amazingly handsome guy.

Nervousness rose inside her again when the car stopped an hour later. "Are we here?"

"Appears so." He placed their glass in the holders. "There's lots of reporters and cameras outside. Hold on to my arm, smile and look straight ahead. I'll wave as we make our way to the hotel. Don't say anything or look at the cameras." Tyler consumed her with his eyes. "Gretchen sure can pick dresses, can't she?"

She gazed down shyly. "I wanted to thank you..."

"No need." Tyler put a finger on her lip. "It's my pleasure to make you the most beautiful woman in the world." He turned to the driver. "Ready when you are, Joe."

The door flung open and they were thrust into a roaring sea of reporters. Flashes filled the air and though ropes and police lined the way to hold back people, she still feared a stampede. Tyler flashed his gorgeous smile and waved. Lauren focusing on the wide hotel steps straight ahead, trying to remember to grin. She had watched such scenes on TV. Now she was clinging to the man all the girls screamed for. Unbelievable.

She breathed a sigh of relief when they arrived at the hotel door. The silence inside was refreshing.

"That wasn't so bad, was it?" Tyler joked as they made their way to the ballroom.

"Not at all. Does this mean my picture will be all over the gossip magazines tomorrow?"

"Without a doubt. Don't worry, I'll leak a hot story about us."

He laughed at her wide eyes and explained he would introduce her as an old friend. "That's the best way to get around gossip. It's a phrase with so many meanings most people don't care to know the story behind it."

Lauren wobbled in her heels climbing the winding staircase. She tightened her grip on Tyler's arm to keep from doing a face plant.

"Mac does this fundraiser every year. After dinner he plays songs people bid on. The highest priced song is played last."

"Creative way to make money. You pay for dinner as well?"

"A thousand a plate."

Lauren choked. "I'll have to write this down as my most expensive concert."

"It will probably be the most memorable, too."

No doubt about that.

They entered the ballroom. Chandeliers, covered chairs, and huge floral centerpieces spoke of the formality of the event. A grand piano was the focal point of the stage.

"It's beautiful."

"Not nearly as gorgeous as you." Tyler gently touched Lauren's necklace and her earrings. "By the way, I love the pearls."

Lauren straightened at his remark. "They were a graduation gift from my dad."

"They make the dress."

"Good evening, Mr. Stevens," the host greeted them. "I'll show you to your table."

As they weaved through the tables, Tyler explained the food would be horrible, but they'd go out afterward. Finally they arrived at their table, front and center.

He scanned the room, informing Lauren of whom others were.

Three other couples sat at their table including a senator and his wife, a musician, and an obscenely rich couple, as Tyler described them.

"They're everywhere in Hollywood because they can afford to be, but they earned their money the easy way: investments." Tyler paused to stand and shake the hand of a senator. When he sat, he turned toward Lauren. "Tends to be the same people each year, like a reunion. All people that love Mac and believe in the cause."

"What charity is it for?"

"Foreign orphans. Mac distributes the money around the world. They build orphanages, buy necessities for them. He started it a few years ago."

"Sounds like a great guy."

"I met him when I first moved to LA. He's like family to me, the one person I trust."

"Don't you trust Mitch?"

Tyler chuckled. "As long as I make money for Mitch, I can trust him. I just have to make sure he doesn't get too greedy."

"I hope they don't send the leftovers to starving children," Lauren muttered, surveying the remains of her overcooked steak, soggy vegetables, and brick hard potato.

Her eyes widened when the waiter placed chocolate mousse in front of her. When her dish was empty, Tyler switched his full dish with hers.

"I'm not a big chocolate fan." He winked.

Lauren shook her head. "Whatever." She devoured his dessert as well.

Once dessert dishes were cleared, the waiters passed out slips of paper with ultra-strong coffee.

"So, what's your favorite song?"

Lauren shrugged. "I don't think I know his music."

The lights began to dim as the announcer introduced Adam Riley.

"Oh, my gosh!" Lauren gasped. "Adam Riley!"

"So, you do know his music?"

"Of course! Who doesn't?"

Tyler raised an eyebrow. "Apparently you didn't a couple minutes ago!"

"You kept calling him 'Mac'. You confused me."

Tyler handed Lauren the pen and paper. "Write your favorite song."

Lauren thought before writing and gave it back to Tyler, who scribbled something on it before motioning the waiter.

"Good evening, ladies and gentlemen." Adam announced from his piano bench on stage. "I'm so glad you could make it tonight."

Lauren's heart raced. Adam Riley.

Why are you surprised? After all, you're here with Tyler Stevens.

"You're a fan?"

She turned to Tyler. "You're friends?"

"He wants to meet you after."

First Tyler Stevens, now Adam Riley. I have to be dreaming.

Adam shared his vision of refurbishing run-down children's shelters in Russia with the audience. Lauren cringed as he described the unsanitary conditions. The fundraiser was to bid on your favorite song. Adam would play the top twenty songs according to the bid.

Tyler leaned over to her. "Your song will be played. Be patient."

Waiters scrambled among the tables collecting the remaining slips while Adam interviewed various people at the tables.

"And the dashing Mr.Stevens." Adam ended at their table. Tyler stood and waved when the spotlight shone on him. "What movie is Hollywood's most handsome bachelor working on?"

"A police adventure to be released next spring." Tyler's voice was smooth as Lauren's palms sweat out of nervousness for him.

"I'm glad you could make it tonight." Lauren's heart skipped a beat when Adam winked at her. She smiled, astonished he even noticed her.

Returning to the stage, he settled down on his bench. Once he read the top slip of paper the music began.

The music entranced her. His hands glided across the keys with intensity and emotion. She caught tears welling inside her several times. It wasn't until Tyler placed his hand on her back that Lauren remembered he was beside her.

Astonishment overcame her when Adam picked up the last piece of paper with a smile.

"One of my favorite songs for my favorite friends. To Tyler and Lauren. I hope you have enjoyed the evening."

Tyler slid his hand in hers. Lauren's heart skipped a beat when Adam stared at her during the song. She imagined this was how Cinderella felt when she danced with the prince.

"Good night, ladies and gentleman!" Adam rose to his feet as the applause began. "Thank you for your contribution. God bless!" With a wave, he ran off stage.

Lauren applauded an empty stage. "He was amazing." She turned to Tyler. "Thank you for bringing me."

Tyler smiled. "The night has just begun." He grabbed his jacket and led her towards the stage.

"Where are we going?" The others were exiting through the doors they entered earlier that evening.

"To get some real food."

The guard standing in front of a side door by the stage opened it for them. "Good evening, Mr. Stevens."

"Good evening." They walked down a seemingly deserted hall.

"Hotels have back passages for food servers, performers, and movie stars, of course." Tyler nodded at a waiter that passed with a tray of food. "Mac has played here for the past three years. I think I know where I'm going."

The last door opened to a loading dock behind the hotel.

Tyler glanced around as they walked on the platform. "It should be here any minute." Lauren tightened her wrap around herself, trying to warm herself.

He turned when her teeth chattered. "Forgive me." He removed his jacket and placed it around her shoulders.

"Thank you. They don't make these dresses with warmth in mind."

Tyler laughed. "It's just a girl's way to scheme a guy out of his jacket."

"Oh, really?"

Tyler put his arm around her. "You had a good time tonight?"

"Amazing. I can't believe you're friends with Adam Riley. And you put in the highest bid for my song." She turned toward him. "You didn't have to."

"It was worth every penny to see your face when he announced it." Tyler brushed her cheek with the back of his hand.

Lauren took his hand in hers. "I can't wait to tell my dad! He is a huge fan of Adam's."

Tyler raised his eyebrows. "Great, maybe he'll like me more."

Wheels screeched and a black limo flew around the corner. Tyler led her down the ramp. "Act Two!"

"Mr. Stevens, Miss Drake." The driver bowed as he opened the door.

"Good evening." Lauren's jaw dropped to see Adam Riley in the seat across from her, lifting his glass of champagne at her entrance. "Glad you could join us Miss Drake."

Her eyes widened as he gently kissed her hand.

Tyler slid beside her. "The night is full of surprises." Tyler poured them champagne.

Adam Riley! "Thank you for having me, Mr. Riley." *Deep breath. Try not to be too awestruck.*

Adam put her hand back into her lap. "You can call me Mac."

"Mac?"

"The names our parents give us usually do not have as much meaning as the names our friends give us. Everyone should have a nickname."

Lauren raised an eyebrow as she looked at Tyler.

"Zeus," Adam answered. "Pretty appropriate for the most famous among the stars, wouldn't you say?"

Lauren nodded, as Tyler handed her a glass. "Adam takes it upon himself to give everyone nicknames. He takes that stuff about Adam naming things seriously."

Adam was thoughtfully examining her. *What is he thinking?* Lauren nervously took a drink.

"Angel." First to Tyler, then Adam turned back to her. "You are an Angel, with an amazing story. I can't wait for it to be revealed."

Chills ran up Lauren's arms. *He's known me five minutes and thinks I'm an angel? And my story...*

"Did you enjoy your song?"

"It was beautiful." Lauren smiled. "The whole concert was amazing."

"You did it perfectly," Tyler agreed. "How much did that one set me back?"

"Just a movie or two." Adam patted him on the back. "But remember, it's all for the children."

Lauren was confused. "You don't know what you bid?"

Tyler shrugged. "I just wrote highest bid plus ten."

$10,000? Lauren shifted her face down. *I don't understand this world of wealth. Why would he do that?*

"I've known Tyler for five years and you are by far the most beautiful woman he has dated." Adam sipped his drink. "And I'm sure the most interesting. This is the first time he's bid in the top five."

Lauren lifted her face slowly towards him. "Thank you, but I'm sure most beautiful isn't true. I've seen some of the women he's dated."

"True beauty shines from within." Adam argued.

"She's smart." Tyler filled his glass again. "Holds a good conversation."

Lauren laughed. Tyler looked at her and smiled.

"That shouldn't surprise you. You said you've seen the girls I've dated."

"I'm sure her father had better intentions for sending her to college than to entertain a pompous movie star." Adam chimed in.

Tyler lifted his empty flute to clink Adam's. "Good one, my friend."

Lauren held tight to Tyler's arm as they weaved through the crowd following Adam, greeting people in line they passed.

It's such an exclusive club, but then again, they are famous. "Do you come here often?"

"Why not?" Tyler shrugged. "It's Mac's place."

"Really?" *Singer, charity organizer, nightclub owner. What next?*

Tyler smiled and waved to a group of girls in the line that shouted his name. "He's owned it about three years. Business is always booming."

When they got to the door, Adam leaned in to Lauren. "You are twenty one, right, my dear Angel?"

"Twenty three and proud of it."

"Ah, to be young again."

"Good evening, Mr. Riley, Mr. Stevens." The broad doorman removed the red velvet rope for them to enter. "Great to see you."

"Thanks, Hank." Adam slapped the mammoth man on the back. "This is Miss Lauren Drake."

Hank extended his hand with a smile. "Great to meet you, Miss Drake."

Half his size, Lauren felt tiny greeting him.

Every two steps Adam and Tyler saw someone they knew and stopped to shout greetings over the blaring music. Lauren scanned the crowds, spotting the feature band on the Late Night Show last week, an actress from a movie she saw a few months ago, one of the widely known directors and his young girlfriend.

Tyler's magnetic pull for gorgeous women made Lauren a little uneasy. After shooing off the eighth girl, he grabbed Lauren, pulling her against him.

"Act like you like me," he said in her ear.

She wrapped her arm around his neck and leaned in close. "Just friends, remember?"

"With potential." His words increased her heart rate.

Two songs had played before they made their way to the second floor. There was a table set back by itself with the sign "Reserved for Mac and Friends" above it. Waitresses immediately scribbled their orders and hurried off to fill them. Lauren and Tyler retreated into the plush booth. It was high enough to see the entire dance floor on the first floor. She watched the dancing on the bottom level for a while before moving her gaze back to Adam, socializing with several people a few feet away by the upper level railing.

"He has an interesting set of friends." Tyler loosened his bowtie. "Social class, race, profession or sexual orientation make no difference to him. He's never too good to be someone's friend."

As Adam talked to others he put his arm around them, hugging or patting their back. He was so outgoing, caring. So real.

"What?" Embarrassed to realize Tyler had been staring at her the entire time, she shook her head and reached for the water the waitress set in front of her.

"C'mon." Tyler playfully pushed her arm. "What's going on in that brain of yours."

"There's a man in the Bible, Paul, that learned how to relate to all people so he could be a better witness. It's a pretty amazing characteristic for someone to have."

Tyler stared into her eyes. He gently ran his hand down her cheek as he leaned in towards her. "You intrigue me." His breath was warm on her ear. "I want to kiss you so bad…"

She felt her blood race from head to toe. She closed her eyes and inhaled to clear her mind. The smell of his cologne fogged it more. She scooted back from him, putting her arms out to keep him from following. "That's a new experience for you, isn't it?"

He sipped his drink, raised his eyebrow as he crunched his ice before replying. "Yes it is."

Fresh salads and a platter of appetizers were placed before them. They had begun to eat when Adam appeared with a woman in her late thirties, dressed in a short purple skirt, Angora sweater and stiletto heels.

"Angel, I'd like you to meet Heidi."

"I hear you're a teacher." Heidi shook her hand vigorously. "That is so neat!"

The remainder of the night, Adam continued to introducing people to Lauren and although her attention was on several other things, she noticed Tyler focused on her alone.

The trio piled in their limo and within minutes Tyler was snoring.

"He's intrigued by you." Adam offered Lauren a water bottle from the fridge. "He's never dated someone so genuine."

"We're not really dating. We're just friends."

"Stand your ground, Angel." He gave her a reassuring nod. "It takes a lot to stand up for what you believe in around here."

"Tell me about your ministry." Lauren kicked off her shoes and settled back into the seat. "I want to know all about it."

He told his stories of the orphans with compassion, remembering their names and backgrounds. He spoke of singing to them, playing with them, missionaries sharing the word of God with them. Completely lost in his stories, she was surprised when they arrived at her house.

Adam gently kissed Lauren's hand. "It's been a pleasure, Angel. I trust we will see each other again."

"I'd like that. Thank you for everything." Lauren smiled.

Adam nudged Tyler. "Prince Charming, Snow White is leaving us now. Walk her to the door."

Tyler rubbed his eyes and yawned. Stepping out of the door held by the chauffeur, he helped her out.

"Sorry about that." Tyler walked her up the path.

"Don't worry. I had a great talk with Adam."

"Was he trying to pick up on you?" Tyler slipped his hand around her waist.

Lauren smiled removing his hand. "He was a complete gentleman." She turned to face Tyler. "I had a great time. Thanks again for inviting me and the dress…"

Tyler placed his finger on her lips. "Telling me you will see me again is thanks enough."

Lauren smiled and embraced Tyler. "I would love to see you again."

As they broke from their hug, Tyler moved for a kiss, but Lauren dodged him.

"Good night." She disappeared into the house.

The porch light switched off. He inhaled the crisp night air and walked dejectedly back to the limo.

"And she was off, without a kiss." Tyler sighed, sliding in across from Adam.

Adam slapped Tyler on the shoulder. "Well, Zeus, I have to admit, she is a fine woman. She will be worth it, if you can make it."

Tyler nodded as he leaned back and closed his eyes. "I'm wondering, about both."

Chapter 8

"Guess whose picture is on the front of the entertainment section?"

Lauren rubbed her eyes, processing Shelly's words. She reached for the glass of water on the nightstand.

"It's my best friend looking incredibly beautiful in the arms of Tyler Stevens."

After quenching her thirst, Lauren sank into her pillow, massaging her pounding head.

"You're famous!" Shelly screamed.

"I didn't go to bed until after three a.m. Please use a quiet voice."

"Yes, Teacher," Shelly mocked. "The article says you're Tyler's newfound love."

"Bring it over at noon." Lauren closed her eyes. "We'll have lunch."

In the center of section E was a photo of Lauren heading up the steps with Tyler at the banquet. The heading read "New Love for Tyler Stevens".

"Reports are Tyler Stevens met his new love last month while shooting his latest action film, which will be released this fall. 'This could be the one,' he told a trusted friend. The two attended Adam Riley's charity ball Friday night at The Grand. They were inseparable all night."

Lauren shook her head as Shelly read. "It's all lies."

"It's awesome! You sound like a movie star. Besides, you were at the dinner."

"And we were inseparable because we sat at the same table. At least they don't know my name."

"You could call and tell them the real details."

"No way! Please don't tell anyone."

"Of course, as long as you tell me everything."

Lauren gave Shelly a play by play of the entire evening, answering all of Shelly's questions. She was recounting the ride home when her phone rang.

"Hey, it's Tyler. How are you?"

"I slept in, so I'm good. How about you?" She winked at Shelly who bit her lip to keep from screaming.

"I've had worse mornings. It would've been better if I woke up next to you."

"So," Lauren changed the subject, "we made the entertainment section."

"Really? Have I fallen head over heels?"

"Apparently you think I might be the one."

"Oh, yes, I told a trusted friend that last night."

Lauren laughed.

"Mac is coming over for dinner. We'd both like you to join us."

"That's fine, but I have church in the morning."

"Bring the sparkling cider and be here around six tonight."

"See you then." Lauren put her phone down with a smile.

Shelly shook her head. "Unreal. My best friend and Tyler Stevens."

"Just friends, Shel. We're just friends."

"Tell me about the banquet." Richard sat on her bed that evening as she put on her make-up.

"You won't believe whose concert it was! Adam Riley!"

"Really? I bet he was great."

Lauren turned to her father. "He was. They're good friends. And Tyler placed the top bid on my song. It was so beautiful, Dad. We went to Adam's club after and he introduced me to all his friends. He thinks it's great that I'm a teacher. All night long he bragged about me."

"I never would have guessed they were friends. Adam Riley seems down to earth, humble."

"Tyler invited me to dinner at his place with Adam tonight."

Richard rubbed her shoulders. "I like the idea of you hanging out with Adam."

Lauren frowned at her father.

"It's Tyler I don't trust, not you." He kissed the top of her head. "Although you do need to keep a handle on going out dancing and such."

"I know, Dad. I'll watch it."

○○

"Tabloids aren't worth worrying about. Most people don't take them seriously and they print whatever they like, saying it's from an unnamed source." Tyler turned to conversation more serious after he and Adam made jokes through dinner about the press.

"Funny they can make up a whole story about someone without even having a name." Lauren smiled at the piece of cheesecake Adam served her.

"That, my dear Angel, is a good thing." Adam sat beside her with his dessert. "Once they do, life changes. You won't be able to go anywhere without people staring, coming up to you. Your life is no longer your own."

Tyler patted Lauren's hand. "Don't worry. You can hang here for the rest of your life. I'll take care of you."

"That's sweet, but I have an interview next week for a full-time teaching position."

Adam and Tyler glanced at each other. "That's great, Angel. I hope all goes well." Adam took a bite before continuing. "Tyler says you have church tomorrow."

"Bright and early. I'm the Director of Children's Ministry. Sunday School at eight a.m. and then Children's Church at nine thirty."

"Sounds like a lot of responsibility for such a young woman."

"I took it on as a second job a few years ago. I had taught in the elementary class since high school, so when the position opened, Pastor asked if I was interested."

Adam smiled. "I'll never forget my fourth grade Sunday school teacher, Miss Sandy. Forties, short brown hair, and glasses. She was so passionate she cried every time we prayed."

"You attended church as a child?" Lauren grew excited over their common bond.

"Every week. Haven't been in years, but God and I are good friends. Once you're famous, it's difficult to go anywhere in public, especially to do something private like worship."

She turned her attention to Tyler. "Have you ever gone to church?"

"Nah." Tyler began clearing the dishes. "Too subdued for me. So, what's your other job? You said the church was your second job."

"I've worked closing shift at the church preschool since my freshman year in college. Two to six p.m. worked with my class schedule."

"There's excitement for you," Adam laughed. "Chasing little ones."

Lauren sighed. "I also get the privilege of cleaning. Vacuuming, mopping, sanitizing the bathroom."

"It's an honor to shape young minds." Adam patted Lauren's arm.

"You still work there?" Tyler put leftovers in the fridge without covering them.

"I can't afford to quit. It takes care of my car payment."

"What about the church?" Tyler sat back down at the table. "You get paid for that?"

Lauren laughed. "I'm on salary, so it probably amounts to $2.00 an hour."

Tyler nodded thoughtfully. "You went to college for how long?"

"But when I'm a teacher…" Lauren paused. "I'll still make a pathetic amount of money. But I'll have lots of breaks."

"And you'll be improving our world by teaching young minds that will one day grow to be leaders," Adam reassured her.

Tyler laughed. "And Mac and I will continue helping people escape from it."

Lauren raised her eyebrows. "And make a bundle doing it. Funny how that works."

As Tyler walked Lauren to her car, the gentle breeze made her shiver.

"Sorry for the talk about money." He wrapped his arm around her. "I didn't mean any disrespect."

Lauren nodded. "We come from completely different places, socially and economically."

Tyler opened her car door. "But you're forgetting, you might be the one."

Adam flipped through channels with the remote control as Tyler sank into the sofa.

"What is it about her? Is it odd that I enjoy hanging out with her even though we're not having sex? She won't even kiss me."

"Lauren is intelligent, sensitive, and compassionate, all rare qualities around Hollywood." Adam turned to Tyler. "The draw is Christ, my dear Zeus. True followers are few and far between. God's love radiates through them. It's a beautiful thing."

"She is a beautiful thing." Tyler closed his eyes, her beauty burned into his mind.

༄

As she drove to the interview, Lauren mentally reviewed the state standards, curriculum taught in the district, and classroom management ideas. Dressed in her professional three-piece skirt suit with her portfolio in hand, she entered the office confidently with a smile. This was the district she wanted. She had student taught with them and subbed for them. A job offer would be the perfect beginning to the summer.

After checking in with the receptionist, Lauren sat and flipped through her portfolio to pass the time. After a few minutes, she glanced up to find the receptionist staring at her. She smiled and picked up her phone.

No big deal, stay calm. Suddenly, another woman entered from a door by the front desk. She spoke to the receptionist, keeping an eye on Lauren the entire time.

Lauren put her head down and closed her eyes. *Oh, Lord, please let it not matter.*

On the way back to the assistant superintendent's office, every woman stared at her. The newspaper, folded to reveal her picture with Tyler, sat on the desk closest to the assistant superintendent's office.

"How was your interview?" Beth jumped to her feet when Lauren entered the room. She shook her head, slowly removing her sunglasses to reveal her red, puffy eyes.

"Nap time!" Beth turned off the TV and herded the kids to their mats.

"They recognized me." Lauren sat in the doorway of the two rooms as Beth rubbed the back of the last awake preschooler. "I looked great, felt confident, until the receptionist started staring. All the women in the office watched as I walked by. Then I saw Saturday's paper. I know they told the assistant superintendent. He showed no interest in me whatsoever."

Beth checked to make sure the child was asleep before moving closer to Lauren. "Why is it bad that they recognized you? Were you mean to someone?"

Lauren took a deep breath. "Promise you won't be mad that I didn't tell you?"

Beth wrinkled up her forehead. "I won't be mad. What didn't you tell me? And why?"

"The guy I've been seeing?"

"Yeah?"

"It's Tyler Stevens."

Beth's left eyebrow raised. "Tyler Stevens, the movie star?"

Lauren nodded.

"Are you kidding?"

Lauren shook her head.

"I thought he worked for your dad?"

"I told you I met him through my dad. Dad put in his pool. I picked Dad up at his house one day and met him. Tyler invited me to see him film at the mall, I had dinner at his house after I finished student teaching and we went to a charity benefit together. The reporters took pictures of me, which ended up on the front of the entertainment section." Beth stared motionless as she continued. "The secretaries recognized me and it ruined my chances of getting a job."

"I'm so sorry." Beth came over to hug her.

Lauren hung her head down and rested it on her knees. Tears rolled down her face. "This was my dream. Now it's crushed."

"Is there another district you could try?" Beth tried to encourage her.

"I've applied and haven't gotten called. It would end up the same." Lauren dried her tears on her t-shirt and sighed. "I don't blame them. Can you imagine if reporters found out? They can be total freaks. I guess I'll work here until they fire me or I'm too old to chase these little ones."

"I think we all feel that way sister. Don't worry, the reporters will never find you here!" Beth walked over and to get Lauren tissues off the counter. "Now, are we done being sad, because it's big news that you are dating a movie star. I want details or I might have to be mad at you for excluding me from your life."

Lauren smiled, wiping her tears. "Actually, I've been dying to tell you about it."

"Tyler Stevens." Beth put out her left hand. "Teaching." She put out her right hand. "Five years from now you will still have your teaching credential but you might not have Tyler Stevens. Think of all the memories you will have. When all the hype settles down, maybe you'll get hired."

Lauren nodded as Beth continued. "Who knows? Maybe you'll end up marrying Mr. Hollywood and never work another day in your life. You could get into acting too and…"

"You're going off the deep end now." Lauren laughed.

"Point is, you have no idea what God has planned."

"That's for sure."

Lauren called Tyler before the kids woke up.
"How you doing?" he asked when he answered the phone.
"You owe me dinner tonight."
"Why is that?"
"Our picture lost me a teaching job." Lauren said.
Tyler sighed. "Your interview. It didn't go so well?"
"I think you owe me dinner," Lauren stated again.
"I'll pick you up at 7 p.m. We can go wherever you want."

"Oh, Lauren." Tyler took her hands after she explained the interview. "I'm really sorry."

"God has a plan for good and will somehow work it out. I just didn't want to sit at home tonight and be depressed." She tilted her head and sighed "I may as well spend time with you since you ruined my life."

"Ouch." Tyler laughed. "There's a line I haven't heard in years and never thought it would come from you. You seem so mild mannered."

Lauren lifted her eyebrow. "Perhaps my mild mannered teacher days are over before they have begun."

The rest of dinner Tyler lifted her spirits with stories of his week. They were having such a good time Lauren didn't even realize people were staring until they walked to the car.

"I hope you're ready for your new life." He led her past the people pointing, snapping photos with their cell phones.

"Bring it, baby." She smiled, taking his hand in hers.

The night found them on the edge of the cliffs. Tyler grabbed a brown bag of something he had stopped to buy along the way. He helped her out of the car.

"Have a seat." Tyler motioned to the hood of the Corvette. She closed her eyes, inhaling the salty sea air, smiling at the rushing waves crashed on the rocks below. Peace slowly overcame her.

He slid beside Lauren with the small brown bag. Lauren laughed, taking her favorite chocolate brownie ice cream and a spoon from Tyler.

He held up his spoon. "But you have to share."

"Did you know this is my favorite?" She pulled off the lid.

Tyler leaned back on the windshield. "The great Zeus knows all."

"Thank you." Lauren scooped the first spoonful and passed the carton to Tyler.

"Anything for you." Tyler took his bite and held it so they could both partake.

She leaned back against the windshield with Tyler. The stars twinkled above as the ocean roared below. "It amazes me. God created all this and then cared enough to make me."

"You don't believe in the big bang theory, huh?" Tyler chiseled at the ice cream.

Lauren narrowed her eyes. "Do you?"

"Nah." Tyler gazed at the stars. "I figure if you believe in that we are all just sophisticated monkeys."

Lauren dug at her dessert. "Not an attractive thought, is it?"

"I don't have a problem thinking God is out there and created me. I have a problem believing He wants to have anything to do with me."

"But why would God make you if He didn't want anything to do with you?"

Tyler ate a bite. "Maybe we're like TV to Him. Something to watch, get His mind off work. But I do think my science teacher came from a monkey."

Lauren laughed. "That must be a pre-requisite for science teachers." They were silent for a minute before Lauren continued. "I hope my students see me as caring and sincere."

Tyler shook his head. "Funny that fame and fortune mean nothing to you. All you care about is helping others."

"What do you care about?" Lauren offered Tyler the ice cream.

"Money. Fame. Fortune."

"Money doesn't necessarily bring happiness."

"Has for me."

"You need to find other long-term things to make you happy."

He handed her the carton with a sigh. "I guess love would. But first I need to figure out what love is."

Lauren slowly worked at the ice cream as she spoke. "The Bible says love is patient, kind, doesn't envy or boast. It is not proud, rude, or self seeking. Love does not delight in evil, but rejoices in the truth. It believes all things, hopes all things, endures all things."

"Every day I receive letters from girls claiming to love me. Any relationship I have is about physical pleasure."

Her stomach turned at his brutal honesty. *His beliefs are so far from my own. Lord, how will this work?*

Putting the top on the half eaten container of ice cream, Lauren placed it back in the bag. "So, why am I here?"

"I like being with you."

Lauren nodded. "Thanks for taking me out tonight."

"I'm glad you told me to." Tyler brushed his hand to Lauren's cheek. "Did I mention tonight how beautiful you are?"

Her heart raced at his touch. Closing her eyes and resting her cheek on his soft hand, the rush of the waves and cool breeze brought peace upon her.

He wrapped his arms around her and she sank into them. His heartbeat relaxed her. She moved her hand over his muscular chest. He ran his hand up and down her arm, warming her.

I gave up my career for him. He cares. He really seems to care about me.

Tyler kissed the top of her head. "Let's go to my beach house and hang out. We could sit by the fire on the deck, snuggle under a blanket."

She lifted her hand to his cheek. He turned to kiss it. The sound of the waves intensified as he turned to her lips.

Lauren suddenly realized where her thoughts were taking her and pulled away. "I need to go home."

"C'mon." Tyler gently kissed her face, pulling her close to him. "Not so soon."

Lauren put her hands on Tyler's chest and gently pushed him away. "Tyler. No."

He sat up. "You can't deny that you want me."

Lauren slid off the hood. She walked across the cliffs to a deserted spot and sat down facing the ocean. *Oh, God, help me. I'm afraid I won't be able to control myself. Help me be strong.*

"I enjoy spending time with you." Tyler sat behind her. "I find you extremely attractive and I can't keep my hands off you. It's got to be worth something."

"I'm flattered." Lauren stared into the dark void. "I'm attracted to you, but I won't change my mind."

Tyler took her hand. "Your ice cream is melting."

Instead of sarcasm, she found sincerity. Tyler helped her up and she followed him back to the car.

Lauren crawled into bed, exhausted. She reluctantly opened her Bible to the book of Mark. Yawning and rubbing her eyes, she began to read in chapter one.

"When Jesus was walking by Lake Galilee, he saw Simon and his brother Andrew throwing nets into the lake because they were fishermen. Jesus said to them, 'Come and follow me and I will make you fish for people.' So Simon and Andrew immediately left their nets and followed him."

The tears came as she prayed. "Lord, I've worked so hard. I don't understand…"

Come, follow me

"I trust You, Lord. Please, take my life and make it Yours. Lead me wherever You desire me to go."

She imagined Jesus wiping her tears and holding her tight as she fell asleep.

Chapter 9

"You know what sounds good?" Lauren reclined on Tyler's leather sofa. Tyler channel surfed as Adam read a book.

"That new horror movie with what's his face?" Adam suggested.

"Are you kidding?" Tyler spat with disgust. "Dean Hardy, that snobby, over paid ..."

"As I was saying," Lauren raised her voice, "you know what sounds good to me?"

"Probably that nighttime drama with the cute twenty-year-old." Adam continued reading.

Tyler flipped through the channels. "You've really been into nature shows lately."

"Chips and salsa," Lauren shouted. "I want chips and salsa."

"Put it on the list." Tyler motioned to the kitchen. "The maid can get them tomorrow."

"I want them now. I'm having a craving."

Adam glanced up with one eyebrow raised. "A craving, huh?"

Tyler turned to Lauren. "That's not fair. I asked first and I'm pretty sure I said please."

Lauren stood. "Whatever. You two stay here and enjoy yourselves. I'm going to find an open Mexican restaurant."

"Run to the store." Tyler focused back on the TV. "It's not that hard. I've done it a few times."

"I want the hot, salty tortilla chips with the thick, home-made salsa. It's not the same as Tostitos and Pace's."

"Picky, picky." Adam stretched as he laid down his novel. "Next thing you know, we won't be famous enough for you."

"Come on, you guys," Lauren pleaded. "Let's do something besides sit at home deciding what to watch. Aren't you tired of being couch potatoes?"

"I'm actually enjoying myself. How 'bout you Mac?"

"Couldn't be happier."

"Fine." Lauren grabbed her purse. "See ya."

She was pulling out of the driveway before they came out of the house to join her.

"You two protecting my house next month while I'm gone?" Tyler scooped chunky salsa onto the hot tortilla chip. The three of them and one couple were the only people in the restaurant.

"How long are you gone?" Adam crunched the ice from his drink.

"Four weeks, give or take."

"We could do some serious damage in that amount of time." Adam winked at Lauren. "Think Dad will be okay with you staying at Tyler's?"

"As long as he's out of the country," Lauren laughed. "You, Mr. Riley, can do no wrong. He would entrust the safety of his daughter to you any day of the week."

Adam nudged Tyler. "See? I could teach you a thing or two about getting along with the parents."

"Yeah, well, I never thought I'd go for the pool digger's daughter." Tyler turned to Lauren. "No offense."

Lauren grinned. "Never thought I'd hook up with a self-centered, egotistical…"

"Just clean up after yourself and don't break anything," Tyler interrupted.

"Don't worry." Adam patted his back. "We'll make sure the maid comes before you return."

"I want to take you shopping this week," Tyler stated when she dropped them back off at his house.

"For what?"

"A new cell. I need you on my network so it won't be expensive calling you."

Lauren started to refuse when he spoke again.

"You also need one you can text with. I don't want to wait weeks for your response."

Lauren hit his stomach with the back of her hand. "I do fine with what I got."

Tyler laughed, rubbing his stomach. "Think of it as saving me money. You'd be doing me a favor."

Lauren batted her eyelashes at him. "Well then, anything for you, Mr. Stevens."

༄

"I'm outside on the patio," Adam called when Lauren entered the house.

Jazz was playing softly on the stereo, lights in the family room and kitchen were dimmed and a spicy, mouth-watering aroma wafted through the screen door.

"Is that carne asada I smell?" Lauren smiled at the sight of Adam in front of the barbecue.

"Si senorita," Adam responded in his best terrible Mexican accent. "You bring the chips and salsa?"

"Yes, sir. Fresh from the corner Mexican restaurant." Lauren found bowls in the cupboard to pour them in. "It's been a long day."

"Oh yeah? Did you have a producer on you all day about finishing your new album in three weeks?"

"How did you know?" Lauren emerged from the kitchen.

"Well, my day was equally terrible." Adam flipped the meat.

"It was?" The table was set neatly with two place settings and all the toppings for the tacos. She arranged the chips and salsa in the middle of the table. "Did you have to put up with two-year-olds screaming all day, three-year-olds not quite making it to the toilet and four-year-olds hitting each other and yourself?"

Adam laughed. "I have the bruises to prove it."

Lauren stretched and relaxed in the chair, kicking off her shoes. "Thank the Lord for Fridays and relaxing with friends."

"Amen to that. So, how do you like your meat cooked? Well or very well?"

"That's perfect." Lauren's stomach grumbled. "Let's eat."

Adam talked about this person and that song. Lauren watched his every gesture, listened to his every word. She felt herself smiling long before he noticed.

"What?" Adam rubbed his chin and nose. "Is something hanging?"

"You are so handsome, smart and caring. Why don't you have a girlfriend?"

Adam took a bite of his taco. "I had my party years and came to realize the only type of relationship worth having is one that is significant and caring. My career and travels limit my possibility for settling down."

"Would you give it up for the right woman?"

"Until now I have only known women in love with Mac the Musician. I would give it up in an instant for someone that found love and comfort in Adam the person."

Lauren smiled. "He's a pretty great guy. Any woman would be happy, and privileged, to have him."

Adam scooped salsa on a chip. "And you? Not even Zeus, the master of love, has stolen your heart yet. Why is that?"

"I can't commit to a non-Christian. The Bible says it's wrong and I have experienced the effects of it in the past. I won't compromise my beliefs for any man."

"If Tyler became a Christian tomorrow?" Adam raised an eyebrow.

"I would want to know he did it for himself and not me. Then I'd take it slow. Any man worthy of me will wait."

"Cheers to that." Adam raised his glass. "I like a woman firmly planted in her beliefs."

"I haven't always been." Lauren watched the chunks of ice float around her drink. "I wish in so many ways I could take back my mistakes. I promised God I would start over and wait. I want to do it, for God, my husband-to-be and myself."

He sipped his drink before speaking. "I was raised in the Christian church, accepted Jesus at a young age. My brother and parents died in a car accident when I was sixteen. I turned to the church with my sadness and doubts. Instead of helping me through it, they shunned me for questioning God and His plan." Lauren saw a void in Adam's eyes. "Families brought meals for a while, but no one offered me spiritual or emotional support. That's when my heart hardened."

Lauren pondered Adam's statement. "Against religion or God?"

"Mostly the religious people. I stopped praying for a while because all I could say was 'Why?' I just grew frustrated when He didn't answer."

"It's a shame when people ruin church for others." Lauren lowered her gaze. "When my mother passed, our congregation supported me and my father and helped us keep it together."

"You don't speak of your mother much."

"A part of me wants to pretend it's not real, like she's just away and will come back one day." She traced the rim of her glass with her finger. "Sometimes I'm afraid the more I talk about her, the more I'll miss her."

Adam nodded. "I understand."

Lauren closed her eyes to push back the tears. "I know I'll see her again, but I miss the closeness I had with her. I miss telling her about my day, getting her advice."

"Nothing can replace a mother's love."

"No. My dad is wonderful, but it's not the same."

"Tell me about your father."

Lauren automatically smiled. "He's a great man. He struggled with depression and drinking after her death, but he pulled himself together. He's hard working and honest, faithful to God." Lauren paused for a minute, looking in Adam's eyes. "I know he'll always be there for me."

"Not very many people have that with their parents."

"I worry about him sometimes. I want him to be happy, but I know he still misses my mom. It's been four years now and he's never dated. He still has that look in his eyes most of the time that he's thinking of her, wishing she was there."

"I'm sure it's hard. He thought they'd be together for the rest of his life. It takes time." Lauren nodded as Adam spoke but remained quiet. "Tell me about your work at church." "Everyone is grateful of the wonderful job I do, but few are willing to help. I spent every break this week calling people to find teachers for Sunday. All I got was excuses. I can't do it alone."

"They shouldn't expect you to. That's taking advantage of you."

Lauren looked down quietly at her water with a frown.

"What's wrong Angel?"

Lauren rested her forehead on her hand. "It's been this way for months now. I figured I would leave the ministry once I got a full-time job. But since that didn't work, I'm stuck needing the money. It's exhausting, worrying about everyone and everything, running around picking up the pieces for others. I go months without attending church. I need to be fed too."

Adam stood up and walked behind Lauren. He gently began to massage her shoulders and neck.

"These shoulders are too small to carry the weight of the world. Angel, you're too young to let your life go by without enjoying it." She felt the tension in her shoulders slowly released at his gentle but firm massage. "I would love to say I will take care of you, but the truth is, you need to take care of yourself." Adam's words immediately brought tears to her eyes. "Make sure you are communicating with God. Maybe He called you to something else and you were too busy to listen."

Adam continued for several minutes working out the knots in her shoulders. "Your faith reminded me of the relationship I had with Him. I thank you for that." Adam gently took Lauren's hand in his and kissed it. "That's why I call you Angel. I honestly believe God sent you to get us on track with Him."

She looked up at him. "Us?"

"Me, Tyler, heck, maybe all of Hollywood."

Lauren frowned. "That's an awful high standard to live up to."

"Don't worry." Adam gently stroked her cheek with his hand. "You do it quite naturally."

At two a.m. Lauren got up to go to the bathroom. When she settled back into Tyler's bed the distant sound of a piano mesmerized her. She followed the melody downstairs to the entertainment room. Snuggling with a blanket on the couch across from Adam and his keyboard, she watched his fingers glide across the keys. Amazing grace, how sweet the sound. She closed her eyes, allowing the spirit of God to fill her. Adam's singing was quiet but powerful. At first Lauren was intimidated by his beautiful voice, but as she entered the presence of God, she had to sing. For a half hour Adam played old familiar hymns and they sang. The last was Lauren's favorite. By the time the song was done, tears rolled down her cheeks.

"Funny how you never realize how far you are from God until you come back." Adam slowly turned to face Lauren, wiping the tears from his cheeks. "At eighteen I moved to New York. The only peace I felt was in front of a piano." Adam moved to the couch beside Lauren. "Bartending allowed me access to the piano before or after my shift. One night the owner heard me and asked me to play the next evening. Within six months I was playing six nights a week. I sent money back to my grandma and sister, making my situation more glamorous than it was so my grandmother would be proud and not worry."

Adam lifted Lauren's feet and allowed her to stretch her legs out over his. "At twenty, I got a gig playing in a small, but well-known bar. After several months, a man in his late thirties would come often and always tip big." Adam rubbed Lauren's feet as he spoke. "One night he dropped his business card in my glass. He was a big time record producer interested in hearing me in his studio. He introduced me to all the important music people and I signed a record deal with him. We worked such insane hours, I moved into his penthouse to make it easier. He included me in his life of partying and he lavished me with gifts. My own apartment, new clothes, fast cars and eventually a grand piano. One night he made a pass at me. His offer didn't seem so bizarre after all he had done for me."

Adam walked toward the kitchen.

Oh Lord, what do I say? I don't believe it. Not Adam. I don't know what to do...

Confess your sins to each other and pray for each other so that you may be healed.

He returned with two bottles of water, handing her one.

"It was like living someone else's life that year. I stopped talking to my grandma and sister. I took care of them financially, but I couldn't stand to call." Adam took a long drink. "I cared about him and we had great times together, but I didn't believe our relationship was right. A year after we met,

I went on tour to promote my second album and swore I'd never come back."

Lauren took his hand in hers.

"I made up excuses when he called why I couldn't talk. I respected him professionally, but I had to be done with our relationship. I settled in LA after my tour and began a new life. The money flowed and I signed with a new record producer. After several months he tracked me down. He screamed at me over the phone, asking where my loyalty was. I told him I had moved on, that I wanted a normal life. When he began to cry, I realized that was normal for him."

Tears appeared in Adam's eyes. "Three years later a friend from New York called to tell me Jim was dying. I spent three days by his side. He was skin and bones, too weak to do anything on his own. We sat through the night talking, laughing and I saw the generous, caring man that had been my best friend and was grateful for the man and singer he helped me become."

Adam wiped a single tear that fell. "He died of AIDS on that third day."

Lauren's heart dropped. Tears welled up in her eyes.

"I've been tested. God was with me, despite my disobedience and rebellion. I went back to LA a changed man, giving up old habits, determined to start anew. God gave me a second chance and I was grateful."

Lauren wiped the tears from her eyes. "It's good you realized you needed to change."

"I wasn't being Christian, just careful. I only prayed when I needed things, did good for Him with my fundraisers, but didn't make it personal. The last month I have read my Bible and prayed everyday. I feel God working in my life and heart again."

A life changed, for Your glory. Joy filled her as she hugged him. "God is good."

"All the time." Adam embraced her tightly.

༄

"Who's that beautiful blonde sleeping in my bed?" Tyler's chipper voice made her head pound.

"That would be me." She rubbed her eyes. "What time is it?"

"We just finished shooting. Late here, early there."

Lauren moaned as she looked at the clock. Her eyes burned.

"You and Mac party all night?"

"We stayed up late talking." She yawned.

"About me, no doubt."

Lauren laughed. "Get over yourself, Tyler." Lauren snuggled the blankets around her. "How's Africa?"

"Hot and smelly. Lots of bugs."

"Seen any lions?"

"A couple. Elephants and giraffes are everywhere."

"Are you taking pictures?"

"Yes, Mom. I'll send you some later. How are you?"

"Good." Lauren closed her eyes. "Glad it's the weekend. I'm tired of kids. I think I need a vacation."

"Come to Africa," Tyler encouraged her. "It seems like an amazing place. Lots of sightseeing, if you have time."

"Don't tempt me."

"But I'm evil," Tyler joked. "Isn't that what I'm supposed to do?"

"According to my father, yes. He thinks I'm staying in the guest room. He would flip if he knew I was in your bed."

"Even though I'm not there? It's not right," Tyler argued.

"It's the thought that counts." Lauren rolled over and pulled the sheets around her.

"Oh, really? And what have you been thinking?"

"That I need to go back to sleep until my eyes stop burning."

Tyler laughed. "One more question."

"What?" Lauren rubbed her temples.

"Do you miss me?" Tyler's serious tone surprised Lauren. *Was he insecure?* "Of course. It's not the same without you here."

"So, what did you and Mac talk about all night?"

"Honestly, Tyler, jealousy doesn't become you. You said one more question. I'm going back to sleep now. Text me when it's morning."

She uncovered her Bible while digging for her hairbrush. *Adam gave me great advice. I need to start listening to God.*

Sitting on Tyler's bed, she was reading her Bible when Adam knocked on the door.

"Good morning. I was beginning to wonder if you were getting up this morning."

Lauren smiled. "Just taking my time. After all, it's Saturday."

"Yes, it is." Adam lay across the foot of the bed. "Everything okay?"

"Fine."

"I was worried after last night. I didn't know how you'd react."

Lauren shut her Bible. "No, I appreciate you sharing with me. It means a lot to know you trust me."

"It's not something I publicize, but I felt I should tell you."

"It can be healing to share your experiences, especially with another Christian. You can encourage and pray for each other."

Adam nodded, looking down at the bed. "You don't think any differently of me?"

"I respect you more, for going through all you have and still being close to God."

Adam looked up, his eyes meeting Lauren's. "How about pancakes for breakfast?"

"Only if they have chocolate chips in them." Lauren smiled.

Adam needed a birthday gift for a friend and Lauren, with her shopping expertise, offered her services for the low fee of lunch. Along the way Adam insisted on purchasing Lauren an outfit here and a dress there to show his appreciation. She didn't want him to buy her so many clothes, but everything he asked her to try on she loved.

"No, Adam," she insisted at the fifth store. "You've bought me enough."

"Don't hurt my feelings. I'm making up for all the birthdays I missed."

Lauren shook her head, surrendering the sundress to him.

On their way home, Adam turned to Lauren. "I had fun today."

"Me too." She put her hand on his shoulder. "What do you say we get all dressed up tonight and go out to dinner?"

"Sounds like a date."

"One condition. I pay."

"I don't think so, Angel."

"Yes. After all you bought for me today I think you can let me buy you dinner."

Adam frowned. "I'm an old-fashioned kind of guy."

Lauren grabbed the back of his neck and shook his head playfully. "Get over it!"

In between putting up her hair and doing her make-up for dinner she filled Tyler in on the events of the day. The pictures he sent of giraffes and elephants cracked her up.

"Hot plans tonight?" Tyler texted.

"Dinner with Adam," she responded.

"Better not look too sexy," Tyler warned.

She checked herself out in her new olive-colored dress in his bathroom mirror. She ran her hands down her waist.

"Saving the best for you" Lauren smiled as she responded.

Adam was in the kitchen getting a glass of water when she found him.

"Well?" She spun.

"A perfect fit." Adam straightened his tie. "I'm not sure that I deserve the company of such a beautiful lady."

"Oh, I'd say you're handsome enough." Lauren took his arm.

They had just started looking over the menu when the manager appeared at their table with a bottle of wine. "Mr. Riley." He extended his hand. "It is a pleasure to have you in our fine dining establishment."

"Thank you." Adam shook his hand. "It's our pleasure to be here tonight. My friend, Miss Drake, has been raving for some time about your restaurant."

The manager turned to Lauren. "Why, thank you." Then he turned back to Adam. "I have taken the liberty of bringing you our finest wine. Of course, anything you and Miss Drake desire tonight is on the house." He opened the wine and let Adam smell the cork. After the manager poured the wine and left them alone, Lauren chuckled.

"I guess I should take you out more often."

"Sorry." Adam shrugged. "Can't help being famous."

"Dessert. Ice cream. My treat."

"Agreed. I'll stay in the car."

"I'm fine." Lauren put out her hand as Adam started to pour her another glass of wine. The waiter had taken away their empty plates a few minutes before.

He set the bottle on the table. "How is it that a beautiful girl like you didn't meet the perfect guy at your Christian college?"

"I was so terrible shy, I went through most of my college years without speaking to anyone in my classes, let alone boys. A friend set me up my senior year. He wasn't a Christian, but gave me the love and attention I craved. I fell head over heels for him. After a month he had me convinced someday we would get married."

Adam looked down into his glass as she continued.

"After six months Mr. Wonderful moved on. The kicker was he'd never broken up with his previous girlfriend. We were polar opposites, but my heart was broken. I had given myself to him thinking he would be the one. Shelly and I started clubbing, and though I told myself each guy would be different, they all ended up the same. I was the one hurt by my stupidity. Praise God for protecting me from being hurt and from diseases."

"You've been tested?" Adam asked.

Lauren nodded. "It still haunts me. I see their faces, how I dishonored myself and God."

"Have you asked God's forgiveness?" Adam took Lauren's hand. She nodded. "Then it's Satan bringing it back. God has forgotten it, Angel. He has no recollection of it."

She sighed. "Now you know the skeletons in my closet."

Adam squeezed her hands. "I think it's time we buried them, don't you think? Let's go by your house, pick up any memorabilia of your past, stop by the store for our ice cream and have a bonfire at Tyler's beach house. What do you say?"

She nodded slowly. "Let's do it."

An hour later they fed the blazing fire old love letters, pictures, diaries, and phone book pages as they passed the quart of chocolate brownie ice cream between them.

"This is Andy." She held up the last photo in her box. "The last guy I dated, a Christian that helped straighten out my life. He accepted me for who I was. A part of me thought we might end up together."

"What happened?" Adam passed her the carton.

She dropped the picture in the fire, taking the ice cream from Adam as the fire curled the edges and burned it. "He became a missionary. Went off to save the world."

"You didn't want to go with him?"

Lauren shook her head as she handed it back. "There are enough people around here that need to be saved."

"Amen to that." Adam lifted his full spoon. "Cheers. To God, Who forgives and forgets. May we do the same."

"Cheers." Lauren raised hers. "And to friends that help us along the way."

∽

Adam snuck in the classroom as Lauren taught Sunday School. The second graders were on the edge of their seats as she dramatically told the story of Elijah and the prophets of Bali, cheering when God sent fire from heaven.

"They really like you." Adam helped clean up crayons and papers after the students left.

Lauren gathered her Bible and lesson. "They're a great group of kids. I've known some of them since they were two. Almost seems we've grown up together."

"You're a great teacher. The way you involved them in the story and relayed it to them at their level was awesome."

"God gives us all gifts." Lauren smiled humbly.

Adam waited in Lauren's locked office while she delivered the snack for Children's Church and checked on the teachers. She returned right before the service. Once worship began they slipped into the back of the sanctuary.

Lauren respected the fact that Adam didn't want a big to-do about him being at church. They hoped if they walked in late and left before dismissal, no one would notice.

Peace filled her as they worshipped together. Usually Sunday morning was a stressful time for her, but having Adam around calmed her. It was after the service when they were picnicking in the park that she shared that with Adam.

"Thank you. That's quite a compliment." They started eating their sandwiches before Adam spoke again. "I had reservations about going to church, but I enjoyed it today. Hearing the sermon, the music, it brought back the good memories and feelings."

"Good. Maybe we can go to church together more often."

Adam smiled. "I'm not sure. That might cut into my sleeping in on Sundays."

Lauren laughed. "Oh, yeah. I forgot, Mr.-All-I-need-is-three-hours-a-night."

"It sounded like a good excuse," Adam teased. "I could handle going to church more regularly. Maybe we should break the news to your pastor next week. It could turn into a circus if word gets out."

"Good point. We'll do that." She finished her turkey sandwich and put the trash back in the basket before she lay down on the blanket. She smiled at first and then sighed.

He gently brushed the hair away from her face. "What's the sigh for?"

She opened her eyes and turned toward him. "Only one thing is missing to make this the perfect weekend."

"What's that?"

"Tyler. I wish he wasn't so far away."

Adam grinned. "He'll be home soon."

Adam offered to go with Lauren to talk to Pastor Jim, but she thought it would be better if she went alone. When she arrived at church that evening at five thirty, the door to his office was open.

After exchanging greetings, Lauren sat on the couch across from him. "Did you get to hear the sermon today, or were you in Children's Church?"

"I was there. In fact, I had a friend visiting church today."

"You did?" Pastor seemed surprised. "And you didn't introduce me?"

"That's what I wanted to talk to you about." After keeping it a secret for so long, it seemed weird talking about it. "His name is Adam. Adam Riley."

"Adam Riley," he repeated. "The musician?"

Lauren nodded slowly.

"How did this come about?"

Once she explained her meeting of Tyler and then Adam, Pastor Jim questioned her about being tempted to be impure.

"I've been very straight forward with Tyler about my stand on pre-marital sex. He's accepted it. We're just friends."

"I'm proud of you for taking a stand."

"Adam would like to attend church here, but he's afraid of the press finding out."

Pastor patted Lauren's arm. "I will do whatever is necessary to give him a place to worship that is free from distractions."

Lauren grinned. "Thank you. We appreciate it."

"What about Tyler? Will he be worshipping here also?"

"Right now he's in Africa. I've been praying for him. I don't believe he knows the Lord yet."

Pastor Jim nodded. "Just remember, God doesn't want us yoked with unbelievers."

"I know." Lauren smiled. "I appreciate your concern."

"You know I care. I am always here for you."

"Thank you, Pastor." She stood. "Off to choir practice."

He gave her a hug before she left. "God will bless you if you follow His commands, Lauren. Remember that."

Lauren leaned back in the front pew of the sanctuary staring at the cross.

"Thank you, God, for today," she prayed quietly. "Thank you for Adam and the relaxing weekend we had together. Thank you for the privilege of leading the children." So many little things had gone wrong at practice, but it didn't bother her. Last week she had been so stressed she raised her voice most of the time. Tonight she laughed when they turned the wrong way during the dance and knocked each other over. They were so precious singing about Jesus. That was all that mattered.

The door of the sanctuary opened. Lauren turned, surprised to see Adam.

"What are you doing here?"

Adam sat in the pew behind her. "I showed up a while ago. After I spoke with Pastor Jim, he took me to the sound room to watch. I loved it."

Lauren laughed, shaking her head. "We were definitely not at our best tonight."

"They were adorable," Adam argued. "Tone and pitch don't matter quite as much when you're so cute."

"Is that your personal philosophy?"

"Hey now." Adam pushed her playfully.

"Did you have a good talk with Pastor Jim?"

"Yes. He's a great man. I'll tell you about it over ice cream."

"You know the way to a woman's heart." Lauren took his hand to help her up.

"I told him it's been a while since I attended church and I enjoyed myself today," Adam said in the ice cream parlor. "He agreed that I should be able to attend church freely and it should be an experience of worshipping God, not screaming fans. Next week he said he'd gently present it to the congregation. At the end of the service, I agreed to play some hymns."

Lauren laughed. "I love when Pastor Jim 'gently presents' something to the congregation. They're in for some lecturing."

"We all need a good lecture now and then, right?"

"I'm getting pretty good at giving lectures. I tell you, preschoolers don't listen very well."

"Pastor Jim mentioned his concern about you not teaching elementary school."

Lauren dug into her sundae. "It's more disappointing than anything. But it's a choice I made."

"It's illegal for them not to hire you based on your popularity. I have a lawyer and I'm sure…"

Lauren shook her head. "I don't want to go that way. It's not worth forcing them to give me a job." Lauren sighed. "The biggest disappointment is I wanted to move on my own. Working at the preschool even full time wouldn't be enough to pay rent and my car payment. God's timing is perfect, right?"

"I guess we should be flattered that you would give up your dream career for our friendship."

"I have the rest of my life to teach." Lauren scooped up her ice cream. "Some days I think you and Tyler might disappear from my life as quickly as you came."

He took her hand in his. "We'll be here for a while, trust me. I think we are growing attached to you."

Just then her phone rang. It was Tyler, proving Adam's point.

Chapter 10

Monday morning Lauren was up at four fifteen to shower, dress and to open the preschool at six a.m.

"You look beat," Beth said when she arrived.

"Thank you." Lauren smiled tiredly. "I thought I was hiding it well."

"Out with Mr. Hollywood late last night?"

"Actually, he's in Africa. Adam and I spent the weekend at Tyler's house."

"Oh, hanging with Mr. Music while your man is away. He's probably keeping an eye on you for Mr. Hollywood," Beth teased.

"You know, they have names. Tyler and Adam."

"Right," Beth laughed. "Because they are normal people like us."

"They are."

"And what did the normal people do this weekend, those that weren't in Africa?"

"We barbecued, talked about our lives, went shopping, out to dinner. Adam even came to church with me."

"Well, that is pretty normal," Beth agreed, "If you throw in laundry, dishes and cleaning."

Lauren smiled slyly as she started out of the room. "That's what the maid is for."

At recess, Lauren stayed inside picking up while the kids were outside with Beth. She called Adam to see if he wanted to have lunch together.

"Adam's phone." Someone answered after the second ring.

"Hi, this is Lauren."

"Ah, Lauren dear, this is Michael, Adam's assistant. How are you, beautiful?"

"Fine." *Have I met Michael? Why does he act like he knows me?*

"Adam's singing at the moment, but he should be done in a few. Can I have him call you back, dear?"

"Sure. Thank you."

"No problem, sugar. He'll talk to you soon."

"I just talked to Michael, Adam's assistant," Lauren announced to Beth as she walked outside. "You're right, they aren't normal people."

Beth smiled. "Glad you're coming to terms with that. I just can't figure out why you're still around here wiping noses and bottoms."

"I need a job."

"Oh, please." Beth shook her head. "You mean to tell me Tyler hasn't offered to take care of you in his little mansion on the hill?"

"I'm not that kind of person, Beth." Lauren set her cell phone on the picnic table while she tied a little boy's shoe. "I can take care of myself."

"Love the new phone." Beth picked it up for an examination. "Mr. Hollywood get it for you?"

"Yeah, so he could text and call for cheaper when he's gone."

Just then, Lauren's phone rang. Beth grinned.

"Lauren's phone," she answered. "This is her assistant, Beth, speaking."

Lauren tried to grab it away, but Beth moved too fast.

"Not too bad, Mr. Riley. Lauren and I are catching a few rays before it gets too hot today." Beth winked at Lauren who was shaking her head in disbelief.

"Please hold and I'll check."

Beth smiled, handing the phone to Lauren. "I like him. Quite a funny guy."

Lauren sat at the table. "Sorry about that."

Adam laughed. "I guess I deserve it, having Michael answer my calls. They just don't allow me to have my phone while recording."

"I'm sorry. I didn't know…"

"No big deal, Angel. You ran away this morning before we could talk."

"I had to open. I didn't want to wake you up when I left at five a.m."

"I appreciate that. I should be done here around two. How about lunch?"

"Sounds good." Lauren smiled.

"Can you be back at Tyler's by one thirty? I'll have a limo pick you up."

"Sure. Thanks." Lauren hung up and shook her head. "Yeah, not normal."

"Promise me one thing." Beth's tone turned serious as she took both Lauren's hands in hers. "If you ever marry rich and famous, hire me as your personal assistant. I'm really good with hair, make-up. I can keep your schedule, make plans for you."

"You don't want to be stuck here forever wiping noses and bottoms?" Lauren laughed.

Beth smiled at her. "Certainly you could pay me more than ten bucks an hour and I would just have to kiss your butt, not wipe it."

The excitement hit when they pulled into the recording studio parking lot. When the limo driver opened the door, a short man in his early thirties with blonde hair quickly approached the car.

"Hi, Lauren." He extended his hand. "I'm Michael. It's truly a pleasure to meet you. Adam speaks so highly of you."

"Thank you." She felt her cheeks blush.

"I'll take you inside to him. You'll need to wear this." He put a pass around her neck that read VISITOR.

The hallways of the studio were wallpapered with recording artists' pictures and platinum and gold records. Michael pointed at Adam's as they passed. She tried to count how many platinum compared to gold, but Michael's brisk pace prevented her from taking everything in. Every person that passed them greeted Michael and smiled at Lauren.

He opened one door and another. Suddenly they were in a dim room. She heard Adam singing before she saw him through the glass window. He played the piano on the other side of the glass and sang. The people sitting at the sound board wore headphones and adjusted this and that.

Adam Riley, famous singer. His concerts sell out in less than an hour, his albums are top sellers. And we spent all weekend hanging out. No, he's not ordinary.

His singing entranced her though she hadn't heard the song before. Adam played with his head down, sang with his eyes closed. When he finished, he sighed, shaking his head.

"Okay, Mac," one of the guys spoke into a mic. "That's a wrap."

Slowly Adam stood and stretched. His frown turned into a smile when he spotted Lauren. "There's the most beautiful woman in the world."

The men at the soundboard turned to look at Lauren for the first time. Adam breezed into the room and introduced Lauren to everyone before whisking her away.

"I thought I'd never get out of there," Adam whispered once they were halfway down the hall.

"I love your new song."

"I did too, until I sang it for hours." Adam nodded at another singer that waved as they passed. "It turned out good. I guess I wasn't in the working mood today."

"Me neither. It's hard to be motivated when you have to get up so darn early."

"What time did you go to work this morning anyway?" Adam placed his arm around her and veered her to the side to avoid people passing them at high speed.

"I opened today, so I had to leave at five fifteen."

"Aren't the children still asleep at that hour?" Adam teased.

"Some of them are pretty out of it. The younger ones are actually very active at that time. I'm the fortunate one to open Mondays and Wednesdays during the summer."

"Sorry I kept you up, but if you would have just lost the card game, you would have got to bed earlier."

They arrived at Adam's car as his cell phone rang.

"Well, hello there beautiful!" Adam opened the door for Lauren as he greeted the person on the phone with enthusiasm.

He climbed in the driver's seat. "Tomorrow's no good I'm recording all week. Maybe by Friday. Noon? Sure, that sounds fine. I'll call when I land."

Adam excitedly pulled out of the lot. "A good friend is in Vegas from back east. I'm going to see her on Friday."

"That sounds like fun."

Adam turned to her with a mischievous grin. "Come with me. We'd have a great time. You would love Georgia."

"Georgia Tates?" *I shouldn't be surprised.*

"We were pals in New York. You have to go. Her concerts are always fabulous."

Lauren sighed. "I can't. I have to work. We're short-handed right now."

Adam was quiet while brainstorming. "What if you open? Could you leave by twelve? I could schedule our lunch for later. The flight isn't that long."

"Of course, because you have a private jet."

"Of course." Adam stopped talking as Lauren shook her head. "What?"

"I was trying to convince Beth today that you and Tyler are normal people, but you're not. It's finally hitting me how rich and famous you both are. I don't know that I fit into your world."

"C'mon, Angel, you don't think you 'fit in'? I thought you had as much fun as I did this weekend."

Lauren seemed frustrated. "It's not you, Adam. It's the whole Hollywood scene. That's not me. I have a great time with you, but all the wealth makes me a little uncomfortable. I grew up learning that you had to work hard for your money."

Adam chuckled. "And I don't work hard?"

"You do. I didn't mean that," Lauren said. "It's just growing up we had food on the table, but seldom went out to eat. I had nice clothes, but we didn't shop in the fancy stores. Family vacations were camping because a hotel was too expensive. I never realized this as a kid, but now I understand it. I know teaching will be enough to pay my bills, but that's about it. I'm not meant to have a lot of money."

As they parked in front of the restaurant, Adam turned off the engine. "None of us are, Angel. Sure, I have people to bring me lunch, clean my house, and drive me places. But I work long hours during production and tour. Sometimes my head pounds from all the decisions I have to make in a day. Every penny I make belongs to God. At night I thank Him for His blessings and ask Him to guide me through the next day." He gently took her hand in his. "Money makes life a little easier, and I love to spoil others with gifts."

Lauren squeezed his hand. "I'll ask Beth to switch shifts on Friday. I can probably leave by eleven."

"Great. We'll have a wonderful time."

Adam excused himself to go to the restroom after the waitress seated them. Shannon, the director, answered when Lauren called.

"I have the opportunity to go out of town this weekend. I was wondering if I could open on Friday instead of closing."

"Fine with me. You just have to convince Beth to give up her early weekend. You want to talk to her?"

"Sure." People had been staring at her since she walked in with Adam. She took a deep breath and sat up straighter.

"What's going on girlfriend? You calling from the limo phone?"

"No, from a fancy restaurant. Can you switch shifts on Friday?"

"What's so pressing that you can't close? Mr. Hollywood coming home?"

"Adam invited me to Vegas on his private jet to have lunch with his good friend, Georgia Tates."

"Oh, my gosh!" Beth laughed. "It keeps getting better, doesn't it?"

"I think so. I know you want me to go and have a great time. I'm trying to get over the whole rich and famous thing."

"That's right, make the most of it. Just remember, when you need a personal assistant, I'm the one suited for the job."

"Without a doubt." Lauren shook her head at the ridiculousness of the thought.

⁓

A hostess served drinks and snacks throughout the flight. Lauren had the remote to the music playing in the cabin. It seemed the flight had just begun when they were landing. A limo picked them up on the runway and they were off to meet Georgia. "We're eating lunch at the hotel. I figured you would want to take a nap right after."

Lauren smiled and nodded. She was exhausted, having hardly slept the night before because of the anticipation.

The limo parked in front of the most prestigious hotel in Vegas. Lauren's heart beat faster. "This is where we're staying?"

"Nothing but the best for my Angel." Adam smiled. "It is my favorite hotel on the strip. Have you ever stayed here?"

"Can't say I have." Lauren smiled, thinking of the cheap hotel on the strip that she stayed at with her dad years ago.

"I only booked one room. I figured you wouldn't mind sharing. Separate beds, of course."

"As long as you don't snore."

"There's the most handsome man in the world." Georgia rose at the sight of Adam, giving him a hug and kiss on the cheek. "Another year older and yet you look twenty-one. Happy birthday, my friend."

"You're too kind, Georgia. Thank you. You look marvelous, as always." Adam stepped back. "Georgia, I'd like you to meet Lauren."

Georgia took both Lauren's hands in hers, looked her over. "Ahh, you're right. She is more beautiful than I." She kissed each of Lauren's cheeks. "It is such a pleasure to meet you, my dear."

"The pleasure is mine. I love your music." Her sweetness and beauty was astonishing. After they sat, Lauren turned to Adam. "You didn't tell me it was your birthday."

Adam smiled. "You didn't ask."

Georgia made Lauren feel she had known her forever. As she told stories, she would often look at Lauren and say "You remember him" or "You know she's such a doll." Lauren smiled and nodded, not knowing whom she was speaking of.

"Tell me about you, Beautiful." Georgia turned her full attention to Lauren halfway through lunch. "I want to know everything. I know you have an inspiring story."

Adam smiled. "She certainly does."

Lauren smiled shyly. "I was born and raised in LA. My father owns his own pool business, my mother passed away from breast cancer during college. I have my teaching degree and work at a preschool and as Children's Ministry Coordinator at my church." She paused, looking at Adam. "In my spare time I enjoy hanging out with a singer and movie star that pretend they're regular people like me."

Georgia turned to Adam. "Funny, smart, spirited." Then she turned back to Lauren. "I have always admired teachers. Every person can look back to at least one teacher that touched them, inspired them to become who they are or do great deeds. Mine was third grade, Miss Brown and eighth grade English, Mr. Estes."

"Mr. Pile, seventh grade math." Adam took a drink of his iced tea.

Lauren smiled. "I agree. Someday I hope to be an inspiration to children."

"Sounds like you already are, dear." Georgia gently patted her hand. "We may affect a few people, but by teaching children, you are changing the world. That is far more important than any song we will ever write or sing."

A bellboy met Lauren and Adam to escort them to their room after lunch.

"Hope you're not afraid of heights." Adam held Lauren's hand as the private elevator zoomed to the top of the hotel. Lauren took a deep breath and smiled when the elevator doors opened directly into their two-bedroom presidential suite.

Silly girl, imagining a hotel room with two beds.

"Hope it's big enough. The grand presidential suite was already booked."

"I can make do." The chandelier in the entryway mesmerized Lauren. A grand marble table in the entryway welcomed guests with an enormous fresh flower arrangement. The walls throughout the suite were covered with beautiful mirrors and paintings. The entertainment room itself was bigger than the entire downstairs at her father's house. It had a built-in cherrywood entertainment center that held more electronic equipment than she owned. High back upholstered chairs, matching sofas, a fully stocked wet bar and a baby grand piano filled the main room. Off to the side was a small kitchen and a dining room table that sat eight.

A king size four-post bed was the focal point of the master bedroom. It was furnished with two nightstands, a desk, a sofa, and plasma TV. The bathroom included fresh cut flowers, double sinks with gold fixtures, a huge shower and Jacuzzi tub.

"Wow." Lauren plopped down in the middle of the bed, feeling as if she was in a dream.

"What do you think?" Adam followed her in and sat on the couch.

"Amazing." She scanned the room. "Absolutely amazing."

"Your suitcase is in the closet." Adam pointed to the walk-in. "I would've had him unpack it, but I didn't know if that would offend you."

"I can't take this room." Lauren sat up. "You're paying. You should get the master suite."

Adam shook his head. "Nothing but the best for my Angel. Besides, I don't like rooms this big. Too much to distract me from sleep."

Lauren leaned her head down on the pillow. "I'd fight you, but I'm too tired. Wake me up in a few hours?"

Adam tossed a blanket over her. "Sleep well, Angel."

The faint sound of the piano reminded her where they were. Rubbing her eyes, she wrapped the blanket around her and groggily walked into the other room.

Adam sat at the baby grand, playing and singing softly. She lay on the couch, listening. It was her favorite song, the one Tyler bid for. Funny to think not long ago she watched him, thinking how great it would be to know him.

You are amazing, Lord. Thank you for bringing Adam into my life. Thank you for the blessing of his friendship.

When he was done playing, he turned toward her. "The concert is in a few hours. Do you want to freshen up while I order a snack? Georgia would love to have dinner with us after."

"Sounds good." Lauren liked not having to make decisions. "I'll be out in a little while." As she walked away, Adam called, "There's a dress for tonight in your closet."

A beautiful black off-the-shoulder, modest cut floor length gown awaited her. A wrap was on another hanger, along with a bag of accessories. She opened the bag and took out a heart shaped note.

The note read "Have a wonderful time. Gretchen." Lauren smiled. It was nice to have someone know her taste.

༄

"Beautiful," Adam said when she emerged an hour later all done up.

Lauren smiled at Adam in a tuxedo. "You, sir, are quite handsome. You know, it's your birthday. I should be the one giving you gifts and surprises."

Adam took her hand in his and gently kissed it. "Your company is the best gift. Please, not another word or thought about it."

He led her over to a table set up by the window. Strawberries and chocolate for dipping, cheese fondue with bread and vegetables, caviar and crackers.

"A little snack for my lady." Adam handed her a glass plate.

"Oh, my. I better not spill on my dress."

"The chocolate is dark," Adam teased. "It will blend in."

Lauren recognized a few movie stars and other singers around them in the front row. Adam greeted everyone like an old friend.

"They all think they know me," he whispered to her. "Honestly, sometimes I forget who I'm supposed to know. Guess that's a sign of old age."

Lauren laughed. "You are not old. You're too handsome to be old."

"I'll take that as a compliment."

Lauren looked back at him. "But how old are you, anyway?"

Adam smiled and put his arm around Lauren. "I'm feeling twenty-four tonight."

"The concert was amazing," Lauren told Georgia enthusiastically in her dressing room afterward.

Georgia stared into the mirror as she brushed her hair. "Oh, thank you, darling, but the bass boy was off. Did you notice, Mac? Oh, it's so hard to find good musicians nowadays."

Adam smiled and kissed her cheek. "Your voice was so beautiful I hardly noticed the bass."

"Oh, well. Off we go." She linked arms with Adam. "I only have one night in Vegas. It's young and I'm getting older by the second. Shall we?"

At dinner, Georgia asked Lauren about her work at the church. Georgia shared her own religious experience from her teens and twenties.

"I still thank God every day for all He has given me, but I guess it's been a while since I dusted off my Bible."

Lauren smiled. "I love that God has something new to reveal to me every day."

Georgia squeezed Lauren's hand. "That's the key, isn't it dear? We have to keep looking. It's easy to get distracted along the way."

Gretchen returned to her room after dinner. Adam took Lauren out to experience the glamorous side of Vegas.

Limos took them to back entrances where they were escorted to exclusive gambling rooms. Most dressed formal and all looked very relaxed. No one flinched when their money was taken away and everyone cheered when they got paid off.

Their last stop was the craps table in their hotel. Chips started at $100 and Adam threw three or four down at a time, letting them ride when he won. Lauren watched with wide eyes as his pile continued to grow.

He handed her the dice when they came around. "You can do it, Angel."

She had no idea what she was doing, but she tossed the dice across the table. Adam cheered, slipping her the payoff chip with a smile. $5000. "This one's for you." He gave her the dice again. "One more time."

Her winning streak ended the next roll, but Adam took her hand with a smile as they walked away. "Let's cash out your money."

Lauren shook her head. "I'm not taking this, Adam. It was your money to begin with. Besides, my last roll lost you money."

"No arguments," Adam insisted. "I'm having too much fun. Now cash out and buy me a drink."

Lauren smiled. "Yes, sir. As long as we can find ice cream, too."

"How old are you?" Lauren dug into her sundae as Adam sipped his beer.

Adam grinned. "It's killing you, isn't it?"

Lauren pulled out her phone. "I guess I could look up your bio on the internet…"

"Thirty-five." Adam stared into his drink. "Ten years too old for you."

"I don't think you're too old for me. Do you think I'm too young and immature for you?"

He reached for her hand, locking eyes with her. "Never, Angel. You are more mature than most the people I know. I've learned age should never determine a friendship."

Lauren held up her water. "Cheers to that."

"So, do we come back to Vegas in April for your birthday, or would you prefer to go somewhere else?"

"How do you know when my birthday is?" Lauren raised an eyebrow.

"I've done my homework on you."

"When is Tyler's birthday?"

"June 14th." Adam sipped his drink with a smile. "I think he might have turned twenty one again this year."

Adam's phone beeped. Pulling it from his pocket, he laughed after reading the message. Then he pushed it over to Lauren.

"Happy birthday old man. Have a great one but keep your hands off the girl."

Lauren laughed as she replied to Tyler's text message. "Don't worry. He's being a gentleman."

Adam leaned against the back wall of the elevator as they zoomed to their room.

"Thanks for convincing me to come." Lauren squeezed his hand.

"I appreciate your company." Adam smiled.

Lauren smiled and gently kissed his cheek. "Happy birthday, Adam."

Adam closed his eyes and nodded. "Yes it is, Angel. Yes it is."

⁂

They had every intention of leaving Vegas Saturday night until Lauren saw the billboard when they were shopping that afternoon.

"That's one of my favorite Christian bands!" She screamed, pointing to the advertisement.

"Really?" Adam pulled out his phone. "They're playing tonight. Want to go?"

"Yeah!" She jumped for joy until she remembered. "Tomorrow is church. I can't."

"Private jet." Adam was dialing his cell phone. "We can leave tomorrow morning."

"It's probably sold out." Lauren's lip protruded in disappointment.

He smiled at Lauren. "That's sweet. Did you actually forget who I was?"

Ten minutes later, back stage passes and front row tickets were confirmed.

The band seemed as excited to meet Adam as Lauren was to meet them. After a while of Adam being the center of attention, he turned it back to them. The band gave Adam and Lauren autographed CDs. When they found their seats in the front row, she looked at him with a huge smile.

"Thank you so much…" He put his finger up to her mouth.

"Anything to make you happy, Angel."

"Thank you for tonight." Adam was the first to speak as they walked to the limo.

"I appreciate you taking me." Lauren linked arms with him.

Adam stared at the ground as they walked. "I really want to be different, to live for God and do things His way."

Lauren smiled. "Maybe it will be easier if we have each other to encourage along the way."

"I think so." Adam smiled. "Thanks for bringing me back to God."

Tears came to Lauren's eyes. "I'm humbled God would use me in such a way."

⁌

They boarded the plane at six a.m. Lauren was at church by eight thirty preparing the snack for children's church. The entire morning went smoothly. Every teacher showed up and there was even an extra volunteer in the nursery. She met Adam in front of the church at ten thirty and they snuck in the back during the sermon.

Adam poked her as she started to nod off. "What, were you partying all weekend?"

"We are all children of God." Pastor started gaining momentum halfway through the sermon. "And as children of God, we have rights. One which is the right to worship freely with other Christians in the house of the Lord. I am so glad that I live in a country that I can come to church on Sunday and worship God freely."

"Amen." Several people raised their hands in agreement.

"Rich, poor, man, woman, and children, we can all come together as one to praise our Lord!"

"AMEN!" the audience shouted as Lauren squeezed Adam's hand.

"We should be able to lift our hands, shout His name, fall to our knees, and praise Him without worrying what others will say. I want to think we are a congregation that views others as children of God, all equal because He loves us all the same. We all have the right to serve Him, praise Him and worship in His house!"

People rose to their feet as they applauded in praise and agreement.

As Pastor led everyone in prayer, Adam walked to the stage and sat at the piano. He played slowly, growing in intensity during the prayer. Sighs and mumbles could be heard as the church opened their eyes after prayer, but Adam smiled as he played old, familiar hymns. They were so beautiful they brought tears to most everyone's eyes as they sang along. After church there was a line of people wanting to shake his hand and welcome him to the church.

"It felt good," he told Lauren on the way home. "It felt right."

Lauren smiled. "That's why even though working at the church is often a headache, it's a blessing because I'm giving back to God. I have such a feeling of accomplishment most days."

Adam nodded. "I understand now."

༄

Beth teased her when she was dragging on Monday morning, but she hung on Lauren's every word during playtime after lunch when Lauren started at the beginning, leaving nothing out.

"Mark my word, someday you will be on *Lifestyles of the Rich and Famous.*"

Lauren shook her head. "I come to work chasing preschoolers for little more than minimum wage, I live with my father who pays for my medical and car insurance, and then on the weekend I jet off to Vegas, eating at the fanciest restaurants, staying in a suite, and going to concerts with the best seats at a moment's notice. It makes no sense."

"Enjoy it for the rest of us, girl. Make sure to share all the details so we can live through you."

She was quiet for a while before speaking again. "The best part was the concert last night. The music was awesome. He thanked me for bringing him back to the Lord." She paused as she wiped her eyes. "I'm beginning to understand a part of God's plan for me. Bringing others to the Lord is more important than teaching."

Beth grinned. "Amen, sister."

Chapter 11

Sunday morning Adam and Richard were in the front pew for the Children's Musical. Lauren, full of energy, led the children in the songs, reminding them of their places to stand, and helping them with lines. Some of their mistakes seemed like a part of the show and were hilarious. They received a standing ovation at the end.

After service, Richard and Adam treated her to lunch.

"Cheers." Richard held up his iced tea. "To the newest, upcoming director."

"Here, here." Adam clinked glasses.

"Oh, come on." Lauren looked down, somewhat embarrassed. "It was God that pulled it together, better than I ever could have."

"It was wonderful, sweetheart," Richard commended her. "You put your whole heart into it and it showed. The children obviously had a great time doing it."

Lauren smiled. "That was the best part. Half of them came up to me after and asked if we could do it again. Funny thing is we've been practicing for so long I don't know what I will do with all this free time."

Adam smiled. "We could jet down to Vegas for the day."

"I'd settle for dinner and a movie tonight." Lauren laughed. "I think I still haven't recovered from our little adventure. Guess I'm getting old."

Adam and Richard chuckled as they shook their heads.

༄

Tyler texted Lauren less during the day. It was a physically challenging role, long days and too hot, he typed. She knew he was tired and frustrated when he used profanity in his messages. After she scolded him for it, she encouraged him that he would be home soon.

On days Lauren opened she and Adam had a late lunch, sometimes with his friends. Lauren came home a few nights to Adam cooking dinner or take-out. A few times Adam made reservations at his favorite restaurants. Conversation came so naturally with him.

Sometimes at night they would go to the beach, swim in Tyler's pool, or sit together on the sofa, each reading a book. They played cards into the early morning or watched movies. When Lauren fell asleep on the sofa, she woke up several hours later, fully clothed, but tucked into bed.

⁂

The delicious smell of pancakes and sounds of talking awoke her. Rubbing her eyes, Lauren wondered whom Adam could be talking to when she remembered what day it was. She ran to the bathroom, splashed water on her face, and ran her brush through her hair. Then she casually walked to the kitchen as her heart beat faster.

"There's our Angel," Adam said when Lauren entered the room. Tyler turned with a hairy face and a smile. The smile that melted Lauren's heart.

"Good morning, Sleeping Beauty." Tyler's voice was sexier than she remembered. He rose as she entered the kitchen.

She grinned bashfully. "Good morning, stranger." She hugged him tightly.

"Are you glad to see me?" he whispered in her ear.

"Very much so. I missed you."

Tyler kissed Lauren on the cheek. "Good." As they parted, he looked into her eyes and pushed her hair behind her ear. "Glad I wasn't the only one."

Lauren rubbed her hand over his scruffy face. "Forget to shave?"

Tyler looked at Adam. "I fly all day and night to be here before she wakes up and she complains about a little five o'clock shadow?"

Lauren rubbed his whiskers again. "It's okay. You're still kind of cute."

"Hot chocolate chip pancakes," Adam announced, placing Lauren's plate on the table.

Lauren smiled as Tyler laughed. "Adam has been filling me in on all your preferences, like chocolate chip pancakes and ice cream before bed."

Lauren sat down at the table. "He took very good care of me while you were gone." She turned to Adam. "Thank you."

Tyler shared fascinating tales all morning of the animals, the people, traveling from site to site. They had a few weeks of filming in the studio, but he had the week off before they started up again.

Lauren showered about eleven o'clock. She emerged dressed from the bathroom to find a clean-shaven Tyler on his bed. His eyes opened slowly as she walked towards him. "The sheets smell like you."

"Sorry I didn't change them."

"I like it." He reached his hand out to her. "Will you be here when I wake up?"

"Of course." She pulled the sheet up to tuck him in. "I'm glad you're home," she whispered as she kissed his cheek. A smile appeared on his lips as she left the room. She joined Adam, who was reading in the family room on the couch. She was beaming from ear to ear.

"Well, guess you're happy?" Adam teased her.

"All is well with my world." She smiled.

༄

The whole week they were inseparable. They spent the days doing whatever occurred to them at the moment.

Shopping, movies, and walks along the beach. Tyler told her stories about elephants, lions, and angry directors and producers. Lauren shared stories of preschoolers and adventures with Adam. It took a while to break him of his foul language again, but she socked his arm every time he cursed. By the second day, he would dodge her after using a bad word. Then he'd apologize when she frowned. On the third day he censored himself, which made her smile.

༄

One afternoon they relaxed in the sun on the balcony of Tyler's beach house, sipping virgin margaritas at Lauren's request, and munching on chips and salsa.

"What would you do tomorrow if you couldn't be an actor?"

Tyler thought for a while. "Maybe go to school to be a drama teacher. Maybe go into business doing something." Tyler smiled as he lifted his glass. "Or sell my mansion and sit on the balcony of my beach house drinking margaritas all day."

Lauren sipped her drink. "A few months ago you would have said that would never happen."

"It's all luck." Tyler scooped up salsa with his chip. "I was lucky enough to get a break. I will never forget what it was like to be hungry and jobless."

Lauren reached for a chip of her own. "What about God? Don't you think He has anything to do with it?"

"I never asked Him for it."

"The Bible says 'All good and perfect things come from above.'"

Tyler smiled. "That would be you. I can admit you are a gift from God. What would you do besides teach?"

Lauren laughed. "That's the question of the summer. God's teaching me patience. I'm keeping myself open for His plan. Maybe someday I would open my own school."

Tyler smiled. "You're a smart woman. You'll be successful in whatever you choose to do." Tyler stared at her for several minutes before Lauren finally spoke.

"What?"

"I never thought I would meet a woman as beautiful as you with brains too. I didn't see myself dating a college graduate, let alone a school teacher."

Dating? Are we dating? "Well, I never saw myself with a movie star."

Tyler squeezed Lauren's hand. "What a pair we make."

༄

Back to work meant changing dirty diapers, running after children and trying to get two-year-olds to sit down and sing the same song at the same time. By five o'clock the cleaning was done and Lauren was left with the kids watching movies. Though exhausted, she had a smile on her face as she thought of Tyler. He called every night when he got done shooting and they would talk for hours.

While she enjoyed the preschool, her church position was wearing her down. It was disheartening when people broke their teaching commitment week after week. She was teaching two or three Sunday school classes together and Children's Church. When Lauren led Children's Church, Adam didn't feel comfortable sitting by himself. She wanted to sit with him during service being fed. She needed that.

Frustration also arose with the children. After teaching a lesson on kindness, she saw kids fighting on the playground. It also made Lauren sad that some of the worst-behaved children had parents very involved in ministry. She prayed about it daily, asking God to help her do the right thing.

After dinner at Tyler's house one Saturday night, he began making plans for Sunday.

"I could only get paroled from church for one week."

Tyler took Lauren's empty plate to the kitchen. "If you don't want to do it, why do it?"

Lauren sighed. "It's a commitment I've made."

"Don't you get paid for your work?" Tyler called out to her.

"Yes."

Tyler returned to the dining room table. "Then it's a job. You can quit your job. People do it all the time."

Lauren frowned. "But they count on me. There's no one else to do it."

Tyler sat beside her, taking her hand in his. "You're a wonderful, hard-working person. No offense, but you're not the only person that can do that job for, what did you say, two dollars an hour? If you quit, they'll have to find someone."

"I need the money."

Tyler frowned. "I believe it was you that once lectured me about the dangers of working solely for the money. Didn't you tell me a person needs to enjoy the work as well?"

"Thank you, Mr. Spiritual Advisor."

"Heck, you can take over my maid's job. I'm sure I pay her more than two dollars an hour. I'd even let you be a live-in." He winked.

Lauren shook her head. "Pretty sad to think the woman that cleans your house and does your laundry makes more money than I do teaching young children and leading them spiritually."

"But your reward will be in heaven, right? Isn't that what you Christians say?"

"Who are you? And where did you put Tyler Stevens?" Lauren pushed Tyler. "Come to church with me and Adam tomorrow. You might enjoy it."

Tyler smiled. "One step at a time."

Chapter 12

The snack list read apple slices and cheese chunks. Lauren opened the church refrigerator to find a bag of apples and a block of cheese.

Oh well, at least I don't have to run to the store this week.

As she began cutting apples, she overheard two older ladies chatting away in the Fellowship Hall as they set up the coffee and donuts for Sunday School. Emma's soft sweet voice reminded Lauren of her grandmother and she had come to know Martha's raspy voice well.

"My son, John, came over yesterday," Emma said. "Seems he's got mixed up with another non-Christian girl. I tried to remind him of the last one he dated and how mean and self-seeking she was. He said 'Oh, Mom. Why is it you only remember the bad ones?' I said 'Trust me, dear, if you brought home a good one, I would remember!'"

Lauren chuckled as she moved on to the cheese.

"Well," Martha started in, "I spoke with my daughter this week. Her oldest, Betty, is going to that university up north. It seems there is a person in Betty's dorm building that has …AIDS." Martha whispered AIDS. Emma gasped. "Can you believe the administration won't say who it is? This person could be living next door to my granddaughter. It could even be her roommate!"

"The nerve of some people." Emma's pitch rose. "It's not right endangering so many people like that."

"I told my daughter she needs to call that college and threaten to take Betty out of that school if they don't release the student's name. It's wrong to let those people walk around like they are normal. I told her Betty needs to stay clear of that person. Who knows what could happen if they became friends!"

Christians are supposed to be loving and accepting. Adam hangs out with non-traditional people of society. He sat beside his friend as he died from AIDS. That's what Jesus would do.

"Everyone deserves a friend," Adam told her a few weeks before. "I count it a privilege to be friends with someone that has no friends."

Christianity was not always best proclaimed by those who attended church.

She put the snack platter in the fridge and thought about the children of the church that everyone wanted taught, but no one was willing to teach. She sighed. "I love you, Lord. Please renew my heart and show me Your work that needs to be done."

Two teachers neglected to show, so Lauren combined classes again. To top off the morning, a fight broke out on the playground before Children's Church between two third graders. When Lauren explained the incident to the parents, one family gave excuses for their son's behavior; the other grabbed the boy's arm and left.

Lauren joined Adam in service toward the end of worship. She doodled on her note page while Pastor spoke, trying to forgot the judgmental words, but her mind replayed them, along with the fight on the playground and every frustration from the last several months.

I'm done, Lord. I'm done.

Twenty minutes before church was over one of the teens told her they needed help with the preschoolers.

"Don't wait for me," Lauren whispered to Adam. "I'll call you later."

Lauren prayed while she cleaned the rooms, trying to make sense of it all. Tyler's advice played over in her head. "It's a job, you can quit. People do it all the time."

Lord, is that what you want? Is it time for me to go?

Pastor Jim surprised Lauren when he came into the children's room as she was locking the doors. It had taken her forty-five minutes to clean up today because there were so few volunteers and such a huge mess.

"How'd it go today?" Jim sat on one of the tables.

She sat on a table a few feet away from Jim. She took a deep breath before she began.

"I'm feeling a bit overwhelmed." She paused, waiting for Jim to interject something. But he sat quietly, so she continued. "I love the children and this church, but my heart isn't in the ministry lately. Maybe I've done it too long."

"Would it help if you had an assistant?"

He cares so much, for me and the church. How can I tell him I'm burned out, used up?

Speak the truth in love...

Tears swelled up in her eyes. "It's been a great two years and I appreciate your support and guidance. I don't quite know what God wants me to do, but He's calling me out of this ministry. I think instead of leading I need to be fed for a while."

They both stood and Jim embraced her. "Then I say God bless you Lauren for all you have done for our children. You are an amazing woman of God. Stay in tune with Him and I know He will continue to do great things through you."

Lauren offered to continue for two weeks. Jim smiled and kissed the top of her head. "No one could ever replace you, dear. If you need to be done, you need to be done. But I would like you to return next week so we can honor you in church."

Lauren held it together until she got home. Then she sat on her driveway and wept. Relief washed over her, as did frustration. She'd heard twenty percent of the people do eighty percent of the work in a church. She had nothing left to give.

As she studied the Bible through the week, she felt peace about her decision. It was time to sit at Jesus' feet and be fed for a while. Her father attended the service the following week when they honored her. As she said her farewells, Lauren knew she would not return to this church she had called home.

⁓

"It's hot!" Adam complained. "And there's sand everywhere!"

"That's because we're at the beach." Lauren set down her ice chest and laid out her towel on the sand.

Tyler plopped down on Lauren's towel. "Where's the swim-up bar?"

"You agreed we could do whatever I wanted." Lauren put her hands on her hips. "It's my first Sunday without commitments. I'm not going to sit here all day listening to the two of you whine." She grabbed the lounge chair Tyler carried and moved closer to the water.

"When you mentioned beach, I assumed you meant the beach house." Tyler laid down.

"The beach house." Adam perked up. "There's a great idea."

Lauren leaned back in the chair and closed her eyes. "Either drop the attitude or pick me up in a couple hours."

"Might as well make the best of it." Picking up his chair and cooler Adam moved closer to Lauren.

Lauren sat forward and pulled off her sundress, handing suntan lotion to Adam. "Do you mind?"

Adam accepted it with a smile as Tyler protested. "What about me? I'll do it!"

"Sorry." Lauren moved her hair off her back. "Adam was closer."

"Like it's fair to go out in public like that..."

"This is a beach," Lauren interrupted him. "I'm wearing a bathing suit. Go to sleep and we'll wake you when you start burning.

"So, this is what a normal person does on Sunday." Lauren relaxed as Adam smeared lotion on her back. "For years Sunday has been about going to church."

"You never explained why you left." Adam massaged her shoulders.

Lauren sighed. "That Sunday I quit, I was so tormented. There was no peace in my soul. I felt physically sick by the attitude, hypocrisy. I realized I was only there because it was comfortable, but God called me to move on long ago. Some people will think I'm slipping away from God and falling into sin…"

"Do you believe that?"

"No." Lauren faced Adam. "I actually feel like I'm listening to God. I thought I'd have a teaching job by now, but I don't. Clearly God wants to take my life in a different direction. I don't know exactly what He has planned, but I need to focus on building my relationship with Him. He's giving me the privilege of time, so I'm studying and reading His word several hours a day."

Adam handed her back the lotion. "Remember Angel, He lives in your heart, not in a building."

Lauren hugged Adam. "Thanks, Mac. That's what I needed to hear today."

⚘

For a while she church shopped. Occasionally her father or Shelly went with her. Adam went with her one week and people stared so much they left early. She attended big churches so she could be one among the many.

"It's frustrating," Lauren told Adam when he called one Sunday night. "I want to find the right church, I just don't know where it is."

"I'm sorry I can't go with you. I'd like to, but I want it to be a private thing."

"I don't get it. How do people like you worship?"

"They don't, I guess. Or maybe they build their own churches." There was a pause before Adam chuckled. "How about that, Angel? What if we built our own church?"

Lauren laughed. "The Church of Adam and Lauren? Kind of bizarre, if you ask me."

"No, silly. A Christian church where well-known people are the norm."

"So, you exclude the common people? Exclusive churches go against God's plan."

Adam got quiet for a while. "I don't know how it will work, but I'll figure it out."

"You could be in charge of worship and I could do children's ministry. Heck, maybe Tyler could preach…"

"Mark my words, by this time next year we will have a church to worship at."

"Alrighty then." Lauren lay back on her bed. "I'll stop looking and wait for you to build me the perfect church."

Chapter 13

September, a time to decorate the classroom, make nametags and write up lesson plans. Instead five years of college only gave Lauren the right to substitute occasionally. Whispers when she walked through the staff lounge forced her to eat lunch in the classroom. She made her way to the preschool every afternoon to mop floors, change diapers, and read stories until six p.m. She received so few hours most weeks she thought it would be better to quit. The other teachers knew her secret and respected her privacy, but once the parents found out, she was done.

"You don't belong here anymore." Beth leaned in the doorway of the bathroom.

Lauren looked up from scrubbing the toilet. "The problem is I don't know where I belong."

"With the rich and famous, girl. You're too upscale for us."

She returned to her chore. *I'm poor and my five minutes of fame cost me my dream career. I don't belong anywhere.*

༄

The next week a call came for a two-week assignment in third grade. The first day Lauren found the teacher left descriptive lesson plans and the class was well behaved. There was even an adorable red-haired boy, Charlie, that helped at the end of every lunch. Lauren appreciated him filing and passing out papers and he loved the attention. He chattered away about his cool video games or what he saw on TV the night before.

On Thursday of the second week, Charlie was quiet all morning. At lunch, he came in and put his head down on his desk.

"Are you okay?" Lauren glanced up from her desk.

When no response came, she went to his desk and knelt beside it. "Want to talk about it?"

Slowly he raised his head, tears streaming down his face. "I don't feel so good."

Lauren felt his forehead. "Are you sick? Do you need to go home?"

"No!" Charlie's eyes widened as he shook his head vigorously. "No." He rested his head back on the desk. "I'm okay."

Lauren stared, not knowing what to say. Nausea overcame her when she saw a bruise, just underneath his sleeve.

"Did you hurt yourself?" *Please, let it be an accident...*

"No." He frowned.

"Did someone hurt you?" Lauren crouched beside the desk. *Lord, give me the courage to handle this.*

The seconds felt like minutes, but finally the answer came. "I didn't do my chores. Dad hit me."

"Once or more than one time?"

"A lot." Charlie stared straight ahead at the white board.

"Does this happen often?"

"When he drinks."

Lauren put her hand on his. "I need to take you to the nurse."

Charlie wiped his tears and nodded.

Lord, take care of him. Protect him. Lauren put her arm around him as they walked through the hall. *Father, work this out, somehow, for Your glory.*

Charlie tugged her hand at the bottom of the steps to the office. "Will they take me away?"

She bent down to look in his eyes. "I don't know, but no one has the right to hurt you like this. You've done nothing wrong." She paused for a moment. "Do you want this to stop?"

Charlie nodded.

"Then we need to do this." Lauren squeezed his hand.

"You'll stay with me?" He wiped a tear from his eye.
"Yes." She started up the steps. "We'll do this together."

"Child Protective Services came after school and took him away." She rested her head on Tyler's shoulder. "He acted so brave, but I knew he was scared. He shouldn't be taken away for what his father did."

"That's awful." Tyler squeezed her tight. "I'm sorry you had to go through that."

"It's just not right." Lauren sobbed. "He's so sweet, so innocent. I don't understand."

"No, it's not." Tyler rested his head on hers.

"Lord, my heart aches for Charlie," Lauren prayed that night in bed. "I want so badly to help your children, but sometimes I feel so helpless. If I had my own class, I could really make a difference…"

Trust in the Lord with all your heart and lean not on your own understanding.

"I trust You, Lord." She pulled her covers up to her chin. "I trust You."

સ૭

She stared at Charlie's empty seat through the day, praying for him each time. God's way wasn't easy, but if she had her own class, she wouldn't have been subbing and the abuse might have continued. God had brought her to this place to help him.

As she turned off the lights at the end of the day, she sighed. "I don't understand it, Lord, and it makes me sad, but take me where You need me. I'm Yours."

She was done searching. It was time to let God lead her.

Chapter 14

The costumes Adam chose for Tyler and Lauren were delivered October 30th. Tyler's Zeus costume included a toga, lightening bolt, and laurel-wreath. Lauren's costume was a simple white dress that shimmered in the light with gold trimmed wings and halo.

"Adam, it's gorgeous." She called as soon as it arrived.

"I'm glad you like it." He coughed as he spoke. "I had it made just for you."

"Are you okay?"

"I think I have the flu. I'll have to save my fig leaf to wear next year."

"I'll come over and take care of you."

Adam coughed again. "No, I don't want you getting sick. Go to the party and take care of our Greek God. I have a girl coming over to Tyler's tomorrow night to do your make-up and hair."

"You are so great. I promise to tell you all about it."

"And a picture. I need a picture of my angel all made up."

She admired herself over in the floor-length mirror in Tyler's bathroom after the make-up artist had worked her magic. Her face shimmered, soft golden curls framed her face with the rest of her hair pulled up in a crown of curls beneath her halo.

I'm beautiful. Tyler will be proud to have me on his arm tonight.
Avoid every kind of evil.

Lauren closed her eyes and took a deep breath. *I'll be fine. I'm a witness to him.*

"Knock, knock." A very hairy Tyler entered the room. His toga costume showed off the best parts of his tan, muscular body. Lauren couldn't help but laugh at his full, wavy beard and overgrown head of hair.

"What's so funny?"

"Nothing." Lauren smiled. "You look great in a dress."

Tyler smiled when Lauren twirled for him. "You're the hottest angel I've ever seen." He took her hand and pulled her against his chest.

"And exactly how many have you seen?" Lauren pushed him away as he went in to kiss her neck.

"Only you, dear." He kissed her hand. "I only have eyes for you."

"Zeus! Zeus!" Men across the house screamed, bowing as they entered.

"That's right," Tyler shouted. "Let the party begin. The great Zeus is here." Cheers broke out across the room. Lauren nodded politely as Tyler greeted others. The costumes confused Lauren, keeping her from remembering who people were. There were typical 70's outfits, Dracula, men dressed like women. Her favorite were those dressed as other stars. Marilyn Monroe, Elvis, James Dean, and Robert DeNiro were a few present.

The backyard resembled a night club, a rock band played on a stage, a packed dance floor, tables and chairs around the floor, and two full bars.

"Beer or wine?" Tyler approached the closest bar.

Do not imitate what is evil but what is good.

"Water would be great." *Lord, you're right, I don't belong here.*

The women flocked to Tyler, their hands all over him though Lauren stood beside him.

"I miss you, Ty. You don't call me anymore." Elvira pawed his chest.

"Yeah. I've been busy." He walked away with Lauren, leaving the nasty look and whispering behind.

Lauren pulled Tyler to the dance floor when *Blue Suede Shoes* began playing. She didn't mind his attention being divided between her and random people that happened by and shook his hand. As long as she kept dancing, she didn't have to attempt to hold a conversation with anyone.

Bryan Wilson, Tyler's top competitor for gorgeous young actor, found them after a few hours. His dark brown hair, large muscles, and personality fit his Tarzan costume well.

He slapped Tyler on the back. "The boys are discussing skiing in the kitchen. Need your input."

"Certainly." He winked at Lauren. "I'll be right back. Bryan will take care of you."

Before she could object, Bryan took over on the dance floor. She chuckled watching the aspiring actresses rub up against him. He smiled, enjoying the attention. When a slow song began, Bryan pulled Lauren close before she could escape.

"Seen any good movies lately?"

"Your last one was great." Lauren stroked his ego a bit. "Lots of action."

"You know, I do all my own stunts." Lauren listened to him build himself up for the rest of the song before excusing herself. She stopped at the bar for more water before making her way to the house.

Though reggae music blared in the dark entertainment room, she could still hear moaning and groaning from various parts of the room. Wrinkling her nose at the stench, she weaved through the room, stepping over pieces of costumes and clothing that littered the floor.

Do not be overcome by evil...

By following the light, she finally made her way to the kitchen. Tyler and other men stood over the kitchen table. He was laughing, rubbing his nose.

She froze, feeling as if the wind was knocked out of her. One of the guys nudged Tyler.

"Angel." Tyler motioned for her to come in. "Come join the fun."

She dashed toward the door.

"C'mon." Tyler followed her.

"I'm leaving." Nausea rose inside her.

"The party's just started." He caught her arm. "Don't be a party pooper."

...but overcome evil with good

Lauren glared at Tyler. "I don't need drugs to have a good time." Lauren broke away from him and walked out the door.

"It might loosen you up."

Lauren stopped at the edge of the porch and turned to face him. "You disgust me. I thought you were different. All night I've been grateful you weren't like the rest of them. Obviously I was wrong."

"Go ahead and judge us. After all, you're perfect, right? That's what you mean, 'Not my type of people'. You're too good for us."

Lauren ran off to find the limo.

She stared out the window the entire way home.

How foolish of me to think he was different. My father tried to warn me...

Her head pounded. Nauseous from the smell of smoke and alcohol she sank back into the seat, concentrating on breathing.

Tears streaked her face as she brushed her hair on her bed after a long hot shower. She stared at her phone. Though she was grateful her dad was out of town, loneliness began to overtake her. She wanted to call Adam. It would have been different if he were there.

The scene of Tyler in the kitchen came back to mind. The floodgates opened as she wrapped blankets tight around her.

"Lord, I don't understand why You've brought me here. I've given up so much."

Visions of the women staring as she walked by for her interview, the people gawking at her in the store flashed in her mind.

I've ruined everything. Nothing will ever be the same. My dreams are shattered.

Lauren cried until sleep finally overtook her.

༄

"So." Adam called the next morning. "How was it?"
Lauren knew tears would come if she talked about it.
"Angel? Are you there?"
"I came home early."
"What happened?"
Lauren took a deep breath. "How are you feeling?"
"Better. Do you want to meet?"

"So, what have you been up to? I didn't talk to you much last week."

Lauren stared into her hot cocoa as he sat down with his latte.

"Chasing preschoolers, changing diapers, scrubbing toilets." Lauren looked over Adam. "How are you?"

"Much better. After being miserable for three days I finally have an appetite."

"That's good. You need to put on some weight."

Adam grinned. "I'll take that as a compliment." Adam took a sip of his drink. "Do you want to talk about the party?"

"Didn't Tyler fill you in?" Lauren diverted her attention to the people walking down the street.

"He told me he made a mistake and I should see how you were."

She sipped her cocoa. "He did drugs, then proceeded to tell me I was stuck up because I wouldn't join in." She closed her eyes, trying to prevent the tears. "It was awful, Adam. He was awful."

"He admitted to saying mean things and feels bad hurting you."

Whispering "excuse me," she headed for the door.

"Hey." Adam caught up to her on the street. "I didn't mean to push."

"I don't understand him." Lauren wiped the tears from her eyes. "One minute he is so into himself no one else matters. The next day he's worried about me. How can he be like that?"

Adam led her to a nearby bench. "Tyler tends to not think until it's too late. I'm not making excuses, but for six years he hasn't been accountable to anyone for anything. It's a new world for him. Honestly, I didn't think he'd last two weeks with you."

Lauren rested her forehead in her hands. "Lately I feel the whole world is against me. I sacrificed my career for Tyler and now he's proven not to be someone I want to be around. A couple photographs and my life changed forever."

"God is on your side. And so am I. Stand by what you believe. I have seen changes in Tyler I never thought would occur. Pray for him. Mediate on the Word and let God lead you."

Lauren buried her face in Adam's shoulder and let her tears flow.

༄

Tyler hadn't stopped thinking about her. The horror in her eyes, the shock on her face. He never meant to cause her pain. The high was followed by the reality that Lauren wasn't there.

"How pissed is she?" he asked when Adam called.

"Hurt, sad mostly. Frustrated at your inconsistent behavior."

"I'm such a jerk."

"Yes, you are."

"Do you think she'll forgive me?"

"Act fast and remain humble. Leave your sweet talk at home. She needs more than an apology. Show her you want to be different."

Tyler nodded, not having any idea what that meant.

༄

I'm such a failure. Dad warned me. Tyler hurt me before, proving insensitive and conceited. Why did I think he'd change?

The music blared in an attempt to drown out the negative thoughts in her head. Darkness replaced the sunlight that had filled her room hours earlier. She remained curled up on her bed, crying hysterically.

We know that in all things God works for the good of those who love him.

How is any of this good? Five years of hard work, wasted. I'll never teach again. I can't even go to the grocery store. And if this story gets out, I'll have to relive the nightmare.

Shelly left another message. Embarrassment, maybe even pride, stopped her from reaching out. Her own foolishness caused the pain.

No one can understand, no one can help. I'm falling apart. I'm in so much pain. She rubbed her thumb over the veins in her wrist. *What's the point? Life as I know it is over.*

The doorbell startled her. Drying her swollen eyes, she ran her fingers through her knotted hair and walked downstairs without turning on the lights. Every time she inhaled, her heart hurt.

It will take a minute to get rid of whoever it is. Lauren rubbed her wrists. *Then I'll be done with it all.*

Shock overcame her to see Tyler standing on her porch, head down, staring at a huge bouquet of carnations. A frown replaced the smile he usually wore.

"I'm sorry I hurt you so badly. I never realized how unimportant all that was until you left." He placed his hand gently on her cheek. "I care about you, Lauren. I care enough to change. I give you my apology and my word that I won't use drugs again." Tyler laid the carnations in her arms. Their eyes met. "I understand if you don't trust me, but I did want to say I'm sorry."

Lauren closed her eyes, inhaling. The sweet fragrance of the flowers washed over her. Could she trust him? She wanted to believe him. She was in such pain. She wanted it to end, to be happy again, like she was during the summer. He apologized…

"Tyler!" She ran to him as he walked to his car and threw her arms around him. "I forgive you. No more drugs?"

"No more." He kissed her neck.

She tightened her grip on him as the tears broke forth. "Please don't go."

Chapter 15

She heard a bird chirp outside as the sun began to heat up her room. He slept peacefully. Was he sincere? Would he keep his promise? Was she naïve for believing him?

All night he held and comforted her as she wept. Dark thoughts plagued her mind as she spiraled downward emotionally. She was scared and knew she couldn't be alone.

The red and white carnations overfilled the vase on her desk. Had he remembered her comment about liking carnations more than roses because they lasted longer?

Quietly she slipped out of bed and downstairs to shower. As the water heated up, she stared at herself in the mirror. Dark circles were under her red, puffy eyes. Staring at her wrists, she rubbed her thumb on her veins that carried blood through her body. Her heart hurt.

I'm so tired. I need rest. If only I could be done with it all.

Tears came as negative thoughts bombarded her. The burden was almost unbearable. She closed her eyes and took a deep breath. "Lord, help me," she whispered.

"Good morning, sunshine." The smile that usually made her heart leap and palms sweat made her frown. Tyler wore the same clothes from last night and his favorite beat up, green John Deere cap.

"Hi." Lauren took a glass from the cupboard and got water to avoid looking at him. "I was going to wake you after my shower."

"I figured." Tyler poured himself a cup of the coffee he had made. "How are you today?"

"Do you want me to make breakfast?" She avoided his question with her own.

"Sure. Or we can go out. Whatever." Tyler lifted her head, forcing eye contact. "You okay?"

"I will be." Lauren held back the tears.

"I meant all I said last night."

Lauren slipped away from Tyler. "It's not all about you. I got down on myself, not having a job and everything." The tears came again. She covered her face, trying to hide them and her shame. She wanted to keep it together, but she was falling apart.

Tyler hugged her tightly until she relaxed.

"Today is your day. Whatever you want to do." He dried her face with his shirt. "Let's start with breakfast. Should I make you chocolate chip pancakes?"

"A huge, ooey, gooey cinnamon roll sounds good." Lauren's head was still resting against Tyler's chest.

"Pardon me for asking, but where does one get a huge, ooey, gooey cinnamon roll?"

Lauren looked up at Tyler. "The mall."

"To the mall we go." Tyler tipped his hat at her.

Lauren polished off the last bite of her cinnamon roll before Tyler spoke. "How about we go shopping?"

Lauren's gaze shifted to her plate. "I don't need anything."

Tyler reached across the table, taking Lauren's sticky hands in his.

"Please."

"I can't afford anything Tyler." Lauren felt the tears coming to her eyes. She was so tired of crying, yet she just couldn't stop.

Tyler smiled. "Maybe I want to get a gift for my friend. It would help me to feel less guilty if I could make your day wonderful." Lauren wanted to argue with him, but she didn't have the strength.

She held Tyler's hand all day. He was holding her up, giving her strength. Tyler surprised her with his good taste. There were only a few outfits she disagreed with. Several hours and bags later, a smile appeared on Lauren's face.

"That's what I was looking for." Tyler brushed his hand against her cheek. "I was hoping it would come out sometime today."

"Thank you." Lauren leaned her head on his shoulder.

"My pleasure." Tyler kissed the top of her head. "Anything to see you smile."

"I think you need a new hat." Lauren scanned the various caps as they walked by a baseball hat stand. "What's your favorite team?"

"But I wear this when I want to go unnoticed. With this hat I'm a nerdy hick. With this one-" He replaced it with a Dodgers hat.

Lauren nodded. "You look like Tyler Stevens."

"Exactly." He put his hat back on and took her hand as they went into the bookstore.

Tyler searched for coffee while Lauren browsed the Christian section. She stopped at her favorite author. Taking his latest off the shelf, she plopped herself on the floor and began to read.

"There you are." Tyler ducked into her row ten minutes later. He lifted his cap that was pulled low on his forehead. "A group of teenagers recognized me. It's ridiculous to have the magazine section next to the coffee shop. Teeny boppers hang out there."

She raised an eyebrow. "Such a hard life, avoiding screaming teens."

"Try it for a few days and get back to me. I do think the hat fooled them." Tyler sat cross-legged next to Lauren. "What did you find?"

Lauren flashed the cover at Tyler. "My favorite author, Sam Jones. Every time I pick up one of his books, he seems to write about what I'm going through."

He sipped his coffee. "So this one is about how to forgive your loser boyfriend when he makes bad judgment calls because of Hollywood peer pressure?"

Boyfriend. The word lingered. "It's about staying true to God when things aren't going how you expected. I never thought of my life without teaching, and I definitely didn't think of my life with a movie star. Hopefully, Sam can help me understand God's will."

Tyler grabbed the book from her hand and headed for the cash register. "Let me know what he says about your future with the movie star."

They sat close to each other on the balcony of his beach house, a blanket across them. She devoured her new book as he listened to the music, staring at the ocean. As the sun began to set, Lauren rested her head on Tyler's shoulder.

"I'm sorry I've been such a mess. I've been feeling overwhelmed lately."

"No apologies." Tyler kissed the top of her head. "It feels good to be needed." They sat in silence for a while before Tyler spoke again.

"You really shouldn't feel overwhelmed, Angel. Can you admit that maybe we're more than friends?"

She didn't want to say it, but she felt it.

"Guess what, honey? I'm rich. If you're my girlfriend, I'll take care of you. I'll pay when we go out, buy you expensive things. Just be happy and smile."

"I appreciate your generosity, but I went to college to start a career and be independent, not to have a rich boyfriend take care of me."

"I'm sure you will find a way to put your degree to use. For now, sit back, relax, and enjoy." Tyler gently leaned his head on hers. "You tell me what you need or want and it's yours. A condo, a car…"

"I could use a haircut." Lauren pushed back her overgrown bangs.

Tyler laughed. "We can start small. I'll send you to my hairdresser tomorrow." He wrapped his arm around her. "I'll show you being with me can be the happiest place on earth."

Breathing in the salty sea air lessened her anxiety. Closing her eyes, she allowed God's peace to wash over her.

Be still, and know that I am God.

Chapter 16

The second week in November she got the call.

"Hello, Lauren. My name is Frank Moore. Mitch Duncan, Tyler Stevens' manager, passed your number on to me."

"What can I do for you?"

"Well, a lot, I'm hoping. I'm the manager for child star Paul Miller. We are in desperate need of a teacher for him. Mitch told me you are a credentialed teacher?"

"Yes, I have my teacher credential, but I'm not currently teaching."

"That's perfect," he shouted. "Would you be interested in being on the set and overseeing Paul's studies between scenes? Pay is 500 a day with a bonus at the conclusion of filming."

She couldn't have heard right. "I'm sorry. Did you say $500 a day?"

"That's been approved by his parents. If that figure isn't acceptable, I could see if they will negotiate."

"No, that's fine." Lauren tried to cover her shock. She made $100 a day subbing for at least twenty kids, sometimes thirty-two. "I didn't think I heard you right."

"Great! Can you start tomorrow?"

This was insane! "Don't the parents want to meet me, interview me?"

"No need. You come very highly recommended."

"What are the hours?"

"Arrive around eight a.m. Generally we're done around four. Paul is only allowed to work six hours a day. Study time is built into his breaks, so you need to be available all day on the set." Frank seemed to be walking very fast from the sound of his panting. "The limo will be there tomorrow at seven a.m. and I'll brief you on the way."

"Well, I need to get out of a prior commitment…"

"Great. The driver will call you for your address. See you tomorrow, Lauren."

༄

"You've got to do it," Beth reassured her at the preschool that afternoon. They had been in the office talking for twenty minutes after the kids fell asleep. "See, girl. This is the life you were meant for."

"I can't just quit."

Beth laughed. "None of us would mind the overtime. Shannon will be ecstatic to hire an eighteen-year-old at minimum wage. As long as I don't have to do toilets, I'm happy."

Lauren laughed. "Never thought of it that way, but I guess you're right."

Suddenly Shannon, the director, came in the office.

"Hey." She walked to the desk. "I forgot the checks to deposit."

"See," Beth whispered walking by Lauren, nudging her. "It was meant to be."

Lauren sighed as Beth walked out of the office. "I was hoping to talk to you. I received a call today from the manager of a child star. He offered me a job being his on-set teacher.

"That is awesome." Shannon congratulated her.

"They want me to start tomorrow. I don't want to leave you high and dry…"

Shannon smiled. "I feel fortunate we've had you so long." She hugged her and smiled. "Don't think twice about us. We'll be fine." She paused and then shouted, "Hey Beth. How do you feel about split shifts?"

"Love the extra pay. Bring it on!" Beth responded.

"What do I wear?" Lauren asked Tyler that night on the phone.

"Some little black sexy thing," Tyler teased.

"I'm serious, Tyler."

"Don't be stressed out." Tyler assured her. "What do you wear when you teach?"

"A dress, usually, or slacks."

"That's fine. Seriously, Lauren, it's no big deal. You'll probably end up sitting around most of the day, maybe talking to him between shots."

"Well, Frank said-"

Tyler chuckled. "What they say and do are completely different. It's all politics. Besides, I've heard the kid's a menace."

Lauren sighed. "Thanks for the encouragement. I really appreciate it."

"Sorry. Welcome to my world."

ᑫᓬ

"The kid's a brat. No one likes to deal with him, especially his parents." Frank talked fast, half out of breath most of the time. "All I need is for you put up with him and pretend to teach him something until the film is done."

"How many teachers has he had?"

"Three during this movie alone. We even went a while without, which is a huge no-no."

Lauren's heart sank. It sounded like babysitting, not teaching. She stared out the window as Frank answered his cell phone.

Lord, be in control. Give me strength.

Though people rushed about, most took time to stare at her as they passed by. She walked fast, keeping up with Frank as he darted among people. She felt overdressed with everyone else wearing jeans or shorts.

Look professional and people will treat you as such, Lauren imagined her favorite college professor saying as she pulled out her favorite dress that morning.

"Paul, this is Lauren Drake, your new teacher," Frank introduced her when they found him in make-up.

"It's nice to meet you." Lauren extended her hand. Paul ignored them, studied his script as the makeup woman rubbed foundation on his skin.

"Well." Frank placed a hand on Lauren's back. "Have a great day. I'll check on you later."

"What's your favorite thing to do?" Lauren attempted a conversation.

When he didn't answer, she repeated herself.

"I'm busy studying my lines," Paul snapped.

Lauren backed off, sitting in a nearby chair.

Ten minutes later when it was time for his hair, Paul turned his attention to the TV.

"Do you like sports?"

"I'm watching TV. Can't you just leave me alone?"

Lauren calmly walked over and shut it off.

"HEY!" Paul screamed. "I was watching that!"

She smiled sweetly. "Now that I have your attention, let me introduce myself. My name is Miss Drake and I'm your teacher. I'm not here to have you talk back to me or tell me what to do. I'm here to help you learn. It doesn't matter how many teachers you have had or how you have treated them, today we start over. I will honor you and expect the same from you. Honor means treating others as special, doing more than what's expected and having a good attitude." The makeup lady tried to keep a straight face. Paul stared at Lauren dumbfounded.

She sat across from Paul. "What do you like to do in your spare time? Do you like sports?"

After a minute, Paul answered in a defensive voice. "I play video games. Sports are stupid."

"Remember, good attitude." She smiled. "What's your favorite subject in school?"

"None. I hate school!"

She frowned. "That's not a very good attitude. Which do you dislike the least?"

Paul shrugged. "Math, I guess. I like to figure out how much money I make."

"Great. Maybe we can do that later today."

After his hair was sprayed, he bolted out the door.

"You did good." The woman offered her hand to Lauren. "I'm Tammy."

Lauren shook hands, smiling weakly. "Lauren."

"Very impressive." Tammy grinned. "I've watched that little punk bully around the last three teachers. It's been terrible. Stick to your guns and you might actually make it."

When Lauren caught up to Paul he was talking to an older man.

"I'm Donald, Paul's father."

Lauren smiled, shaking his hand. "Lauren Drake."

Donald smiled. "My son already hates you, so you must be doing a fine job."

"Dad!" Paul sneered at his father.

Donald patted his back. "You need a tutor. Miss Drake seems nice. The director threatened to stop filming if you lose another teacher. And if that happens, your career could be over."

Paul shot his father a piercing look before stomping off.

The rest of the day Lauren followed Paul around smiling, patting him on the back, congratulating him on good scenes. He glared at her without a word. At lunch Lauren excitedly filled her plate with lots of good things to eat from the Italian buffet. Paul took three pieces of pizza and a soda.

"What other actors have you taught?" Lauren was impressed Paul acknowledged her.

"You are actually my first."

Lauren could tell that wasn't the answer he was hoping for when he took a bite of his pizza and diverted his attention elsewhere.

She leaned in close and whispered, "Truth is, I'm Tyler Stevens' friend. I met him before I got a full-time job and now I can't get hired because I'm so popular."

Paul's eyes widened. A grin appeared on his face. "Tyler Stevens? Really?"

Lauren nodded.

Paul shrugged his shoulders. "He seems cool. I'd like to meet him."

Lauren smiled. "I could arrange that."

By the end of the day, Paul read for Lauren from a fourth-grade book she brought.

"I read scripts every day." Paul argued when she suggested he needed to read at home every night.

"It's not the same because it's broken into pieces. Besides, you're reading for the purposes of performance, not for enjoyment or knowledge."

For math, they broke Paul's salary for the film into a daily rate and compared it to what he made on his last film. When Lauren left at the end to the day, Paul actually said, "See you tomorrow."

⁓

Every day got easier with Paul. Lauren bought books she thought he might be interested in. By Friday all his subjects were scheduled out, incorporating writing and reading into science and social studies to make the most of their time.

Tyler joined them for lunch Friday. Paul's eyes widened and his jaw dropped as he shook Tyler's hand. "I love your action movies."

"Thanks. Keep it up, kid. In no time you'll be an action star. But do well in your studies because in the long run your education is more important than acting. You're lucky to have such a great teacher." Tyler winked at Lauren.

Within a few minutes Paul fired questions at him. Lauren enjoyed seeing the kind, brotherly side of Tyler. At the end of the day, Lauren put her arm around Paul's shoulders and squeezed him. "Have a good weekend. Thanks for working so hard this week."

"Thanks. I'm glad you're my teacher. Tell Tyler 'hi'!" and he ran off to meet his dad.

Lauren had a sense of accomplishment she hadn't felt for a long time. She was a teacher again and she loved it.

༄

"We can't thank you enough, Lauren." His father handed her a bonus check at the end of six weeks. "We have seen a tremendous improvement with Paul in his reading, writing, and attitude. We would love for you to work with Paul when he shoots his next film in a few months."

"I'd like that." Lauren smiled and hugged Paul. "It's been a pleasure getting to know you. You're a great guy." She leaned over and whispered in his ear. "Tyler's right. You'll be a big action hero someday."

A grin spread from cheek to cheek as he hugged her back.

༄

"What are you going to do with all your money?" Tyler said at dinner that night.

"Don't spend it all in one place now," Adam said.

"I'm going to pay off my car and insurance for next year. I'll put the rest in the bank."

"No shopping?" Adam teased.

Lauren smiled. "I'll keep out a little for Christmas presents."

Adam lifted his water. "To God's plan."

Lauren clinked glasses with him. "Much better than my own."

Chapter 17

Though the electric blanket was on high, Lauren felt chilled. December 23rd she and her mother would snuggle under a blanket on the couch. With only the lights on the Christmas tree, they would sing their favorite carols and then read the story of Mary from the Bible. They talked about how scared Mary was, but that she trusted God. And He blessed her because of it.

"God has a special plan for you Laurie." Her mother held her tight, kissing her forehead. "He will use you in marvelous ways. Listen to Him and believe His promises, that He will always love you, forgive you and help you prosper. He knows your heart's desires and wants to make them all come true."

Lauren thought it would be easier each year, but it still hurt. She missed her laughter and desired that closeness with her tonight.

The ring of Lauren's phone startled her.

"I didn't wake you, did I?" Tyler said.

"No." Lauren dried her eyes with a tissue. "How was work?"

"Horrid." Cupboards and then the refrigerator slammed shut. "The producers are freaking out because the film is over budget. They want to be wrapped by the first. The director is pissed off at everyone complaining. There's talk of us working on Christmas."

"You're kidding?" Another wave of sadness overcame Lauren.

"No. The camera people are making a stink about it. There's talk of a strike. On top of that, they served Asian food tonight. I've been starving for the last two hours and now nothing sounds good." She heard his apple crunch. "How are you?"

"Tired."

"What'd you do today?" Tyler asked.

"Wrapped gifts, shopped with dad for Christmas dinner." She closed her eyes to hold back the tears. Silence followed.

"Lauren? You there?"

"Yeah." She took a deep breath to calm herself. "I'm just sad."

"Why?"

"I miss my mom this time of year."

"I'm sorry. I'm sure the director will give us the day off. Mac called, asked what I was up to…"

"Invite Adam." Lauren's mood began to lighten. "We'll eat about two o'clock. Dad makes a mean lasagna."

"Lasagna, huh? Not the traditional turkey with all the fixings?"

"Mom started the tradition, being too busy shopping and wrapping to cook Christmas dinner. Dad agreed as long as he could make what he wanted. We ended up with lasagna."

Tyler laughed. "How long ago did this start?"

"Eighteen years ago."

"I'll call Adam tomorrow and invite him. Surely there's something in my contract against me working holidays. I'll check with Mitch."

Lauren hung up the phone, thanking God for turning her sadness into joy.

༄

The morning was filled with presents and her favorite breakfast of cinnamon rolls. Lauren had put away her new clothes and showered when Tyler called to say they were on their way.

"What'd you get for Christmas?" There was so much background noise as Tyler drove Lauren could barely hear him.

"Clothes, CDs. Dad gave me a beautiful pearl bracelet."

"Cool. Our gift is a little big, so you'll have to forgive us for not wrapping it."

"You didn't have to get me anything." Lauren thought of the small gifts she had for Tyler and Adam under the tree.

"It's being delivered. Has it arrived yet?"

Lauren peeked out the kitchen window but the bush blocked her view. "I don't think so." She opened the door as Tyler drove into the driveway with a beautiful baby blue convertible. He smiled when her jaw dropped. "Merry Christmas."

Lauren hung up, walked toward the car in a trace. Adam got out of his parked car. "You approve?"

"Are you kidding?"

"You mentioned the first thing you'd do is get a new car when you got a job." Tyler opened the passenger door for her. "Figured since I ruined that for you, it's the least I could do. We thought you'd look good driving a convertible. Mac had your top of the line stereo put in."

Lauren climbed in the front seat. "This is too much. Way too much."

"Nothing but the best for our Angel." Adam jumped in the back. "I loaded the MP3 player with all my albums."

"Wow." Richard joined them on the driveway.

"We thought it suited your daughter." Adam motioned for Richard to join them. "Let's take it for a spin."

After they both drove it, Lauren and Richard agreed it was worth keeping.

Tyler laughed when he unwrapped the new leather wallet Lauren gave him. Removing his old ripped one from his pocket, he eagerly transferring the contents. "Just what I needed."

Adam thumbed through the leather Bible Lauren gave him with his name engraved on the cover.

"The commentaries are by my favorite author. I think you'll enjoy his writing."

"You're so thoughtful Angel." Adam hugged her.

"Well, it's not a new car."

Tyler gave her a hug and kiss on the cheek. "Thank you."

The boys had the monster TV Lauren bought for her dad set up before dinner, tuned in to the football game to check on the score.

"You make fabulous lasagna, Richard," Tyler commented as they cleared dinner dishes.

"Thank you." Richard avoided eye contact as he packed up the leftover food.

Tyler could hear Lauren and Adam laughing as they washed the dishes. "I'm sorry I was a jerk when you put in my pool. I've found I need to be hard on people so they don't take advantage of me."

"I treat my employees with respect and they do the same with me." Richard looked up at Tyler. "You were a jerk, but I understand money and stardom can sometimes inflate a person's ego, causing them to think highly of themselves and treat others badly."

Tyler froze, holding the butter dish in mid-air.

"I believe you must not be like that now if my daughter cares to spend time with you."

Tyler suddenly felt sixteen, talking to his girlfriend's father who was holding his shotgun. "Yes, sir."

༄

It was cold and dark inside when Tyler arrived home. Turning on the heater, he went to the entertainment room and opened the blinds to reveal light from the full moon. This was the first Christmas that mattered in five years, since he'd gone to his parents' house. Lauren's laughter echoed in his head. The way she and her father talked, completing the other's sentences amazed him. Tyler had been to a lot of houses and parties filled with tons of people and energy. Nothing compared to the warmth at the Drake's house. The love filled his heart with peace.

He dialed the number he should have forgotten by now. They would be in bed, but he wanted to hear her voice. That would make the day complete.

It rang three times before she answered sleepily.

"Merry Christmas, Ma." Tyler fought back the tears.

༄

"Tyler was on his best behavior tonight," Richard commented to Lauren when they were alone that night.

"He respects me, Dad. He doesn't even try to kiss me on the lips anymore. Admit it, he's growing on you."

"I still like Adam more." Richard ended the conversation.

With her new pajamas and her flannel sheets Lauren was warm and cozy in bed. "Happy birthday, Jesus. Thank you for the day You entered the world and for all the blessings You have given me." She drifted off to sleep thinking of her mother holding her tight and telling her about the miracle of Christmas.

Chapter 18

"You are gorgeous." Tyler approached Lauren as she entered the room.

"Thank you." She ran her hand down her green velvet gown and twirled for him.

"I think your dress might be missing something." Tyler picked up a velvet box off the coffee table. He turned it toward her and opened it. Lauren was almost blinded by all the sparkling diamonds on the bracelet. She had picked out the matching necklace from Gretchen when she got the dress.

She gasped, reaching her trembling hand to touch it. "It is so beautiful."

Tyler fastened it to her wrist. "I needed something that would do your beauty justice." He lifted her hand and gently kissed it.

As soon as the band began to play after dinner, Adam escorted Lauren to the dance floor.

"Any New Year's resolutions?" Adam asked between twirls.

"The one I made to Tyler is to allow him to lavish me with beautiful and expensive gifts and not complain." Lauren smiled. "See my new bracelet?"

"Beautiful. And he's right. You do need to get used to it."

Lauren spotted Tyler across the room, laughing and talking with friends. "Some days I think we are so close, but then something inside me makes me wonder."

"Wonder what?"

Lauren looked into Adam's eyes. "If he's the one or if I just want him to be." She rested her head on his shoulder. "Maybe I analyze things too much."

"Not at all Angel. There's no rush. God will let you know."

They danced in silence for a while until Lauren spoke. "How about you, sir? What is your resolution?"

Adam smiled and leaned his head against hers. "To take good care of my angel. Make sure she smiles every day."

Lauren laughed. "When I hang out with you, smiling isn't hard to do."

Tyler spun her around the dance floor. They were laughing, at what Lauren couldn't remember. He was so handsome in his tux. All night he was attentive to her. He watched over her when she was with Adam. The rest of the time he stood beside her, talking to others about her and with her. The way he rested his hand on her shoulder or put his hand on the small of her back made her feel so close to him. When he smiled, her heart melted.

"You were the best thing that happened to me this year." He rested his cheek against hers.

Lauren ran her fingers through the hair on his neck. "You are the best thing that has ever happened to me. The past six months have been an amazing dream."

Tyler's voice was quiet and serious. "I keep waiting to wake up next to your side."

As the countdown began, they stared into each other's eyes. She wanted to say it, but she didn't want to feel foolish...

Seven, six, five...

"I love you, Tyler."

He placed his hands on her cheeks. "May I have permission to kiss you?"

As the crowd shouted "one," Lauren nodded. It was short, but filled with passion.

"Happy New Year, Lauren." He whispered in her ear. "Maybe this will be the best one yet."

Chapter 19

"What'cha doin'?" Tyler's excited voice didn't stir Lauren from lying on her bed, staring at the ceiling.

"Nothing." Rolled over, she pulled her quilt under her chin.

"Adam's here. Come over and we'll go out."

"I don't think so."

"C'mon. We can go out dancing."

"I'd rather stay home tonight." Lauren closed her eyes to push back tears.

"Didn't you hear me? Get all prettied up and come over. It's Friday night. Let's go out."

"No, Tyler." Lauren heard Adam's voice in the background.

"She said 'no.' Something's wrong," Tyler said to Adam.

"Angel," Adam said into the phone, "what's wrong?"

"I don't know. Maybe I just need sleep."

"Then rest you shall have. Pack a bag. We'll be there in about an hour and a half. Tell your dad we're kidnapping you for a few days."

"What are you talking about?" Lauren rubbed her temples.

"We're taking you away for some rest, relaxation and maybe some fun."

"I can't. I have too much to do this weekend."

"It'll wait. Pack warm clothes. We'll be there soon."

She rolled off her bed and kneeled beside it. "God, I need peace. Please come and fill me with Your Spirit."

"Where are you going?" Her father frowned when she entered the kitchen with her suitcase.

"I don't know, Dad. They just told me I would be gone a few days."

Richard shook his head disappointedly. "I think you've been going out too much lately. You know what it does to you."

Lauren raised her hand to stop him. "I feel on the verge of a breakdown. I need time away. I'll call you tomorrow." She kissed her father's cheek. "I love you."

She walked out the door as the boys drove up in Adam's SUV.

"Hey, baby." Tyler hung out of the passenger's window as they pulled into the driveway. "Need a lift?"

"Definitely."

Tyler jumped out of the car to help with Lauren's suitcase. "Please, allow me."

"Jump in, Angel." Adam patted the seat beside him.

"So, where are we going?" Lauren fastened her seat belt.

"You'll find out soon enough." Adam smiled.

"Wake me when we get there." Tyler settled into the backseat and closed his eyes.

They made small talk until they got on the freeway. As Adam sped off into the horizon Lauren became quiet. Almost an hour passed before she spoke.

"I'm bipolar." She slowly turned from the window to look at a Adam's face.

"Really?" he asked without flinching.

Lauren turned back to the window. "I've dealt with depression all my life. After my mom passed away and my first boyfriend left me, I went to my doctor seeking a referral to see a counselor. He prescribed me antidepressants. Over the next several months, I would go out dancing and drinking on the weekends, spend money I didn't have, and often make decisions without thinking. Three medications and seven months later I saw a psychologist. He diagnosed me as bipolar. The manic side was dormant until I took antidepressants."

"Are you on medication now?" Adam took her hand in his.

"No. Manic spells come mostly when I'm excited or have a lot to do and the depression is seasonal. During the good times I don't think about it, but then it comes, paralyzing me. The past several days have been hard because I've been really down."

Adam caressed her check. "You're very brave to face your problem."

A tear fell as she turned to Adam. "Now you know why your Angel's wings are tattered and broken."

Adam wiped the tear away. "Not broken, just broken in. Nothing you could say would make me think any less of you. It doesn't change the fact that you are a genuine, loving person."

"Either you are the most sincere man I know or you just know a lot of good lines."

"I've seen a lot in my life. Circumstances don't make a person bad unless they allow them to. What can I do to help?"

Lauren bit her bottom lip nervously, turning to Tyler asleep in the backseat. "Tell him somehow, sometime. I don't know that I can." Lauren leaned back in the seat. "My dad thinks I've been maniac, making bad choices about going out with you guys. I don't feel out of control, but that's why you need to know. It's easy to slip into my old ways."

"Understood. What can I do for you when you're depressed?"

She squeezed Adam's hand. "Be my friend. Stay with me until it passes."

"I can do that. But make me a promise."

"What?"

"Tell me when you are feeling high or low. No matter what time it is or how far away I am, call me. Can you do that?"

"You really want me to?" Lauren frowned.

"Why is it so hard for you to accept that people care about you? You've given so much to me in the past six months I want to help you. Will you let me?"

"Yes." Lauren leaned her head on his shoulder. "Thank you."

"We'll get through it together."

The altitude, along with Lauren's anticipation, climbed as they headed up the mountain. White powdery snow covered the trees and lined the rocks on the side of the road. Lauren smiled.

"We thought it would be a good weekend for a getaway to my cabin."

Lauren shook her head as she chuckled. "Beach house, cabin in the woods, what's next?"

"Never a dull moment, Angel. Not with us."

༄

"So, you two talk about me the whole way up?" Tyler and Adam unpacked food in the kitchen while Lauren showered. "You didn't spread any nasty lies about me to win her for yourself, did you?"

Adam didn't even look up from his unpacking. "She told me she's manic depressive. She asked me to tell you."

Tyler froze. "You're kidding right?"

Adam took the teapot from the cupboard and began filling it with water. "She has dealt with depression most of her life. She went on antidepressants, which started manic spells. It's leveled off and she doesn't take medication anymore but still has ups and downs. It makes sense actually. All her sad days mixed with her uncontrollable excitement."

Tyler shook his head. "She's psycho?"

"There are different stages of the disease." Adam put it on the stove. "She has a mild form."

Tyler sat down at the kitchen table. "She's psycho."

"Knock it off, Zeus. Don't be so closed-minded. It takes a strong person to make it through so many years of negative self talk. Lauren needs us. This is no time to run."

"She seemed different. Better."

Adam glared at Tyler. "It's only a problem if you make it one. Be mature, for once."

"What's that supposed to mean?" Tyler growled.

"You bail when the going gets tough. If you care about Lauren see past the stereotypes. Appreciate her values. She's concerned with making mistakes she did in the past. When she's manic, she doesn't think rationally. Alcohol encourages that side of her. That's why she wanted us to know." Adam sat beside Tyler. "All that emotion is what makes Lauren special, why she loves so intensely. You need to remember she can also hurt very badly."

Tyler nodded, grabbed his coat and walked out the door.

"The water was nice and warm." Lauren emerged from her room in sweats, brushing her wet hair. "Hot cocoa would be great…"

Looking around the kitchen, she frowned when she realized Tyler was gone. "You told him?"

Adam sighed. "He needs time. It's big news for such a narrow mind to comprehend."

Lauren nodded. Her lip began to quiver as tears began.

Adam approached her with a hug. "Give him time. He's not good with surprises."

Lauren buried her face in his shoulder. "You took it so great I hoped he would too."

Adam rubbed her back. "How about that hot cocoa and a game of cards?"

༺༻

"I think you have skips up your sleeve." Adam laughed as the door opened.

"I'm lucky I guess." Lauren focused on the cards.

"Hi." Tyler joined them at the table.

"Did you find what you were looking for?" Adam played his discard.

"In a way." Tyler gently rubbed Lauren's arm. "I'd like to talk to you."

Lauren took a deep breath before nodding at Adam.

"I was getting whooped anyway." Adam stood, putting his cards on the table. "Good night, Angel. Let me know if you need anything."

"Thanks." She smiled at him, gathering up the cards.

"Adam told me." Tyler ran his fingers over the paisley design on the tablecloth. "It freaked me out. I've never known someone normal having that." Tyler stopped and took in Lauren's beauty. "I love spending time with you, going out, dancing. I don't see what the big deal is."

"That's how I got myself in trouble in the past."

"Bummer I missed those days."

"I was insecure, needy, pretty altogether pathetic."

Tyler stood, taking Lauren's hand to help her up. "I respect you. I think I've shown that. I can't give up drinking altogether, and honestly, I love dancing with you."

"I know the closer we get, it might be difficult for you to accept my terms. If you would rather date other people, I understand."

"Different, not as hard as it used to be." Tyler reached for Lauren's hand. "I enjoy being with you and don't want to give that up."

Lauren smiled. "The last several months have been great. It's just easier when the people around me understand what's going on."

Tyler nodded. "Have I ever seen you manic?"

"The night I came to your house after finishing student teaching. And when I dragged you out for chips and salsa. When I'm manic, I get an idea in my head and I can't let it go. After you returned from Africa, I hardly slept for three days."

Tyler smiled, ran his hand down Lauren's hair. "You're still the best I've ever dated. You're not going to scare me away so easily."

"Thank you." She squeezed his hand. "That means a lot."

Tyler smiled. "C'mon. I'll tuck you in."

Ten minutes later Tyler emerged from Lauren's room to join Adam at the kitchen table.

"You two make up?" Adam typed away on his computer.

Tyler leaned back, putting his feet on the table. "When I left I wandered around thinking, what if Lauren wasn't in my life? I realized I've never been so happy with someone. With Lotus, it was just about sex. I enjoy being with Lauren, even respect her."

A smirk appeared on Adam's face. "Imagine that. Sex isn't everything."

"I have to admit I didn't believe you on that one." Tyler laughed. "Maybe you are smarter than I."

༄

She awoke to the pitter pat of falling rain. Pulling the blankets to her chin, the air chilled her lungs as she breathed it in. There was a faint smell of burning wood as light flickered beneath the door of her room. Wrapping the quilt from the top of the bed around her, she slipped into her cozy slippers. She was greeted by the warmth of the fire burning in the fireplace as she shuffled into the family room. Adam sat on the couch, feet up on the coffee table, keyboard on his lap and earphones on. His fingers tested different cords, scribbling on his pad in between playing. He didn't notice her until she sat beside him.

"How's my sleepy Angel?" He removed the earphones, placing them with his keyboard on the coffee table. "Hopefully you weren't disturbed by bad dreams."

Lauren shook her head. Resting her head against the back of the couch, a sleepy smile formed on her lips. "Remember during the summer when we stayed up late talking or you'd play for me."

"It was a great summer."

"You really don't sleep much?"

"Don't know if it's a gift or a curse. Sometimes I sleep six hours, sometimes two. I never quite know what it's going to be."

Lauren yawned. "It's like that when I'm manic. I'll wake up at two, my thoughts racing and I can't go back to sleep."

"Do you get tired the next day?"

"If the mania continues, I'm fine. It's like I don't think about how much sleep I need."

Adam stretched her feet out across his lap. "Are you manic now?"

She shook her head. "Over tired. That happens when I'm depressed." She closed her eyes. "How long has it been raining?"

"Since midnight. Forecast for tomorrow is snow."

Her eyes popped open. "That's not something you see everyday."

Adam laughed. "Spoken like a true Southern Californian girl."

"No better place on earth."

"You never wanted to move?" Adam asked.

"Thought about it in college. Then I watched the Weather Channel."

"Ever been to the east coast?"

"Farthest east I've been is Missouri," Lauren said. "Hot and humid as all get-out."

"It's amazingly beautiful, very distinct seasons. From the fall trees to the luscious green hills it is God's masterpiece displayed for all to see. The most peaceful times in my life were in upstate New York."

"Would you ever move back?"

Adam had a far-off look on his face. "I enjoy visiting my sister Ruth once a year. Too many memories to live there. Your talk with Tyler went well, I take it."

Lauren nodded and sighed. "I should be used to the initial reaction of shock. There's such a negative stigma attached."

"We all have secrets. What matters the most is how we respond to them." Adam patted Lauren's legs. "Jesus says He will make your burdens light. Lean on Him and walk in faith believing with Him all things are possible."

"I know that in my heart, but sometimes everything gets messed up in my head."

Adam took her hand in his. "I'll be here to remind you. As often as it takes."

༄

The small beam of light through the slit in the curtains woke Lauren. Opening the curtains revealed a picturesque winter scene. White patches scattered on the ground with clumps atop the trees. After tying back the curtains to fill the room with light, she settled in her bed with her Bible, praying for an open heart and mind.

An hour later Lauren emerged from her room dressed and ready to start the day.

"Sleeping beauty awakes." Tyler read the newspaper as he sipped his coffee.

"I'm on vacation." Lauren flicked at his paper as she passed him. "That means taking my time in the morning."

Adam took his coffee cup to the sink. "Would you like breakfast or lunch?"

"Chocolate. Have any chocolate?"

Adam rummaged through the cupboards. "Cookies. How about cookies?"

"Perfect." Lauren took the bag from Adam and filled up a glass of water. "I've decided to move out of my dad's house."

"Really?" Adam joined them at the table. "When did all this come about?"

"During my devotion time this morning. I need space to be responsible. God has given me peace with it."

"How will he handle this?" Tyler folded his paper, laying it on the table. "Do I need to purchase a bulletproof vest?"

"He won't take it very well, but I'll tell him it was Adam's idea so he won't be mad."

"Not a problem." Adam patted her hand. "I'll help you look for a place."

Lauren nodded, biting into her second cookie. "I just need a job to support myself."

"Who needs a job when you have rich friends?" Tyler reached across the table, stealing a cookie from the bag in front of Lauren.

"Thanks, but I'm not a freeloader."

"I could use some help scheduling my concerts." Adam reached for the bag.

"And I need someone to-well, I'm sure I could find a job for you." Tyler winked.

"I'm a teacher. I need to find more successful young stars in need of an on-screen teacher."

"Whatever you say, teach." Adam stood. "We are leaving in a half hour."

"Where are we going?"

"Skiing." Adam filled Lauren's glass.

"Skiing?"

"What do you normally do on a mountain covered with snow?" Tyler laughed.

"I've never skied," Lauren said.

"We have an instructor meeting us." Adam handed her the glass. "Check your closet. Ski pants and a jacket should be hanging in it."

"We'll have a great time." Tyler squeezed her arm. "Trust us."

Lauren successfully skied one small bunny slope and then fell at least twenty times down the beginner slope. Laughter filled the air when Lauren pulled Tyler down while he tried to help her up and then he tripped Adam. Despite the fun, she was ready to be dry and warm.

"See you in a few hours." Tyler kissed her cheek. "Miss us."

She sat in a corner booth where she could see the TV but couldn't hear it. She put her feet up, waiting for her hot chocolate. She closed her eyes. With each deep breath she felt renewed. Life was good. She was very blessed.

༄

"Hi, honey." Richard met her at the door, taking her suitcase. "How was your trip?"

"Good." She followed her father into the living room.

"Are you hungry?"

"Not really." Lauren sat down on the sofa. "I'd like to talk to you."

"What's up?"

Palms sweating, stomach flipping, she took a deep breath. "I did a lot of thinking and praying this weekend. It's time I move out."

Richard nodded slowly. "How will you pay rent?"

"I have money in savings. Paul's parents said they expect to need me again at the beginning of the year."

"You can't pay rent with a hope, Lauren."

"I know, Dad." She stared at her fidgeting hands. "I feel like God is telling me to step out on faith. He will provide the job or jobs I need to pay the rent."

Silence hung in the air like a black cloud as Richard leaned forward, staring at the floor.

"Is this so you can have others spend the night or decide not to come home?"

"I spent a lot of time listening to God this weekend. I'm not doing anything to be ashamed of." She paused before continuing. "I told Adam and Tyler the truth this weekend."

Shock covered his face. "I thought you didn't want people to know."

"They're my friends, Dad. It gave me the opportunity to explain why I need to be careful going out. They understand and agreed to watch out for me."

Richard touched Lauren's cheek. "I love you. In some respects, you just came back to me. I'm not ready to lose you again."

Lauren wrapped her arms around his neck. "Don't think of it as losing me. Think of it as moving our relationship to the next level."

Chapter 20

Lauren lay on her bed staring at the ceiling when Adam called. "You find anything with Shelly?"

"Not really." Two days of apartment shopping with Shelly only frustrated her.

"Good. I talked to a friend today that has a friend, and well, there is a lady named Jean who is looking to rent a townhouse for a reasonable price to a responsible person. I told her we'd swing by tomorrow."

"What's the catch?"

"None, except maybe that it belonged to her mother. She doesn't want to sell it. She's excited that you are a teacher."

Lauren sighed. "I guess we can go look."

"What's wrong, Angel?"

"I'm tired and overwhelmed. I had no idea it would be this difficult."

"Hang in there. I think it's about to get easier."

༄

Between the small talk, Lauren read the directions for Adam. Trees lined the driveway back to a dead-end lot surrounded by the quaint townhouses. It was small, about twenty units, set off from the busy road.

"Very peaceful." Lauren scoped out the neighborhood. "You sure this isn't a senior complex?"

Adam laughed as he parked. "Maybe that's the downfall. Let's find out."

The two-story townhouse had a garage and a small grass area in front. Though the door was wide open, Adam knocked.

"Come in, come in," a voice called. "I'm opening windows. The painters didn't bother leaving the windows open like I asked them to. You definitely don't have to worry about crime here."

A woman in her mid-forties emerged from the back, greeting them in the living room. "Hi." She extended her hand to Lauren. "You must be Lauren. I'm Jean. Adam has told me so much about you." Turning to Adam, she extended her hand. "It's a pleasure to meet you, Adam."

"The pleasure is mine."

She ran her fingers through her already tousled hair, "A little bit about this place. My mother moved in ten years ago. I re-carpeted and re-painted a week ago. The majority of the people in the neighborhood are retired."

"This is your living area." She motioned to a couch and chair. "I thought the person that moved in might need furniture, but you are welcome to call Goodwill." Lauren wasn't wild about the floral print, but with covers they'd be great. "I also left the furniture on the patio off the kitchen." Jean walked over to the back sliding door.

A very small iron table with two chairs was surrounded by plants and flowers. "My mother loved plants. She enjoyed gardening and wasn't going to let the fact that she lived in a townhouse stop her. The kitchen has all working major appliances."

It wasn't as big as some places she had looked at, but Lauren fell in love with it.

After the tour was complete, Jean turned to Lauren. "What do you think?"

"It's wonderful."

"I hoped you'd like it." Jean surprised Lauren by patting her arm. "I need someone responsible to rent it. My husband and I have teenagers that may want to live here some day, so we don't want to sell it."

Lauren bit her lips nervously. "How much?"

"I only need enough to cover the mortgage and repairs. $1000 a month."

"Really?" Lauren tried not to act surprised.

"Any less and I'm taking a loss."

Lauren smiled. "That will be fine."

"Great. You can move in anytime. Mortgage is paid through the month. I need your first check at the beginning of next month."

"You don't want first and last month's rent? A deposit?"

Jean laughed. "Oh, no, honey. I know how hard that is. Promise not to destroy the place and give me time to find someone new before you move."

"I promise." Lauren shook on it. "I can move in Saturday."

"Perfect. It will be a pleasure having you here."

"It's too good to be true," Lauren told Adam over lunch.

"Amazing, isn't it?" Adam was a quarter done with his sandwich and Lauren still hadn't picked hers up.

Lauren glared at him suspiciously. "Do you have anything to do with all this going so smoothly?"

"It's all about who you know."

Lauren stared at her food. "Part of me doing this was doing it by myself. Feeling like an adult because I could take care of myself." She looked up at Adam. "Thank you, but-"

"Oh, Angel, you did it by yourself. What I meant is it was fortunate I knew Barbara who knows Jean."

Lauren nodded. "Everything was either too expensive or in a terrible neighborhood. Today went so smoothly."

Adam raised an eyebrow. "God's will, perhaps. So, we move on Saturday?"

Lauren smiled. "Glad I don't have much to pack."

Adam called Lauren Friday night to tell her he hired movers. "We'd have to rent a truck anyways, might as well get the burly men that go with it. With Tyler out of town, I didn't want to put the stress on your dad.

By noon all of her belongings were in her townhouse. After lunch Shelly, Adam and Richard insisted on unpacking. Lauren was excited to have all the help, but it soon became overwhelming. "Where does this go?" and "I put this here," was shouted from every direction.

Adam smiled, kissing Lauren on the forehead after her father and Shelly left. "Congratulations, Angel. I'll be on my way so you can relax."

"You don't have to go." Lauren didn't mean to sound pathetic.

"I'm sure you want to enjoy your place alone." Adam opened the door.

She bit her lip. "I don't really want to be alone. Could you stay? Maybe we could order pizza for dinner, watch a movie?"

Adam shut the door. "How about pepperoni?"

"Do you love it?"

"I do." Lauren fell sleep a few hours before but didn't mind being woken by Tyler. "How was the opening?"

"Good. Wish you were here. The guy sitting next to me hogged the armrest and ate most of the popcorn."

Lauren chuckled. "Who was next to you?"

"The director."

"I would have liked to have been there. I'm sure it was less chaotic than moving."

"You know what else we're missing this week?" Tyler rustled around, probably unpacking.

"No." Lauren tried to remember what she may have forgotten.

"The Globes. I'm nominated for Best Actor."

"Really?" Lauren felt so lame, dating a movie star and not knowing such an important event, but she avoided the gossip magazines and papers. "When are they?"

"Tomorrow. I didn't win because they didn't ask me to record a speech."

"I would have voted for you."

"Now that you have your own place," Tyler turned on his sweet, sexy voice, "can we have sleepovers?"

"No."

"C'mon, you're not living with your dad anymore. You can do what you want."

Lauren sighed. "I thought you understood."

"I do, sort of." There was a pause. "What about…"

"Good night, Tyler."

"Good night, Angel. Congratulations on your new place. When I come back, we'll celebrate."

⁂

Monday evening Tyler showed up on her doorstep, long-stemmed red roses in one hand and a bottle of champagne in the other.

"Come in." Lauren opened the door. "I'm rearranging things." She returned to the kitchen without hugging him or commenting on his gifts.

Stepping in he closed the door behind him. "I brought you a little something." Tyler set them on the dining room table. She didn't even turn around. "I would've got dinner, but I didn't know if you were cooking or wanted to go out. You didn't answer when I called."

"My battery died." Lauren moved pots from the kitchen cupboards to the floor. "I couldn't find my charger. So I started organizing my bedroom. I got through my desk and came for a glass of water. That's when I realized the dishes and pots and pans are in the wrong place. There's no way I could make dinner like this!"

Her rapid speech amazed Tyler. She was constantly moving, gesturing with her hands.

"Everyone helped me unpack. I would have put the glasses next to the refrigerator and the plates on the other side. The pots should go in one cupboard with the baking stones in the other. And the cookie sheets go with the stones, but I can't find them anywhere!"

Tyler opened his mouth to respond.

"I can't imagine they would have ended up in the bedroom." Lauren dashed passed Tyler down the hallway. "I'm sure I put them in the kitchen box. I know they aren't in the bathroom because I organized that earlier today." He heard her rustling in the other room. "What time is it?"

Tyler went in the kitchen, crouched down and pulled open the drawer underneath the stove. Cookie sheets were neatly stacked inside. "Five-thirty."

"Geez, where did the day go?" Her pitch rose with each phrase she blurted out. "Sorry I'm such a mess. I didn't realize it was getting so late. I need to do laundry." She suddenly appeared with her laundry basket. "Mind if I start a load?"

"No." Tyler held up a cookie sheet. "Found them."

Lauren maneuvered past the pots on the floor to the laundry room. "Where were they?"

"In the drawer under the stove. My mom kept hers there, so I figured-"

"I guess that's a good place for them." She dropped the basket on the floor. "I thought about making dinner, but I really don't have groceries. If you could wait a while, we could run to the store." Her volume increased as the water began to fill the washer. "What do you feel like? We could go out. I might feel like Chinese. Adam and I ordered pizza Saturday night. There's a good place that delivers. They have sandwiches. I love meatball sandwiches. Or they make calzones. Do you like calzones? I guess we can always order pizza."

Tyler returned to the dining table, collapsing into a chair. His head was spinning from her talking.

"So? What do you think?" She closed the laundry room door behind her.

"Are you on something?"

"Excuse me?" She blinked.

"You're talking so fast and you're all over the place, on to a new subject. You're acting crazy."

Lauren sighed. She closed her eyes and massaged her temples. "Not crazy."

Tyler carefully stepped over the piles of pots and pans to get to her. He wrapped his arms around her. "This is what your manic side is like."

A tear slipped down Lauren's cheek as she rested her head against his chest.

Tyler rubbed her back. "Hey, don't get all depressed on me. I can't handle both."

"I'm sorry." Lauren wiped her tears. "There's so much to do, and I want to get it all done."

Tyler caressed her cheek. "Understandable, but one thing at a time." He lifted her head to look in her eyes. "Hi. I missed you."

Lauren smiled. "I missed you, too."

Tyler collected the flowers and champagne, holding them out to her. "Congratulations on your new place."

Lauren accepted his presents. "They're beautiful." She closed her eyes as she inhaled the scent of the roses.

"Now," Tyler pulled out his phone, "I know a Chinese place that delivers. I'll order and then help you put away all the dishes where you want them."

"Sounds good." Lauren sighed. "I'll find a vase and glasses."

"Good." Tyler patted her head. "Remember, one thought at a time."

"Yes, Dr. Stevens." Lauren chuckled. "Thanks for reminding me."

Chapter 21

"I can buy my own groceries!" Lauren called Adam one afternoon when a grocery delivery boy showed up on her doorstep.

"It's easier to buy them online than to tell you what to get," Adam said. "I thought we could have steaks tonight and fish tomorrow. I guess if you don't feel like ice cream, I can eat it…"

Lauren smiled at his kindness.

She loved that the boys would come to her place for dinner and hang out, but she hated being alone at night. Every noise made her heart race.

"Move in with me." Tyler yawned as they spoke on the phone one night. "It would be so much easier."

"I won't live with anyone until I'm married." Lauren stretched. "You know that."

Lauren began to think Tyler had fallen asleep he was quiet for so long before he spoke.

"If I asked, what would you say?"

Lauren's heart raced and her palms started sweating. "Are you asking?"

"No."

"Then why bring it up?"

"You brought it up."

Lauren felt God speak to her heart. Although she didn't want to say it, she knew the timing was right.

"I need to marry someone that believes in God and has accepted Jesus as his Savior. The Bible says it's important that believers marry other believers."

"So, why hang out with me?"

Lauren smiled. "I keep hoping you'll come around."

"That could be a pretty lofty dream. I've cursed God more often than not in my lifetime."

"God forgives and forgets. He wants to make you a new man."

Tyler chuckled. "Don't know that I can handle more change. I appreciate and want your company rather than sex, I enjoy quiet nights at home instead of wild parties. I've given up drugs and only drink occasionally. See what getting involved with a Christian schoolteacher has done to me?"

"Aren't you happy?"

"Yes, Angel, I'm happy. If I wasn't, I wouldn't be talking to you in the middle of the night."

She wanted to be independent, not scared and lonely. She grabbed her teddy bear from the other side of her bed.

"I'll let you go." Tears began forming in her eyes as she squeezed the stuffed animal.

"Are you busy on Valentine's Day?"

That brought a smile to her face. "I don't know, am I?"

"Yes. You and me and a fancy, romantic dinner for two."

"Sounds great." She wiped her tears on the bear's soft brown fur. "Good night."

"Sweet dreams, Angel. Sweet dreams."

꒜

Growing up in LA she had always heard about the "castle on the hill", the biggest Christian church in the city. The sign at the entrance of the parking lot listed the time of the five Sunday services and three Saturday services. Last time she attended church was Christmas. She read her Bible every day, but she felt something was just not right. She craved the fellowship without the fanfare.

Six people greeted her at various locations between her car and church, shaking her hand or patting her shoulder. Light streamed into the sanctuary. The music was loud and contemporary. The usher walked her down the left side, five rows from the front.

"Is it this full at every service?" she couldn't help but ask the usher as he seated her.

"The 7:30 a.m. is usually only three-quarters full."

The three-leveled sanctuary that fit thousands was almost completely full. She had no idea there were that many Christians in her city.

Most of the songs the worship band played were on Christian radio. She closed her eyes and allowed God's spirit to fill her. She instantly felt peace, warmth inside.

The pastor preached a dynamic message from the book of Mark. John the Baptist in the wilderness, in his camel skins eating locusts, people asking "Who is this guy?" Lauren realized that was the question she asked herself.

"Who am I?" she thought every morning, climbing out of bed with no job to go to. She wondered that when she walked with Tyler, arm in arm among the movie stars and now that she lived alone, not accountable to her father for her whereabouts. She asked herself frequently "Who am I, God?"

How great is the love the Father has lavished on us, that we should be called children of God! And that is what we are!

Lauren wasn't crying at the altar call, but she had been touched by God. She was His child and only needed to seek Him.

༄

Tuesday while she was running errands, a call came from Paul's agent. Filming began on Monday. Was she available until April?

"Definitely." Lauren thanked God for the job. She decided to surprise Beth with lunch.

"Did you enjoy your little vacation?" Lauren told Beth about teaching Paul next week. They sat down with the kids to eat. It was a rainy day so they were all inside and full of energy.

"Yes. I went skiing with the boys."

"Didn't know you skiied." Beth shooed a three-year-old back to the other table.

"Neither did I. I'm settled in my new place. You have to come see it."

"Mr. Hollywood shacking up with you?" Beth peeled a banana for little Suzie.

Lauren grinned and answered sarcastically, "No, and I reminded him last week not until marriage."

"So, did he ask you to marry him?"

"Not really, but he did ask what I would say. I explained I won't marry an unbeliever."

Beth turned back to Lauren. "Look at you. Dating a gorgeous movie star and still holding out for salvation. Most people don't have that determination."

"I went to church Sunday." Lauren changed the subject. "God reminded me I'm His child, first and foremost. If I'm following Him, He will make great things happen. Then today, I got the call to teach Paul. That's what I need to do right now. Touch the life of this one guy."

Beth lifted her Coke. "Cheers to you, Lauren, changing the world one soul at a time."

"Even the rich and famous need God. If that's who God wants me to go to, so be it."

Chapter 22

The first day on the set Lauren picked up where they left off. Paul was excited about an adventure book he started reading, so Lauren worked that into her plans for him.

The director thanked Lauren when he greeted her in the morning for the work she was doing with Paul. "I hear he's not nearly the pain he used to be."

At lunchtime Paul was very talkative. First thing he asked was "Why do you always wear that?" pointing to her cross.

"Because I'm a Christian." She smiled. "I wear it to remind me Jesus loves me and died on a cross for my sins."

Paul nodded a little. "We don't go to church, but I know a little about it."

"I'll teach you more about the Bible if you'd like and if your parents don't mind. One of my favorite characters in the Bible is Paul. He was a great man of God."

Paul took another bite and moved on to his next question.

"How's Tyler?"

"Good. He'd love to stop by and have lunch with us, but he's filming again."

"Maybe you can come to my house for dinner one night." He became very excitedly. "I have a huge screen TV and XBox and…"

"That would be fun." Lauren pulled out his math book. "Let's see what you remember about fractions."

༄

Three days before Valentine's Day she came down with a nasty cold.

"You are not canceling on me." Lauren frowned when Tyler raised his voice at her. "I have reservations. I NEVER make reservations, especially on Valentine's Day."

"You didn't make them, Mitch did." Lauren turned the phone away as she coughed.

"Actually, I did the calling."

"I'm resting and taking my vitamins." Lauren rubbed her pounding head. "I'm trying to get better."

※

Valentine's Day she woke up with a fever. She called in sick to Paul's parents, took medicine and fell back asleep. She showered after awakening at noon, but found herself back in bed right after, head pounding and body aching.

"I'm sorry." She rubbed her forehead as she talked to Tyler. "I feel awful. I don't want you to spend hundreds of dollars on a dinner I can't even taste, let alone don't want to eat."

"But we have reservations," he whined like a disappointed child.

"It's the thought that counts." Lauren held her chest as she coughed. "I really appreciate your thought." He was silent for a while, so she decided to lighten the conversation. "You could take Adam if you want."

"Yeah. That might not be a bad idea."

"Just buy me a copy of the tabloids tomorrow when-" Lauren sneezed and put down the phone to blow her nose. "When you make the front page as the hottest new couple."

"You sound like crap."

"That's how I feel." Lauren collapsed onto her pillow. Even breathing was a chore.

"I'll be over about six. We'll kick it at your place tonight."

"I might still be in bed." Lauren closed her eyes.

"My favorite place in the house."

"I bet he proposes." Shelly called Lauren a few hours after she had talked to Tyler.

"No way." Lauren sat up in bed to take more medicine. "He is not ready for that."

"Lauren, you told me he brought it up the other night, and he's making such a big deal about the reservation."

Lauren rubbed her eyes. "He hasn't even said 'I love you'."

"You'd say yes, right?"

"He's not proposing." Lauren put her pillow over her head. "I have to go." Lauren hung up. The thought excited and frustrated her. What if he did?

I can't consider it. He's not a Christian.

The fever caused her to drift back to sleep before dwelling on it any farther.

Tyler arrived at six o'clock, a bag in each hand. Placing a brown bag with a grease stain on the side on the table, he carried the other to the freezer.

She knew it was from the corner Mexican drive-thru before opening it. Building a pyramid with the small salsa cups that littered the top of the bag, she made her way to the food below.

"Since you can't taste, I thought the spicier the better." Tyler closed the freezer. "Maybe it will clear your sinuses."

She finally made it to the large styrofoam container. Opening it revealed carne asade nachos smothered with sour cream and guacamole. Definitely her dish of choice, especially when sick. "Very thoughtful of you."

Lauren sat down at the table as Tyler walked to her stereo. Pulling a CD from his inside jacket pocket, he put it in the stereo and then handed her the case. "Present number one."

With the first beat, Lauren smiled. The newest album from her favorite female Christian artist, Kimberly Moore.

Lauren was shocked he remembered how much she liked her, let alone chose the newest one to purchase.

"Open it." He smiled like a Cheshire cat.

"*To Lauren – Keep walking in His light. In Him, Kimberly.*"

Autographed? "Amazing, Mr. Stevens." Lauren was truly impressed and flattered that he went to such effort.

Tyler took his burrito from the bag. "Yes, that's what they say."

"So, what else do you have in that jacket of yours?" Lauren reached to feel his pocket.

"The night is still young." He pushed her hand away. "Sit back and let it unfold, my dear."

After dinner, Lauren lay with her head on a pillow in Tyler's lap, a box of tissue by her side. She was comfy in her sweats with her quilt around her. They watched the previews before the latest romance movie Tyler bought her, present number two. He massaged her back and neck gently, relaxing her aching body. He was doing a great job of taking care of her.

"Why the big deal about ruining your reservations?" She didn't think Shelly was right, but the curiosity was killing her. *Oh Lord, he's not going to propose, is he?*

"This is the first time in five years I've made plans to go out on Valentine's Day."

Lauren rolled over, looking up at him, surprised. "Really? Why?"

He brushed back Lauren's bangs, his gazed locked on hers. "I've always thought if you go out with someone on Valentine's Day, it should mean something, especially in my line of work. The next day, pictures will be everywhere. This year, I was ready to tell everyone I've found the perfect woman."

Lauren's heart skipped a beat when he reached in his pocket. *Oh God, what will I say? He doesn't believe in You...*

He pulled out a silver bracelet with a heart charm at the end. He smiled as he fastened it on her wrist. "I wanted to give you something you can wear everyday to remind you that you have my heart."

His sincerity touched her heart. Lauren thought she was going to cry, but she sneezed instead. After she blew her nose, she turned to Tyler with a frown. "Sorry I ruined the great evening you had planned."

"If you refused to see me, it would have been ruined. You'll just have to make it up to me by going out with me every night for a week when you're well."

Lauren grinned. "That's some payback. I suppose they have to be fancy restaurants."

"Of course." Tyler smiled. "Nothing but the best for you."

Lauren spent more time staring at her bracelet than the movie. She had dreamt of the day Tyler would profess his love to her for the last several months. Now that it was here, it wasn't as grand as she imagined. Tyler's fame had begun to fade for her. Today he was just a guy, her boyfriend. Someone comfy to lie on. His heart was changing. He opened his heart to her; hopefully, next it would be to the Lord.

Tyler served her a dish of chocolate brownie ice cream halfway through the movie. When it was over, Tyler carried her to bed. She was awake, but didn't mind being taken care of.

"Thanks for the bracelet." She smiled as he tucked all her blankets around her. "I love it."

"I'm glad." Tyler knelt besides Lauren's bed. She could see tears forming in his eyes.

Lauren placed her hand on his cheek. He kissed her gently, leaving without a word.

Five minutes after he left, her phone rang.

"I love you" he blurted out as soon as she answered.

This time she cried. "I love you, too, Tyler."

Chapter 23

A few weeks later Adam called on her way to work.

"Are you busy tonight? I've got something I want to show you."

"Where have you been lately?" Lauren asked when Adam picked her up at her townhouse. "I feel like I haven't seen you much."

"Creating new songs. When I get inspired I have to seize the moment. How was Valentine's Day?"

"Fabulous." Lauren held up her wrist to show him the bracelet. "Did he show you?"

"No, but that's very nice."

"Our dinner plans were ruined because I was sick, but he came over and took care of me. His gifts were very thoughtful. Although I felt awful because I was sick, he made my heart feel good." Lauren was quiet for a minute. She hadn't told anyone yet, but she wanted to. She knew she could say anything to Adam. "He told me he loves me."

Adam focused on the road. "That's great, Angel."

"So, are you taking me to your place so I can hear your new songs?" Lauren asked.

"No. I want to show you something."

When Adam stopped a while later, they were facing flat ground, a construction sight. A chain gate surrounded the property with machines in the middle.

"What's this?"

"The future site for a church for the famous." Adam smiled.

Lauren turned to him with an eyebrow raised. "I don't understand."

"We're building a church where the rich and famous will be the norm and can worship freely." Adam put his arm around her. "I told you I'd build a church for you. It should be done next year."

"You're doing this all on your own?"

"I donated some, found a few other contributors and a Christian non-denominational church to back it. They're already interviewing pastors and other staff members."

Lauren hugged Adam. "Adam, this is so amazing."

"Anything for you, Angel." Adam returned the hug. "I may not be around because I'm recording, but I'm never too busy for you. You can call me anytime. You know that, right?"

"Yes. Thank you, Adam. You are a great friend."

True to Tyler's promise, they went out to a fancy restaurant every night for a week. Lauren enjoyed being pampered and the amazing food. By the third night she didn't even think about how much it cost. The fourth day their photo was on the cover of every tabloid. Saturday night they took a break from the glitter and lights for dinner at Paul's house.

"Thanks for agreeing to this." Lauren massaged Tyler's shoulder on their way. "Paul is a huge fan. He talks about you most of the day."

"I am the best around."

"I want to get to know his parents." Lauren ignored his boastful comment. "He asked about my cross. I'd like to teach him about the Bible if they agree."

Tyler smiled. "You don't give up, do you?"

"Jesus didn't give up. Why should I? The world is filled with people that don't know Him."

"Exactly. There are so many people, you can't tell all of them."

Lauren slid her hand into his. "I tell some, and they tell others. Christians are called to do His work. That means telling others about Him."

Tyler squeezed her hand and sighed. His smile told her he didn't think she was crazy.

Dinner was fabulous. Paul's mother, Melissa, admitted during the meal they had a cook. "I hired a cook before we ever got a maid. I don't have a problem cleaning my house, but there is no way I can cook worthwhile meals. Grilled cheese is fine. Anything that takes more than three ingredients and two steps is beyond me."

Tyler smiled and winked at Lauren. "See, dear, you never need to learn to cook. We'll just hire someone."

"Thanks, honey." She tried to kick his leg under the table.

After dinner the men excused themselves to play video games and talk movies. Melissa and Lauren went to the living room. Lauren updated Melissa on Paul's schooling and discussed goals with her.

"Paul asked me about my cross." Lauren rubbed her fingers over it. "I told him if he was interested and you were okay with it, I would teach him from the Bible."

Melissa nodded. "That would be fine. My husband had a bad experience with the church growing up, so he hasn't wanted to attend, but I still consider us a Christian family."

"I would start by studying Jesus, His life and salvation. Christianity is really about a relationship with God, not religion."

Melissa smiled. "I guess I have some studying of my own to do. I honestly don't know that we have a Bible in the house."

Lauren smiled. "I wouldn't mind picking out some for you. It would be great if you joined our study. Maybe we could do it in the mornings during his make up and hair."

"Sounds good," Melissa agreed. "We could start Monday."

On the way home Tyler talked non-stop, hyped up about the video games he played. She listened for fifteen minutes before she interrupted him. "I'm glad you had fun with your new best friend."

Tyler glared at her. "How was your boring adult conversation?"

"Melissa is interested in studying the Bible with us. We start Monday. I need to get Bibles tomorrow."

"Look at you, little Miss Witness."

Lauren relaxed into her seat. "Maybe I've found my calling after all."

"Good to know our relationship didn't totally ruin your life like you once thought it did." Tyler teased her.

Lauren smiled. "I keep asking God if He wants me to stay with you. He hasn't told me to move on yet, so He must be changing you."

Tyler gently flicked the silver heart that dangled from Lauren's bracelet. "Must be."

∽

Though Paul complained about his mother being there, he quieted down to listen while they read and discussed the scriptures. For weeks they studied the life and miracles of Jesus. When they came to Jesus' death on the cross, Melissa cried while they read the scripture. When Paul left after wrapping up the study, Melissa sat with her head down, wiping the tears from her cheeks.

"Would you like to pray?"

Melissa's eyes met with Lauren's as she took her hand.

As they prayed, the angels in heaven rejoiced and Lauren knew she was where God wanted her to be.

Chapter 24

"You know what time of year it is?" Tyler brought up one evening as Lauren set dinner on the table.

"Well, it's still winter." Lauren served Tyler chicken and rice. "But the groundhog did predict an early spring, which makes sense with all this crazy weather we're having…"

"Awards time, silly."

"I thought the awards were the weekend I moved in." Lauren dished herself food before sitting.

"These are the major leagues. My action flick from last year is up for Best Actor, Best Supporting Actor and Best Screenplay."

"Guess I should know these things about my boyfriend." Lauren began cutting her chicken.

Tyler chuckled. "I like that you aren't a Hollywood snob. It's nice to have a life outside of that. Will you be sitting next to me when they call my name?"

Awards night. Never did I imagine…

"Of course." She pushed the food around on her plate, suddenly not hungry. "Sounds like fun."

"Call Gretchen tomorrow and have her start looking for your dress," Tyler said as he finished his bite. "I'll have hair and makeup people here that day…"

I'm in love with a movie star and the entire world is about to know it.

⁓

The week before the big event Tyler became short during their conversations and didn't have time to see her.

"Is he always like this?" she asked Adam during dinner. "I mean, Best Actor is a big deal, but the stars don't look nervous at the show."

"He's feeling more pressure this year because he was nominated last year and didn't win. I hope he doesn't get it. It will resurrect his arrogance. Once tomorrow night comes, he'll be better."

༄

Lauren arrived at noon the day of the event to be pampered. At three p.m. she emerged from Tyler's room looking and feeling like a movie star. And there was her gorgeous mate in his tuxedo. He had a smile on his face and a beer in his hand.

"You are the most beautiful co-star I have ever had." He extended his hand to her and pulled her close to him. And most of all, I'd like to thank Lauren Drake for being such an inspiration." He spoke into his bottle.

"Oh, please, you will not say my name during your speech."

Tyler took a swig of his drink. "Maybe I'll just say, 'To the love of my life. You know who you are.'"

"That's more likely," Lauren laughed.

Tyler's cell phone rang. He looked at the number before answering it. "Hey, Ma. How are you? Yeah, Lauren's going with me. We're getting ready to walk out the door." He paused for a minute listening and then handed Lauren the phone.

"My mom wants to talk to you."

Tyler shrugged at Lauren's questioning look.

"Hi Lauren, this is Betsy. I wanted to meet you on the phone before I see you tonight."

"Oh. You'll be at the awards?"

Betsy laughed. "Oh, no, dear, we'll be watching on TV. Got all the friends and neighbors here tonight to see Tyler win his award."

"That's great."

"Sounds like you're a nice girl from a good family. Tyler told me about Christmas at your house. That's great of you and your dad to have him and Adam over."

"It was our pleasure. We had a great time at Christmas."

Tyler pulled the phone out of Lauren's hand. "Okay, Ma. The limo's waiting. I'll blow you a kiss from the red carpet." He listened for a minute before saying, "Love you too" and hanging up.

"Shall we, Miss Drake?" Tyler offered Lauren his arm.

As Lauren gazed at Tyler's face, she realized he wasn't the man she first met almost a year before. He was becoming grounded.

Will winning blast him back off into the world of Tyler, where everything revolved around him? Please, Lord, don't let him go back to the egomaniac he once was.

They were in the limo on their way when it suddenly occurred to her. "You have to give interviews, don't you?"

Tyler opened the champagne. "That's right."

"What are you going to say about us?"

"That you are the love of my life and great in bed."

"Tyler!"

He handed her a glass. "There will be reporters all over the red carpet, along with screaming fans. Smile, wave, and hold on to me. We have known each other for about a year and met through a mutual friend. I'm going to introduce you as my girlfriend, Lauren Drake, if that's okay with you."

"Mitch thinks this is a good idea?"

Tyler placed his hand on Lauren's cheek. "Please don't think I was ashamed of you and hiding you from the world all this time. I didn't think you were ready." He gently kissed her lips. It was amazing how it excited her but calmed her at the same time.

"I think you're ready now." Tyler backed away from her lips. "I know I am."

The limo pulled up to the curb. Lauren had to ask, "Will you be terribly disappointed if you don't win?"

"As long as you don't leave me for the best actor, I'll be fine." He kissed her hand then stared into her eyes. "You're beautiful, Angel. Thanks for coming with me."

With that, the limo door opened and the flashing of the cameras began.

"The second hardest part is over," Tyler told her when they entered the theater. "Now we just have to wait."

The noise inside was as overwhelming as the commotion outside. Stars mingled in the lobby, enjoying their beverages before they were seated. Every time Tyler turned someone was patting him on the back. He instantly introduced Lauren, each time Lauren's smile growing wider.

"Are you really that hung up on me?" Lauren teased when they were escorted to their seats.

He kissed her lips gently. "I love you." He hadn't said it since Valentine's Day. Suddenly she had the reassurance she needed.

He held her hand all night. The far-off look in his eyes and his sweaty palms proved he was nervous. Halfway through the show he presented the award for best supporting actress. The fans sitting in the balcony screamed for several minutes before settling down.

He's my boyfriend. All of these beautiful, sexy women and he picked me. I don't understand it, but thank you, God.

"You were born to be on stage," she whispered when he returned to her, kissing him on the cheek. "They loved you. I'm feeling fortunate to be with you."

Tyler smiled, taking her hand again.

Tyler straightened as his name was read. Excitement and nervousness rushed over Lauren.

"And the winner is…"

Oh, Lord, please, only let him win if it won't change him.
She squeezed his hand as the envelope ripped.
"Will Gibbins."
Tyler stood with a smile, applauding. His movie didn't win any awards, but when the cameras turned off and they yelled, "That's a wrap!" he turned and kissed her.
"Let's go party." He smiled.
Once they were in the limo heading downtown for the big party, Tyler leaned his head on Lauren's shoulder.
"Are you disappointed?" Lauren ran her fingers through his hair.
"Only a little." His voice was quiet, drained. "I still have a beautiful woman by my side. I'd rather have you than a gold statue any day of the week."

ལྕ

"You are so famous." Lauren answered the phone the next morning when Shelly's name came up on caller ID. "Your picture is everywhere. I love the interviews 'This is my girlfriend Lauren Drake.' Oh, my gosh, Lauren!"
"I'm kind of living in a dream world right now. Mind if I call you later? I'm still half asleep." Lauren hung up her phone and stretched. From the couch she could see Tyler in her bed. She closed her eyes and drifted back to sleep.

It was noon when Tyler awoke from a kiss on his cheek. He opened his eyes, realizing he was at Lauren's apartment, in her bed.
"You didn't take advantage of me last night, did you?" Tyler rolled over toward her.
She chuckled, sitting on the bed next to him. "Would it upset you if I did?"
"No, I was going to thank you for it."

Lauren ran her fingers through his hair. "I enjoyed diet soda all night and helped you socialize. You passed out in the limo when we left at two a.m. I didn't want to send you home alone."

"Very thoughtful of you. Does this mean you'll sleep with me?"

Lauren messed up his hair. "I slept on the couch, dear, safe from your reach."

She disappeared to the bathroom before he could stop her.

His thoughts took him back to the awards. He was disappointed but couldn't let it show. The fact that the film won no awards was easier to swallow, but he wanted to win.

Lauren's degree, framed on the wall, caught his eye. Next to it was her teaching credential, also framed. A teacher. How had he fallen for a teacher?

On her nightstand were two framed pictures. One of her and her parents at high school graduation, the other of Lauren and Tyler at his beach house on the 4th of July. Adam had taken it. Her worn-out Bible sat on the nightstand as well. He traced her name engraved on the leather cover.

"Thank you, God, for bringing her to me. I don't deserve such an amazing woman."

"So," Tyler wrapped his arms around her waist when she came out of the bathroom dressed, "you okay with a loser of a boyfriend?"

"Actually, I got a few numbers last night, including Mr. Will Gibbins. I might go out with him tonight."

"Don't think you'd like him. I've heard he's pretty full of himself."

"I think you need a shower." She handed him a clean towel. "Then I'll take you out to lunch. Just because."

Tyler smiled. "Glad you're not ashamed of me."

"Besides," Lauren walked toward the door, "I'm starving and there's nothing here to eat."

"He's not a Christian, Lauren." She wasn't surprised at her father's words or tone when he called a few minutes later. "God does not want you unequally yoked. He should not be calling you his girlfriend for that reason."

"I keep asking God to search my heart and move me on if it's not right. I see Him changing Tyler. He's not the arrogant jerk he was. He respects me physically and he asks me about God's Word. I pray for him everyday and see God is softening his heart."

"I'm praying, too," he firmly told her. "You need to slow down. He's not a Christian."

"You know I love you." They were sitting in the corner of their favorite greasy Mexican food restaurant. Lauren had no peace since talking to her father. She knew it was time to say something.

Tyler smiled. "I love you, too."

Lauren took a deep breath. "But you will never be number one in my life. God will always come first."

Tyler nodded as he chewed his fish taco.

"I'm hoping and praying one day He will be number one in your life." She looked into his eyes. "I need a man that loves the Lord."

Tyler swallowed his food. He reached across the table and took her hand. "I know. One day at a time, okay?"

Lauren nodded. Somehow that gave her peace.

Chapter 25

"I tried to call you this morning." Lauren was washing her dishes when Tyler finally called her. "I was thinking we could have lunch."

"I'm at the hospital," Tyler said.

"What?" Lauren almost dropped her plate. "Are you okay?"

"I'm fine. It's Adam."

"What happened?" She wiped her hands on a dish towel.

"He was doing fine until the last couple weeks. It started coming back again."

"What are you talking about?"

"He wants to see you and tell you himself. Can you come meet us?"

"Is he dying?" Her stomach turned when she spoke the words. Her legs felt weak and the room began to spin. She sat at the dining room table.

Tyler chuckled. "Not today. He's hooked up to IVs while they run tests."

Lauren's hands were shaking when she hung up.

Oh, please, God. Please take care of Adam. Please take care of my friend.

"I'd hoped I'd seen the last of it four years ago." Adam spoke to her from his hospital bed. He looked small and helpless with tubes running into his body, wires placed on his chest. Lauren sat beside his bed in a stiff hospital chair. Tyler stepped outside so they could have some privacy.

"I'm sorry to tell you like this." Adam took her hand in his. "You brought me back to life and out of my self-pity mode. I felt so good I didn't want to think anything could get me down."

Lauren squeezed his hand. "I'm here for you, whatever you need."

"Thanks, Angel." A weak smile came to Adam's lips as he settled back into bed.

Too much of my life has been spent watching loved ones deteriorate and die. Please Lord, don't take Adam, too.

The doctor came in the evening. The biopsy was positive. They would remove the tumor and then start him on chemo. Lauren hugged Adam good night and walked to her car with Tyler.

"I called his sister. She's coming from New York tomorrow." Tyler squeezed Lauren's hand as tears formed in her eyes. "He'll be fine, Angel. He's been fighting this for years. He's not about to give up."

She drove straight to her father's house.

"Sweetie, are you okay?" Richard hurried to her when she walked through the door crying.

"Adam has cancer."

Richard led her to the couch where he held her as she cried.

༄

Lauren was getting ready to go to the hospital the next day when Tyler called.

"They are starting chemo today. Adam doesn't want us to come."

"I've been through it before with my mother and grandmother. I'm going."

"He insists that I leave, too. Ruth is by his side. She'll stay with him. We need to respect his wishes."

Tears came as she spoke. "Then what do we do?"

Tyler laughed. "Go shopping. That should cheer you up."

She bought anything she thought would make him smile and keep him occupied. Crossword puzzle books, magazines, books, candy, DVDs, and CDs. Tyler shook his head at all the packages when they went to lunch.

"You are quite the shopper!"

Lauren smiled. "Depression turned into mania, but for a good cause."

Most of lunch was spent with Tyler recapping Adam's first battle with cancer for her.

"He lost all his hair. For about a week after he was tremendously sick, then he slowly regained strength. He toured less than six months later. The press thought he shaved his head."

"It is amazing he has kept it a secret for so long."

"Mac doesn't want pity. That's why he doesn't want us to see him go through this part. I respect him for that."

Lauren nodded. "Chemo made my mom really sick. Being with her and helping her gave me more respect for her. No matter how sick and miserable she was she would ask how I was, tell me I needed to get something to eat or get some sleep. She never stopped taking care of me the whole time I was taking care of her."

Tyler took her hands in his. "He'll be okay, Lauren. He'll be okay."

An overwhelming sense of loneliness covered her spirit like a dark raincloud as they pulled up to her townhouse.

After several minutes she turned to Tyler, tears rolling down her cheeks. "I can't be alone."

Tyler placed his hand gently on her shoulder. "Pack your things. Come stay with me for a few days."

They watched a movie, but instead of distracting Lauren, the anxiety within her continued to rise. She lay in bed sobbing when Tyler knocked on the door.

"Can I come in?" He came in and sat beside her. "Do you want to talk about it?" he asked sweetly.

"I'm just so sad." Lauren wiped her tears. "My heart hurts."

They laid in silence for a long time. The rhythmic beating of his heart calmed her.

"I had a hard year in fourth grade." Tyler stroked her hair. "We lived in Virginia. I hated my teacher, schoolwork, and classmates. I had one friend, my neighbor Joe, and he was in a different class. One day this big thug started picking on me during lunch. He called me names, threw food at me. I charged him." Lauren lay quietly on Tyler's chest listening to his story. "He fell back into a little girl who fell and spilled her food everywhere. I got suspended for two days for fighting."

"Did the big guy get in trouble?"

"Not at all. Mom picked me up and said, 'Wait 'til your father gets home.' When we got home, I ran as far and fast as I could. I was determined to leave and never come back."

"How far did you make it?" Lauren could feel his heart pounding as he recalled the event.

"Into the woods, to my favorite tree. I climbed up and sat in it for at least two hours until Joe came and joined me. After a while he said, 'That really sucks.' We didn't talk about it, but I felt better just knowing that he felt the same way I did." Tyler kissed Lauren on top of her head. "This just really sucks. But we'll get through it together."

They were quiet for a while until she asked, "What'd your dad do?"

"Spanked me so hard I couldn't sit for an hour and grounded me for a week. Then he told me next time to punch the kid and not hurt innocent bystanders."

Lauren took his hand in hers. "Was there a next time?"

"Nah. He moved on to smaller children."

Lauren snuggled close to Tyler and fell asleep in his arms.

Chapter 26

Lauren hated doctor's offices. Always silent, as if people were afraid to speak and the smell made her nauseous. She sat with Adam before his appointment, flipping through the latest gossip magazine as Adam narrated each of the pictures.

"That's really her cousin," Adam whispered about Makena Ross. "Her mother told her she had to take him out, show him the city. Someone takes their picture and suddenly they've been dating for weeks and she's cheating on the boyfriend the writer made up last month."

Lauren laughed. The nurse shot nasty glares their way, causing Lauren to cover her face with the magazine in embarrassment.

Adam disappeared to the back, leaving Lauren's mind to wander back to all the times she waited for her mother, hoping and praying this would be the day they celebrated her healing. Her mother would emerge with a weak smile, tears in her eyes.

Father, let this be different. May this be the day Adam is healed.

Adam was in the hospital for a week. He had been chipper the past two weeks and this morning he had a smile on his face.

"It's gone," he told Lauren on the way to the doctor's office. "I feel great."

Lauren jumped up as Adam walked through the door. "Thanks, girls." He smiled at the serious receptionist.

"What did the doctor say?" she asked as soon as they were out the door.

"I'm great, fabulous." He put on his baseball cap to cover the fuzz on his head.

"Really?"

Adam took her hand in his. "He told me to take a trip to celebrate. Call Tyler. We leave tonight."

Lauren laughed at his spontaneity. "Where are we going?"

"New York, for starters." Adam spun Lauren around. "All of us are between work, so it's the perfect time for my favorite girl to cash in on her birthday trip."

In three hours, they had the SUV packed and a path plotted from LA to New York. They decided to rotate driving. After a late dinner they picked up on the road, Lauren fell asleep in the backseat. Adam offered to drive the first shift.

"What's going on?" Tyler asked when he was sure Lauren was asleep.

"We're taking a trip." Adam stared at the road.

"Why?"

"To celebrate. Lauren told you on the phone."

"What did the doctor really say, Mac?" Tyler stared at Adam, trying to read him. "No lies, remember? Nothing but the honest truth. That's our pact."

Adam sat in silence for sometime. He turned to the backseat to see Lauren sound asleep. "Trust me, Zeus. It will do us all good to get away."

Tyler nodded, turning his attention out the window. "You had me worried, man. I thought this was going to be your last hurrah."

"It's only the beginning, my friend." Adam took a deep breath. "The best is yet to come."

Adam woke Tyler and Lauren to use the restroom. When they returned, Adam was in the front seat with his keyboard.

"Guess it's my turn to drive." Lauren climbed into the driver's door.

"What time is it anyway?" Tyler grumbled from the backseat as he pulled the blanket around him.

"Five a.m." Adam continued playing his keyboard.

"Whose idea was this?" Tyler grumbled.

"Go back to sleep." Lauren started the car. "I'll wake you up for breakfast."

"And coffee," Tyler grumbled, rolling over to face the backseat.

"Are you writing a song?" She pulled out of the driveway.

"Yeah. Give me a while and you will be the first to hear it."

Lauren smiled. "Just let me know."

"It's rough," Adam announced a few hours later, "but here it is."

A song about hope, lost, but found again in Christ. Questioning God's great plan, but realizing His divinity. The pain suffered, but peace that was found.

Tears welled up in her eyes. Chills ran up her arms. "The chemo. It didn't work, did it?"

Adam touched her cheek. He wiped the tear that escaped. Slowly he shook his head. "It's all good, Angel. God has a plan."

Lauren tried to focus on the road, but her hands began to shake and her eyes became blurred by tears. She pulled off at the next exit, driving to the nearest gas station. "You fill up." She quickly exited the car. She hurried toward the restroom as the tears started. She sat in the stall, sobbing.

"God help me. Help me understand."

Ten minutes later Lauren walked out to the car composed, wearing sunglasses to cover her red, swollen eyes. They were parked in a space in front of the convenience store, Tyler still asleep in the backseat and Adam leaning against the driver's door.

"I thought you might need this." Adam handed Lauren her favorite candy bar.

"Thanks. Sorry I freaked out."

Adam pulled her close to him in a hug. "I'm glad you did. It shows me you care."

Lauren squeezed Adam tightly. "Anything you need, I'll be here."

"Thanks, Angel. I appreciate that."

Lauren offered to drive again. She knew it would help her from being over emotional.

Adam tuned in love songs on the satellite radio. He settled back in his seat and looked at Lauren.

"Tell me your hopes and dreams."

"I enjoyed working with Paul and want to work with more kids. I know I can make a difference one child at a time, helping them balance school and career and show them God's love. There has been a tremendous change in Paul." Lauren stopped suddenly. A frown appeared on her face.

"And marriage?"

Lauren sighed, glancing back at Tyler. "He's not quite the spiritual leader I hoped and prayed for. He's not even saved."

"He has undergone major changes over the past year, all because of you introducing God to him." Adam took Lauren's hand in his.

Lauren nodded. "I keep praying. God hasn't told me to give up yet. How about you?"

Adam paused, turning his attention to the passing scenery. "Finish one more album, have it be my best."

Lauren frowned.

Adam gently squeezed Lauren's hand. "Don't be sad, Angel. I've lived a full life. Thanks to you, God and I are buds again." A smile spread across Adam's face as he leaned back in his seat. "As for marriage, I'd ask you if I thought you'd say yes." Lauren smiled and looked over at Adam. "But knowing you and Tyler are together is enough to make me happy." Adam closed his eyes, holding her hand until he fell asleep.

A few hours later Lauren glanced over at Adam as he began to stir. He was staring at the sky.

"You all right?" Lauren's eyes jumped between the road and Adam.

"Heaven. What do you think it's like?"

Lauren smiled thinking about it. "Beautiful beyond belief, filled with the glory of God and His love."

Adam picked up his keyboard, playing while he spoke. "What about that Bible verse when Jesus says there are many mansions? What do you think that means?"

Lauren thought about her response for a moment. "I think it's different for each person. For example, mine would be Victorian with a front porch, swing, climbing ivy and rose bushes."

"Really?" Adam chuckled. "You think God has a place like that for you in heaven?"

"Absolutely."

Adam nodded, turning off his keyboard and leaning back to look at the sky.

Lauren smiled. "What's yours like?"

"My penthouse."

"Nothing more elaborate than you have now?"

"I'd love a Jacuzzi in the middle of it."

A laugh came from the backseat. Lauren glanced in the rear view mirror. Tyler lay across the seat with the blanket to his chin, laughing.

"Prince Charming awakens," Lauren said.

"Not really." Tyler closed his eyes.

Adam turned to Tyler. "What's your place in heaven like?"

"No comment." Tyler rolled over.

"C'mon," Lauren encouraged. "We shared."

Fake snores came from the backseat.

"Fine," Adam said, "don't come knocking on my penthouse door expecting to use my Jacuzzi."

They broke out in laughter as they searched for a place to eat breakfast.

༄

"Tell me about your family."

Tyler thought Lauren was asleep in the passenger's seat because she hadn't spoken for almost an hour. After they had stopped for breakfast Adam had moved to the backseat and Tyler took over the driving. Lauren sat with her head turned toward the window. He was driving along, listening to his MP3s when she spoke.

"Why?"

Lauren turned towards him. "I've known you for almost a year and you successfully avoid the subject every time I bring it up. Then, out of the blue, your mom wants to talk to me before the awards."

"They're your typical American family."

"I doubt that. You're not the typical American. What was your childhood like?"

Tyler sighed. "I attended five schools by the time I went to high school. Ended up in Florida. My senior year they tried to move again and I refused. My parents postponed the move until after graduation. The day after I graduated I took off. Ironically, they stayed in Florida."

"Why did they move so much?"

"Dad was always searching for something bigger and better. He opened a new business in every city. About the time business dried up, he'd pack us up."

"Where'd you go when you left?"

"Worked in a casino as a bartender and saved to head west. I worked as a waiter at nights while I tried to get acting jobs in LA."

"You have a sister?"

"Yeah, four years younger. I didn't want her around much as a kid. She got married a few years ago." Tyler chuckled. "I got drunk and forgot to go to the wedding."

"Tyler!"

"She's so pissed she won't talk to me. She refused my Christmas gift last year. Sent it back unopened."

"Can't blame her on that one. But you stayed in touch with your parents?"

"I hadn't talked to them for about two years. After Christmas with you and your dad, I started to miss Mom, so I called her Christmas night. Now she makes it a point to call about once a month, and I make sure I take her call."

"Do you talk to your dad?"

Tyler shook his head. "I don't need the lecture that acting is not a legitimate profession and I should grow out of it. I think Dad is pissed off because I do something that pays a lot and I'm good at it. He never really figured out what he is good at." Tyler drove in silence for a while. "You and your dad have something pretty special. Most people don't see eye to eye with their parents."

Lauren nodded. "He's pretty great. When I went through my manic stage in college, he never lectured me. Maybe he was afraid if he did I'd leave. I knew he didn't approve, but he just asked me to be honest and let him know where I was."

"What made you change?"

"I met a guy at church and realized a Christian relationship was better."

"Where is Mr. Super Christian now?"

"On a mission field somewhere." Lauren quietly looked out the window. "I cared about him, but didn't see my life in foreign missionary work. I felt God's call to be a teacher."

They sat in silence until Tyler spoke. "Do you regret your decision?"

Lauren turned to Tyler deep in thought. "Not really. We got close, but I never felt a great physical attraction to him. I wanted the relationship to work because there were so many appealing qualities in him, but the chemistry wasn't there. I couldn't imagine spending the rest of my life with him for that reason."

"Then you moved on to the most attractive male in America, yet among the least spiritual."

"But you pursued me, even after I told you I wouldn't have sex and took a stand against drugs. Why?"

Tyler took her hand in his. "You have peace. It feels good to be around you. No drug or sexual experience matches the feeling I get from talking and laughing with you, holding your hand."

"You know where that comes from?"

Tyler grinned. "I thought Jesus Freaks were freaks until I met you. Now I understand it's about love."

"I experience that love from God because I have accepted His forgiveness." Lauren was quiet for a minute while she worked up the courage to ask him the question that was weighing heavily on her heart. "Have you found that forgiveness yet?"

"I know God doesn't hold my past against me. I hope to do better in the future."

"You can't be better unless you have admitted He is God, asked for His forgiveness and invited Him to live in you."

"Sorry I'm not ready to be a 'freak' yet."

Lauren smiled and closed her eyes. *One step at a time.*

"What's your greatest fear?" The three of them lay beneath the stars after their gas break at 10 p.m. when Adam asked the question.

"Dying," Tyler blurted out.

Lauren chuckled. "Living."

"Why are you afraid of living?" Tyler turned to Lauren.

She sighed. "I'm afraid of not being able to handle my depression. Dying is the easy part; I know where I'm going.

It's living that worries me. I never know what each day will hold."

"Dying is a mystery to me. I still struggle believing in something I can't see."

Lauren sat up. "That's one reason I choose to believe. The alternative to God not existing scares me. If God exists, He has a better place than Earth for me. If God doesn't exist, there's nothing to look forward to."

Tyler turned to Adam. "And you?"

"I'm afraid of not finishing all I want to before God calls me home. It's not dying that's frightening to me, it's standing before God, accountable for my life and having Him say 'Well Mac, I see you didn't do this and that.' I wasted half of my life choosing not to hear from God."

Lauren placed her hand on his arm. "No beating yourself up over the past, remember? Take it day by day."

A few minutes later they were racing down the freeway. Tyler drove with Lauren asleep in the front seat and Adam in the back. An hour on the road, Adam woke up coughing.

"You okay?" Tyler turned toward him.

Adam sat up, trying to calm himself and shaking his head. "Pull over," he managed to say.

As soon as Tyler stopped, Adam was out the door.

"What's going on?" Lauren sat up in the backseat.

"I don't know," Tyler admitted. "Adam was coughing. He told me to pull over."

Lauren threw her blanket off and rushed to Adam, who was kneeling in the dirt.

"Adam? What's wrong?" Tyler heard her yell as he ran over to them.

"I woke up and couldn't breathe. I felt like I was choking."

Lauren moved her hand to his forehead. "Adam, you're burning up! How long have you had a fever?"

Adam shrugged. "I got the chills before I fell asleep. I thought I was just cold."

"We need to get you to a hospital!" Lauren grabbed Adam's arm, leading him to the car.

"Whoa." Tyler touched Lauren's arm. "What are you talking about hospital? We'll stay in a hotel for the night. He'll be better tomorrow."

"He's sick, Tyler!" Lauren screamed. "Let's go!"

"I'm fine." Adam looked at Lauren. "Really, Lauren, I'll be fine."

"How can you say that?" Lauren became hysterical. "It could be the cancer."

"What are you talking about?" Tyler climbed in the driver's seat. "The cancer's gone. He's fine."

"He lied to you, Tyler. He's dying. We need to find a hospital."

"Mac," Tyler calmly turned to Adam, "what's going on?"

"I'm not feeling well." Adam settled himself in the backseat. "Let's stop at the nearest hotel and call it a night."

"Are you dying?" Tyler stared at Adam.

"Not tonight, my friend." Adam settled back into the seat. "I think we'll all feel better in the morning."

They rode in silence ten miles to the next hotel.

Lauren checked them in as Tyler and Adam sat in the car. Tyler had a million questions, but knew it wasn't the time. He watched his friend sleeping in the backseat, so pale and restless. When Lauren returned with three keys in her hand, he pulled the car closer to their rooms and unloaded luggage while she tended to Adam.

"What the *#@! is going on?" Tyler screamed at Lauren when he entered her hotel room.

"I don't appreciate your profanity and screaming at me. If you're going to be that way, just leave."

"My best friend is dying. Don't tell me to watch my mouth. What's going on?"

Lauren sat at the edge of the bed and began taking off her shoes. "The doctor told Adam he only has a few months to live."

Tyler cussed again, kicking the bed in anger. "Why didn't he tell me?"

"He didn't want you to worry." Lauren tried to calm him down. "I'm sorry I overreacted. I shouldn't have told you that way." She patted the edge of the bed until he sat beside her. "We called his doctor. I gave him medicine to bring down the fever. If he's running one tomorrow, we'll take him to the hospital. The doctor wasn't concerned. He said Adam's body needs rest, that we should purchase airplane tickets to our destination."

Tyler hung his head. "I don't get it. He seemed fine. I thought he was better."

Lauren squeezed his hand. "Don't give up on our friend. He's a fighter and God is a God of miracles. He might have a wonderful surprise ahead."

Tyler looked at Lauren in disbelief. "Then why did Adam get cancer to begin with?"

"I wonder the same thing but God tells us He won't give us more than we can handle. We only see what is happening right now but God sees the whole picture. He has a plan."

"Well, excuse me, but I think it's a pretty crappy plan."

Lauren stared at the floor. She moved her feet slowly in circles. "Had my mom not died, I would not be so close to my dad. We never talked except to exchange pleasantries when she was alive. My father has also come closer to God through my mother's death."

"It makes no sense to me." Tyler shook his head.

"It's called faith. Remember the love and peace you talked about? Faith is another part of a relationship with God.

It's not always easy to believe, but God has it all in His control. The Easter after my mother passed away, Dad attended church with me. I remember the pastor saying 'One step of faith is all it takes for God to change your life.' My father and I prayed together that God would give us peace and build our relationships with each other and Him. It has been amazing how far we have come."

Tyler sat silently for several minutes before walking out the door.

Chapter 27

Tyler cussed as he sped down the freeway. The windows were down and the air rushed through the vehicle. "Trust what? In a God that inflicts pain and suffering?"

First he heard police sirens. Then he saw flashing lights behind him.

"Nice. Just what I need." Tyler shielded his eyes from the flashlight as he read the name badge on the officer's uniform. "Good evening, Officer Greene."

"Do you know how fast you were going?" The cop pulled on his mustache as he leaned to look inside the car.

"Probably pretty fast, but I have no idea."

"License and registration."

Tyler handed him his license. "It's my friend's car. Do you want me to check the glove compartment for the registration?"

Greene studied the license with the flashlight, then shined the light back to Tyler's face.

"You Tyler Stevens, the movie star?"

"Yes, sir. On vacation from Hollywood."

"You're in that love story filmed in Africa?"

"Yes, sir."

"The missus made me watch it last week." He shined the light in Tyler's face again. "What in the world are you doing out here in the middle of the night driving like a crazy man?"

Tyler sighed. "Having trouble with the missus. I dropped her at the hotel and was hoping to find somewhere to get a drink."

Officer Greene lowered his light and handed Tyler back his license. "Sorry, kid. This ain't Hollywood. Bars close by 10 p.m." Greene opened his ticket pad and handed it to Tyler. "Mind autographing it to Lisa?"

Tyler smiled. "My pleasure." He scribbled away. "Did you like the film?"

"Wasn't the worst love story I've seen. Would've been better with more lions."

Tyler laughed. "Believe it or not, we didn't see a lot of lions. It's hard to find good extras nowadays."

With a tip of his hat, Greene smiled. "Good night, Mr. Stevens. You'd best head back to the hotel and make up with the missus. If there's something I learned in fifteen years of marriage, a little apology goes a long way."

Although Tyler saw the words come from his mouth, he knew they were coming from a higher authority. "Yes, sir. Thank you."

Thirty minutes later Lauren opened her door to Tyler.

"I'm sorry I lost my temper," Tyler apologized.

"I'm sorry you found out that way. I'm sure Adam was going to tell you, in his own time."

Tyler nodded.

Lauren pulled Tyler inside and shut the door. She wrapped her arms around him. His heart hurt thinking his best friend was dying. He didn't know if it was out of frustration or anger, but he began to cry.

"God will work it out. We'll get through this together."

They spent the night together, but this time it was Lauren holding and comforting Tyler.

༄

Tyler delivered breakfast to Adam. "Good morning." He placed the tray on the bed beside a sleeping Adam. Adam slowly opened his eyes.

"Room service. I think I like this vacation."

"How you feeling?" Tyler pulled a chair beside the bed.

"Better. A little tired, but well rested."

"The cute one offered to bring you the tray, but I wanted to talk to you."

"Sure." Adam sat up in bed. "What's going on?"

"You know when we were talking about our fears at the rest stop? You said you felt you wasted half your life?" Adam nodded, buttered his toast. "Do you really feel that way? I mean, you've done so much, made so many albums. People love you. You give to charities. How can you say it's a waste?"

"Anything out of God's plan is a waste." Adam opened his orange juice carton. "Most of my albums were about money and fame. God wants us to glorify Him, not ourselves. There may be a camera in my face everywhere I go, but I don't need to be prideful. God gave me the talent of music and at any moment he could take it away. I need to put Him first, thank Him every day and ask for His guidance. He put us in the spotlight for a reason, my friend. When I stand before Him one day, I want Him to say, 'Well done, my good and faithful servant.'"

Tyler shook his head. "You're giving and caring, yet you make it sound like it's not enough. That confirms my belief that it's impossible for me to lead that kind of a life."

"It's impossible on your own." Adam poured his cereal in the bowl. "I rely on God because with Him all things are possible. When I live each day in His power, I get to know Him better and desire to please Him more." Adam dug into his cereal, while Tyler digested his words. "I know it's hard to understand, but you need to forget your past mistakes. God not only forgives but also forgets. Every day is a do-over."

༄

Lauren came in at lunch to find Adam showered, sitting in his robe in a chair with his feet on the bed watching TV.

"Look at you. Feeling better?" Lauren sat on the bed beside his feet.

"Very much so." Adam took the paper bag out of her hands and started to open it. "So, what did you bring me? I like this food delivery service."

Lauren grabbed the bag back. "Here's your sandwich." She pulled out a grinder. "And chips and juice."

"Thank you, Angel." He opened the chips first.

Lauren placed the back of her hand on his forehead, "Do you have a fever today?"

"No, Mom. Maybe I can go back to school tomorrow."

Lauren glared at Adam. "I'm just concerned."

"I know. We should be able to hit the road tomorrow night."

"I think we should fly. I started checking on fares and it's not too bad…"

Adam frowned. "Getting there is half the fun, remember?"

"I think we're ready for some rest. We made it halfway, which is more of this country than I've ever seen."

"What's Tyler up to?" Adam asked.

"I don't know. I called him to ask if he wanted lunch and he declined. He insisted on taking you to breakfast this morning and I didn't see him after. He had a pretty hard night."

"He's searching." Adam unwrapped his sandwich. "We need to be praying he runs to God rather than away."

༺༻

He stared at the ceiling for hours, replaying it all in his head. Adam choking. Lauren hysterical until they made it to the hotel and then calm and collected. The cop. Crying in Lauren's arms. Mac was his only real friend. The thought of him dying scared Tyler.

"We understand God has a plan for us to prosper and not fail." Lauren words replayed in his mind. Death didn't seem like a good plan to Tyler. It made no sense. If God loved Adam, why would he take him so young?

Was there such a place as heaven? Could there be something better than the here and now? Tyler figured the poor and unloved felt that way because their lives were miserable. They needed something to hope for. But Lauren was just as happy with a new book as she was with expensive jewelry. It didn't seem to matter to her.

You may think you're loved, but no one really knows you. They just love your stardom.

The truth hurt. Even Lauren didn't know the real Tyler, the Tyler that longed to get drunk, high, laid. Any or all would be fine. He didn't remember the last time...

Forget the former things; do not dwell on the past. See, I am doing a new thing!

"That's a lie. I couldn't change, even if I wanted to. There's nothing more than this life, so I need to enjoy it."

Arguing with himself was exhausting. He closed his eyes, welcoming the state of unconsciousness.

༄

Adam's good spirits convinced them to venture out to Ann's Steak House next to the hotel for dinner. Lauren and Adam laughed all the way to the restaurant about the ridiculous TV shows they had watched earlier, but Tyler walked silently. The tension was high after the waitress took their order.

"What's up, Zeus?" Adam patted his arm. "Seems you've got something hanging over you."

Tyler gently swirled the water in his glass. He sipped it slowly, clearing his throat before speaking.

"I've been thinking, about life and death. I listen to you guys talk about faith and God. I want the peace both of you have." He turned to Adam. "You have no fear of death. And

Lauren, you gave up your dream career for our friendship and don't regret it. If I was dying, I'd freak out. If I knew I'd never work again as an actor, I would be pissed off. I don't get how you two can be so happy." Tyler looked down at the table. "I know it has something to do with God, but I just don't get it."

Adam placed his hand on Tyler's arm and gently squeezed it. "That's the first step, man. Admitting it's beyond your comprehension. The second step is surrendering to Christ. The things of this world will pass away so we need to not put our trust in them."

Tyler pushed back his chair, excused himself, and left the table.

"Zeus, wait up," Adam called from behind him on the sidewalk. "You know I'm in no shape to run."

Tyler waited, wiping his tears, allowing Adam to catch up. They walked as Tyler spoke.

"Man, I don't know what's going on. I feel I'm on the verge of a breakdown. I can't control my thoughts."

"God is calling you. He is telling you it's time to surrender to Him."

When they came to the hotel parking lot, Adam unlocked his car so they could sit inside.

Sin, love, forgiveness, redemption, salvation. As Adam spoke, a burden grew in his heart. All that he knew no longer made sense. For the first time in his life, he needed rescuing. A weight crushed his chest, making it hard to breathe.

"Do you want to receive God's forgiveness?"

It's all a sham. You don't need this. You've always done fine on your own.

Tears welled up in his eyes as the other voice came.

Fear not, for I have redeemed you; I have summoned you by name; you are mine.

As he repeated the prayer after Adam, he immediately felt chains released from his soul. He could breathe again, better than ever before. Peace came over him.

⁓

Lauren smiled through her tears when she saw them enter the restaurant smiling. She jumped up to give Tyler a hug.

"I guess you can call me a freak," he whispered in her ear. Lauren laughed and squeezed him tighter.

When they arrived back at the hotel after their fabulous dinner, Adam told them the travel plans.

"Tomorrow we fly to New York. We'll spend several days there. Ruth knows a doctor I'll check with. Then we go international."

"You're up to that?" Lauren asked.

He smiled. "Anywhere in the world, Angel. Where do you want to go?"

She looked at Adam. Then Tyler. They were both grinning.

"I'd love to go to Europe."

Tyler wrapped his arm around her neck. "It's off to Europe."

"Lord, You amaze me." Tears welled up in her eyes as she prayed. "I've hoped, prayed, and now, finally, he believes. Thank you, Father." She wiped her tears and took a deep breath. "Be with Adam. Heal him. Nothing is impossible for You."

Chapter 28

The first day in New York, Ruth escorted Lauren shopping all day and to a spa. She enjoyed hearing stories of Ruth and Adam growing up. During lunch, Lauren asked if Ruth and her husband wanted children.

"We do," her tone turned somber. "We've been trying for six years. It just hasn't happened yet."

"I'm so sorry."

"It's fine. We believe when it's God's time it will happen. And if that's not His plan, that's fine. Some days are harder than others."

Her heart hurt for Ruth, but to see her attitude witnessed to Lauren. That was faith in its finest form.

༄

The second day they went sight seeing to all of Adam's favorite places. He pointed out where he wrote the songs off his first album and the first bar he played at. For dinner they went to Adam's favorite restaurant, definitely the best Italian food Lauren ever had.

As they walked the streets after dinner, Tyler steered Lauren from running into people as she walked in awe of the lights, the people, the traffic.

"It's all so intense." Lauren tried to look in every direction at once.

Tyler suddenly spun her around. Lauren laughed, almost falling to the ground.

"What was that?"

"Trying to make it more fun, less intense."

"I am having fun." She leaned on him. "I'm just trying to take it all in."

Tyler stopped in the middle of the sidewalk, turned Lauren to face him. "I love you." Placing his hands on her cheeks he gently kissed her lips. When they separated, he whispered, "How about taking that in?"

Lauren hugged him. New York with Tyler, in love. Intense, but fun.

༄

Adam had tests run at the doctor's office when they arrived in New York, and the third day the results were in. He insisted on going alone.

Lauren fasted all morning. She sat at the kitchen table, as Ruth did dishes, and read her Bible. When her mind wandered, she prayed until she could focus again. After about twenty minutes, Tyler sat beside her.

"What'ya reading?" He rested his hand on hers.

"Ephesians. Paul wrote it to encourage the church at Ephesus. I could use a little encouragement right now."

He nodded, starting to read over her shoulder. After a minute, Lauren pushed it over to him.

"Would you read out loud? I'm having problems focusing."

Tyler squeezed her hand and began reading. Soon Ruth joined them. Tyler read, occasionally stopping for clarification. After a half hour, he passed it to Ruth and she continued reading. Lauren was taking her turn when Adam finally walked through the door.

"Well?" Ruth jumped to her feet as he entered the house.

Adam smiled. "God answered our prayers."

Tears filled Lauren eyes. *Oh Lord, could it be?*

"It's gone." Adam grinned from ear to ear. "The doctor found no trace of cancer."

Ruth screamed and ran to hug Adam. Tyler congratulated him with a hug. Lauren remained at the table, tears running down her face.

"Really?" she whispered when Adam came and knelt beside her. Relief and disbelief raced through her mind.

"Really, Angel."

"I prayed and I hoped and I prayed…"

"I know." He kissed her cheek. "Thank you."

They celebrated with a formal dinner that night. After they ordered, Adam escorted Lauren out on the dance floor.

"You're gorgeous." Adam's smile hadn't faded since he returned from the doctor.

"Your sister has quite the eye for fashion," Lauren admitted. "Wait until you see the rest of the outfits she helped me pick out." They danced in silence for a while before she spoke.

"It's not that I didn't believe He could heal you. I guess I'm just amazed at the reality of it."

"I feel the same way. Maybe this episode was necessary for me to get another opinion so we could all rest easy and enjoy our trip to Europe." Lauren's smile spread from ear to ear as he continued. "We leave in two days for your dream vacation. Happy birthday, Angel."

She text messaged her dad on the way to dinner. She hadn't spoke to him since Adam's episode out of fear that she would break down. But now she wanted him to celebrate with them.

"Adam is healed. Tyler accepted Christ. Enjoying New York. Europe next."

During dinner he responded. "Guess your trip is all I am praying for. God is good. I love you and miss you."

"God is good," she whispered in agreement. "Thanks, Dad."

Oh, yes, the Spirit can do amazing work.

As the plane took off from New York to Paris, she settled back in her seat and listened to the boys chat. No longer was it gossip or complaints: it was spiritual questions. Tyler asked about baptism and Adam shared with him examples in scripture.

He's growing. Thank you, Jesus, that he is growing closer to You.

༄

She stepped out of the shower, wrapping her towel around herself. As she dried off, she thought of him. It had been an amazing four weeks touring France and surrounding countries. There were wonders and adventures around every corner, and he had been beside her, holding her hand.

Every day she fell deeper in love with him. His subtle tenderness, his sense of humor and caring touch were still the same. But his spirit was different. It was pure, searching, and hungry for the truth. He accepted Christ. He was a Christian. God had meant for them to be together.

She put on her fluffy white robe as she brushed through her wet hair. He was committed to her. She could see it in his eyes, hear it in his voice. When they passed beautiful women on the street he didn't even turn his head. The flirting with waitresses had stopped. He looked at Lauren with a sparkle in his eyes. She didn't have a ring yet, but she knew it would come. Like everything else, he would come around. It was his birthday, tonight was their last night away from the world. She wanted to make it a night to remember.

He was awakened by her massaging his shoulders. He sighed and moved his head to the side. Her hand grazed his cheek. It was so warm and soft. He turned his head and kissed it gently. When he opened his eyes, he was surprised with what he saw. There stood Lauren as beautiful as could be in her fluffy white robe. His eyes widened. "Shouldn't you be getting dressed?"

"I was." Lauren moved around to the front of the couch. "But then I started thinking of you, how gorgeous you are." She leaned in and kissed his lips softly. "And I missed you."

Excitement rushed through Tyler. He closed his eyes, returning each kiss.

He opened his eyes to see Lauren, his beautiful angel. She smiled shyly. He remembered her standing firm against sex before marriage, walking away from him when he did drugs, reading the Bible to him, explaining it…

"I can't." The words shocked him back to reality. He didn't realize he had actually spoke them until he saw disappointment and embarrassment on her face. "I'm sorry, Lauren." He sat up beside her on the couch.

She crawled to his side, kissing his neck. "Yes, you can. I love you. You love me."

How could a man argue with that? Tyler wrapped his arms around her, kissed her passionately, forcefully.

Man, does she want me! Of course she does, every woman does.

"No matter what I do or say," her words came to his mind, "I don't want to have sex again until I'm married. Sometimes it's hard for me to stop. I need your help…"

Tyler sat up again. He ran his fingers through his hair, hoping to knock the sense out of him. He stood up, walking to the window.

"Lauren, I can't." He wanted to so bad, but he knew tomorrow everything would be different. He never wanted her to regret being with him.

He heard her run from the room, slamming the door behind her.

Tyler found Adam at the hotel bar. He ordered a drink as he sat beside Adam.

"You look like crap, man." Adam sipping his beer. "What's wrong?"

"Lauren wanted to have sex." He downed his drink and ordered another.

"Really?"

"I left her half naked and crying." Tyler stared at the bar. "It was probably the stupidest thing I've ever done."

"You can say that again," Adam snapped. "Hey, Mike, can you get me the phone?"

"What's your deal?" Tyler glared at him. "I did the right thing and walked away."

"Tyler, you know her history. You can't reject her and leave her alone crying." Adam dialed her room. "When did you leave?"

"About five minutes ago."

"Don't you ever think of anyone but yourself?"

"You're right, Mac." Tyler shot his second drink. "I was only thinking of myself when I told Lauren to stop undressing me because I couldn't have sex with her. I should have slept with her and not returned her calls."

"Hey, Angel." Adam turned his attention to the phone. "Are you okay?"

"Yeah." Adam looked over at Tyler. "We're at the bar. Come join us."

Tyler replayed the scene in his head. He had done the right thing…

"There is nothing to be embarrassed about. Everything is fine."

But why did he feel so stupid? This was what he had been waiting for.

"No, baby, he cares about you. That's why he left. Not because he didn't want you, but because he did." Adam smiled at Tyler. "He was protecting you, helping you to keep your promise."

Tyler sighed, motioned the bartender for another.

"No, maybe a little manic, that's all. Get dressed and meet us in the bar. We all need to relax and enjoy our last night of vacation. See you in ten minutes?"

Adam hung up the phone, sighing. "I'm sorry for jumping all over you. Remember, Lauren doesn't think the way we do. One rejection throws her into a downward spiral. Someone needs to be there to pull her out."

"Got it, thanks." Tyler stared into his drink.

Adam patted Tyler on his back. "You did the right thing."

"Doesn't feel like it." Tyler massaged his temples.

"Someday it will."

Lauren hung up the phone and searched for something to wear. She chose a comfy sundress from the closet. As she dug for the shoes inside her suitcase, she found her Bible. She picked it up with a sigh. She had been so busy she slipped away from God and His Word. As a result, she almost made an awful decision.

"God, forgive me." She sat on the bed with her Bible in her lap. "Forgive me for not making time for You. Thank You for giving Tyler the sense to leave tonight. Thank You for protecting me and helping me remain true to You."

She opened the Bible with great anticipation. God always had something to say to her. She just needed to take time to listen.

Timidly, she entered the bar. Adam played the piano, coaxing her to enter. She approached Tyler, who was slouched over his drink at the bar.

"I'm sorry." She hugged him from behind.

Tyler took her hand and gently kissed it. "Don't be. I wanted to." He lifted her hand to touch his cheek. "I just don't want it to ruin what we have."

Tyler turned to face her and kissed her cheek. Then he stood. "C'mon." He led her out to the dance floor. Tyler ran his hand down her soft, damp hair. "Sex has been a normal response to every relationship I've had. Tonight as we got closer, I realized I care more about you than that. I want you to be happy, with yourself and me. I don't want you to have any regret or doubt."

She gazed into his beautiful brown eyes and smiled.

Oh Lord, You're making him into the man I need him to be.

"Happy birthday, Tyler." She leaned her cheek against his.

"Thank you. You're the best part of it."

∽

Lauren sat next to Adam when they boarded the plane. "Tyler's no fun. He's just going to fall asleep," she complained. "Was this trip everything you hoped it would be?"

"It was." Adam nodded.

"What's wrong?"

He leaned back into his seat and turned toward her. "Sad it's over."

"Yeah." Lauren sighed. "That's the scary thing about going back. You wonder if things will be the same."

"I think we have all changed a little on this trip."

Lauren held Adam's hand. "Thank you for calling me last night from the bar."

"I promised you I'd be there. I'm pretty good at keeping my promises."

"Yes, you are. I know I can always depend on you." Lauren took off her shoes and put her feet on her seat. She leaned back, relaxing. "I never would have guessed Tyler would stop when we got too close. God's definitely doing a work in him." She squeezed Adam's hand. "Thanks for playing last night. I appreciate it."

"That's my job, to make people fall in love." Adam turned to look out the window as the plane began to take off.

Halfway home Tyler woke up and asked Lauren to sit next to him. "Mitch called last week. The movie I'm filming next month switched female co-stars."

"It was going to be that new girl, Lucy something?" Lauren tried to keep the stars straight, but it was a struggle.

"Right. Now they hired Lotus Khan."

"Oh. Should I remember her?"

"She was my co-star in 'The Night Before Last.'"

She was quiet for a minute. "Weren't you with her for a few years after that movie?"

"Yeah." Tyler squirmed in his seat. "How do you feel about that?"

"Did you live with her?"

"She never officially gave up her place, but we were together most of the time. It was before I moved into my house."

Lauren never thought about other women resurfacing. She figured most of them were insignificant. But this one wasn't. If there were love scenes, she'd be all over him…

"Do you want to work with her?"

"We worked well together." Tyler took Lauren's hand. "It was a long time ago. I've seen her a few times at events. We exchanged pleasantries and that was it. I don't think this will be a big deal."

"Then why mention it?"

"No secrets, no surprises." Tyler kissed her hand.

Lauren found sincerity in his eyes. "I trust you."

"I think I'll get my Masters in Administration," Lauren told Adam and Tyler in the limo on the way home. "I checked into it while I was earning my credential. If I double up on classes I can be done in five, maybe six months. Paul won't be on the set again until next year, so it gives me time to finish."

"Administration." Tyler raised his eyebrows. "Like principal?"

Lauren smiled. "I could go that direction. A part of me would love to open a private school some day."

"Good for you." Adam nodded.

"You might become too busy for your uneducated friends," Tyler pouted.

Lauren smiled, wrapping her arm around him. "You have a new project you're starting and a new faith to build. You shoot during the day, study the Bible a few times a week with Adam and we'll have the weekends together."

"I'm not sure how I feel about you being smarter than me."

"Too late for that," she joked, squeezing his hand. "You've got the looks, I've got the brains. We make the perfect pair."

Chapter 29

The first day jitters began the moment she awoke. It seemed like forever since she had been in the normal world, away from the boys. They met for lunch at their favorite sidewalk café to celebrate her going back to school. After they ordered, Adam and Tyler presented her with a latest fashion backpack filled with all the necessary supplies – pencils, pens, folders, notebooks, a baseball hat so no one would recognize her, quarters for the soda machines and lots of chocolate.

"Since we won't be able to help you with your homework, we thought at least we could get you started off right." Tyler rubbed her shoulder.

Lauren smiled. "That's very sweet. Now I'll think about you during my class."

"What's wrong, Angel?" He squeezed her hand gently as he walked her to the car. "You hardly ate and look pale. Are you sick?"

A frown came over her face as she bit her lip. "What if someone recognizes me?"

"Wear your hat and you'll be fine."

Lauren shoved Tyler. "I'm being serious, Tyler."

He leaned his head against hers. "Don't let it bother you, Angel. You have goals. Don't let anyone take that away from you."

"Not even a zillion reporters?"

"Not even one." Tyler kissed her lips gently. Tyler wrapped his arm around her as they continued walking to her car. "You know you can always pack your bags, move into my palace on the hill and never have another worry. You don't need to go back to school."

"I want to, for myself. Besides, I'm not moving into your palace until we have our fairytale wedding."

"Patience, Cinderella." He smiled. "Good things come to those who wait."

She looked in the mirror at herself in her student uniform – jeans, t-shirt, hair pulled back under her hat. It was a role she slid back into comfortably.

There was a familiar feel as she entered the room with long tables. Half a dozen people were randomly scattered, quietly reading. Lauren sat at an empty table on the end, just in case she decided she needed to escape. She took out her notebook and textbook. When she opened her notebook, she found the boys' notes on the inside cover.

"Knock'em dead, teach!" Tyler wrote.

"Breathe, Angel…you'll do fine" Adam encouraged.

Maybe this is ridiculous. I'll be attending classes Monday through Thursday and studying in between. It would be less stressful to just hang out with them…

She looked up as a girl sat beside her.

"Hi, I'm Cheryl."

Does she recognize me?

She reached out her hand. "Hi, I'm Lauren."

"Nice to meet you." Cheryl shook her hand. "Is this your first class?"

Lauren nodded.

"Mine, too." Cheryl blurted out "I'm kinda nervous. Is that crazy?"

"Not at all." Lauren smiled, knowing she had made a friend.

༄

Tyler shuffled through the house like an old man looking for something he lost.

Tyler found himself entering the guest room. He lay on the bed, closing his eyes and inhaling slowly. The sweet smell of her perfume lingered on the sheets. He turned his head to the side and opened his eyes, thoughts of her still roaming in his head. Then he saw the Bible Lauren had bought to keep at his house on the nightstand. Whenever she had a hard time, was upset or depressed, she would read the Bible. When she closed it, her attitude had changed. She would be content, at peace. That's where her peace came from.

"Okay, God, show me what you got." Tyler opened the Bible and began to flip through it.

"How was it?" Tyler waited until after 10 p.m. to call her.

"Not bad. I made a new friend. Her name is Cheryl. She teaches second grade. She's really sweet, and I don't think she knows who I am."

Tyler laughed. "How about your class? You know, the reason you went tonight?"

"The professor is terrible. He thinks he's so funny, but he's really lame. By the end of the night we were laughing at him, not his jokes. Unfortunately, that boosted his self esteem, encouraging him. It helped to have someone next to me to roll our eyes at him together."

"Some people make jokes when they're nervous. Maybe he'll get better. How about I come over with a quart of ice cream?"

Lauren yawned. "I haven't slept well the past few nights and I'm exhausted." Lauren yawned again. "Thanks again for all the stuff and I loved your note."

"I'm glad it went well. How about lunch tomorrow?"

"Maybe. I have three chapters to read before Thursday. I'll call you when I wake up."

"Good night, Angel. Drive safely." As Tyler hung up he knew their relationship was changing.

The first week Tyler saw her at lunchtime. She would close her textbook while they ate, but an hour later she'd start reading again.

"I'm an incredibly slow reader," she confessed to Tyler one afternoon. "I'm barely getting all my homework done." She spent most of the weekend catching up. He wanted to bring up that he was reading her Bible, but he didn't know how. Her mind seemed preoccupied.

Three weeks into her first class his new movie began production. For the first time in his life, he was nervous. Although the feelings weren't there for Lotus, he remembered them. It was the closest he'd gotten to love before Lauren.

The first day on the set his heart skipped a beat when he saw her. She truly was more beautiful than the last time he saw her. Her long dark hair brushed his arm when she walked up beside him.

"Hello, Tyler." A mischievous smile danced across her face. "Long time no see."

"Lotus." He leaned in and politely kissed her cheek. "You look great."

"Of course. You look a bit, domesticated."

He shook his head and walked away.

⁓

They had passion in front of the camera but stayed away from each other the rest of the time. Lauren came to the set for lunch the second Friday they were shooting. He tried to avoid Lotus, but of course she sniffed Lauren out like a vulture.

"I'm Lotus." She stuck out her hand to Lauren, a sheepish grin on her face.

"Hi, I'm Lauren." Lauren politely shook her hand.

"Nice to meet you. I'd say Tyler has told me all about you, but he's being a bit tight lipped lately. All I know is the gossip I've heard around town."

Tyler pulled Lauren away before the conversation could continue.

"Real sweet lady." Sarcasm laced Lauren's voice.

"Some days I think this was a mistake, shooting with her."

"Why?"

Tyler shook his head. "She's just such an arrogant…"

"Some stars are like that," Lauren teased.

Tyler smiled. "Really? It's shocking people let fame affect them like that."

"You seem relaxed." Tyler massaged her shoulders after they finished eating in his trailer.

"Mmmm." Lauren closed her eyes. "Just finished my finals. I get the weekend off. Back to the grind on Monday."

"We should go out and celebrate. Two classes down."

"The reading about killed me, but I did it," Lauren admitted.

"I've been reading lately."

"Oh yeah?" Lauren waited for the punch line.

"Yeah. The Bible you left at my house."

"Really? What part?"

"Mostly the New Testament. That Old Testament is pretty dry."

Lauren smiled. "Stay away from Numbers. That's a snoozer."

Tyler sat next to Lauren. "I opened it one day and started reading different parts. Then I started at Matthew. It's been interesting reading about Jesus."

"Matthew, Mark, Luke, and John are called the gospels. All include accounts of Jesus' life. It gives you a clearer picture of Him."

Tyler nodded. "I'll get there."

"Yes, you will." Lauren squeezed his hand.

"She's cute." Lotus snuck up behind him later that day. "Schoolgirl, huh?"

"School teacher," Tyler corrected her.

"I didn't think a school teacher would do all the things that please you."

"Oh, darling, you did all that for yourself, not me. It was always about you."

Lotus smiled. "Still is." She leaned over and whispered in his ear, "Give me one night to remind you how great it was."

"In your dreams." Tyler walked the other way.

༄

Monday night at dinner Lauren and Cheryl discussed relationships. Cheryl told Lauren about her boyfriend she'd been seeing for years. She expected a ring soon. Lauren occasionally mentioned her boyfriend, but didn't go beyond that.

"What does your boyfriend do for a living?" Cheryl asked after she had told Lauren about her guy being in the military.

I'm not going to lie. I need to be truthful if I want to be friends. She took a deep breath.

"He's an actor."

"Anyone I've heard of?"

"Tyler Stevens."

Cheryl about choked on her salad. "You're serious?" She looked into Lauren's face, squinting her eyes. "Oh, my gosh. You went with him to the awards last spring."

Lauren smiled and nodded. "I never know how people will react. I really don't want it to affect me getting my Masters."

"Wow. How did you meet him?"

Lauren laughed. "Well, I can give you the two-minute version since we have to go back to class."

Lauren knew her secret was safe with Cheryl. It felt good to have a new friend she could trust.

Chapter 30

Lauren's eyes gently shut and her head nodded. Rubbing her eyes and stretching, she glanced at the clock. 8:30 p.m. The night was so young, yet she was so tired. Once upon a time she and the boys would be heading off to unknown destinations.

Lauren stared at the silver heart dangling from her bracelet and thought of Tyler. It had been two weeks since they really spoke, just had played phone tag lately. They had a great time hanging out at the beach house relaxing after her first round of classes, but her next classes were full of research and reading.

But it's Friday. I have plenty of time to play this weekend and still study for finals.

Lauren found Tyler's number in her phone.

He had been a little standoffish in his messages, probably from stress. Maybe he had gotten off early tonight. We could watch a movie or hang out…

"HELLO!" Tyler slurred loudly. Then he started laughing out of control.

"Tyler?" Lauren didn't understand why he was laughing.

"Hey. What's going on?"

"I thought I'd take a break from studying and call you. I've missed you this week." Her stomach turned. *Something's not right.* "How are you?"

"Oh, you know."

"Ty, you know I get the munchies when I'm high," the feminine voice cooed in the background, but Lauren heard every word clearly. "Your fridge is totally empty. Let's go out."

Tears came to Lauren's eyes as she recognized the whining. "Sorry I bothered you."

"Lauren, wait…"

Her whole body shook as she hung up the phone.

༺

Tyler cussed as he walked to the kitchen.

"Get out." He slammed the refrigerator door.

"What's wrong?" Lotus' pouty face always annoyed him. "I was just saying we should get something to eat."

Tyler slammed his cell on the counter. "Just leave. I didn't want to hang out. I just wanted to get high."

Lotus glanced at the phone and then back to Tyler. "Oh." Her eyes widened. "Was that your girlfriend on the phone?" She placed her hands on Tyler's chest. "Did I get you in trouble?"

Tyler pushed her hands off him. "I'm going for a swim. Be gone when I return."

༺

Lauren stared at the phone in her hand. Her eyes caught sight of the bracelet that dangled on her wrist. *He loves me. I'm just overreacting. He's different.*

After several minutes, she redialed his number. *He's reading the Bible. It wasn't what it seemed…*

"Hello there, Lauren." Lotus answered Tyler's phone on the second ring.

"Where's Tyler?" Lauren's face grew hot at the sound of her voice.

"He can't come to the phone right now. But I do want to thank you for making Tyler hold out for a year. I know we'll have amazing sex tonight."

Lauren screamed with anger and threw her phone across the room.

Adam called her name as he entered her house. She had texted him, asking him to come over. She knew it wasn't safe for her to be alone.

Adam held Lauren as she cried. "I don't understand. How could he be so cruel and uncaring?"

"One thing I could always say about Tyler. He never ceases to amaze me. Do you want to talk about it?"

Lauren recapped both conversations.

"I love him." Lauren felt ashamed as she said it. "I thought he loved me, too."

"Oh Angel. He does care about you, he just doesn't understand commitment. I'm sorry you had to be hurt by his selfishness."

୭∽୧

For three nights Adam slept on Lauren's couch by her request. The third night Lauren came to him crying in the middle of the night. She knelt on the floor beside the couch.

"Angel." Adam rubbed his eyes, trying to focus. "What's wrong?"

"It hurts," she sobbed.

"What hurts?" Adam gently reached out and touched her head.

"My heart. It hurts so bad."

Adam sat up and helped Lauren to the couch. She buried her face in his chest as he pulled the blanket around her.

"I feel so sad," she cried. "I feel so alone."

"I'm here." He whispered rocking back and forth. "I'm not going to leave you. You're not alone."

"I want to be done."

"Done with what?"

"Life. I can't do it anymore. I want to be done."

"It's not time for that, Angel. God's not done with you yet. We can do it, sweetie. We can beat this. God has an awesome future for you. You just need to wait and watch it unfold."

"I can't. I'm tired, Adam."

"Think of all the times you have felt this way. And think of all you would have missed. Graduating from high school, college. Becoming a teacher. Growing closer to your dad. Having candlelit dinners and margaritas with your best friend Mac." Lauren giggled at his comment. "Now, think of all you would miss in your future. Finishing your Masters, finding the man of your dreams, marrying, having children. Do you really want to give that up?"

Lauren wiped her eyes on Adam's shirt.

"I love you, Lauren, as do so many other people. You are a wonderful, beautiful, caring person. God promises He has major blessings for you. You just need to hang in there."

Lauren's crying subsided, her breathing slowed. He ran his fingers through her hair, relaxing her.

"Do you know how beautiful you are?"

Tears filled her eyes again. "Obviously not beautiful enough."

"You are without a doubt the most beautiful woman I have ever known. Beautiful inside and out." Adam kissed her forehead. "He doesn't deserve you, Angel. He never has. Let go of him. Walk away with your head high, knowing you are worth so much more. God has the perfect man for you that will love and respect you for all you are and hope to be, that will treat you like the Angel you are and thank God everyday for the privilege of being by your side. Do yourself and everyone that loves you a favor and don't settle. You deserve only the best."

She closed her eyes, resting in the shelter of his arms.

The next morning Adam found Lauren showered, dressed and sitting at her desk with her books. "I need to finish. He has ruined enough of my life. He won't ruin this, too. I won't let him."

Adam smiled. "You know who to call for a study break. Or a massage when your neck gets stiff from reading."

"Don't worry, I'll be calling you."

༄

Lauren walked into class slowly, with her head down. She sat without a word.

"Are you okay?" Cheryl looked at her.

Lauren shook her head and bit her bottom lip. She opened her notebook and scribbled, "We'll talk at break."

"I don't get it." They were in Cheryl's car driving through fast food for dinner. "A month ago he told me he was reading the Bible. He was learning about Jesus. Then suddenly he's back with his old girlfriend. I don't get it."

"You know, they say those who are seeking or have just accepted Christ are the greatest under attack. It's like the seeds that sprout but the roots fail to grow." Lauren knew God had brought Cheryl into her life because she was a great Christian.

"I was so excited when Tyler accepted the Lord. It seemed everything was falling into place." She quietly looked at Cheryl with tears in her eyes. "I loved him. He said he loved me."

Cheryl put her hand on Lauren's shoulder. "I'm so sorry."

Lauren wiped the tears from her eyes and smiled.

"God does have a plan, though. And it's for good, not evil."

Lauren nodded. "I need to hear that, because right now it doesn't feel so good."

Wednesday morning Tyler called Adam and asked to meet him for coffee.

"How's Lauren?" Tyler stared into his coffee cup.

"Surviving."

The silence that followed was too long and painful for Tyler.

"You know, I didn't mean to hurt her."

"Yeah." Adam chuckled, "You just meant to please yourself. You're all that matters, right? Only looking out for number one, right Zeus?"

"C'mon, Mac, you know I care about her."

Adam glared at Tyler. "If you cared about her, you wouldn't have hurt her. And hurt her. And hurt her again."

"That's my point. I had no intention of hurting her."

Adam shook his head. "Correction. You didn't intend on getting caught. Was that slut worth it? Was she worth losing the best woman that ever came into your life?"

Tyler looked down again at his coffee. "I got scared man. You know."

"Yeah, I know what it's like to be scared. Every day I'm scared. Scared that I'll get sick again, that I won't be able to sing. Scared that Angel will carry out those nasty thoughts that live inside her head." Adam took a deep breath. "But I don't run. I hold her until she falls asleep and pray to God He will keep me well long enough to take care of her. That's the difference between us. You run and I stay to pick up the pieces." Adam stood and threw five bucks on the table. "But there's a difference this time. I won't let you go back to Lauren. You don't deserve her."

"But you do, right?" Tyler asked sarcastically.

"That's for God to judge. One thing is for sure, I will never hurt her the way you did."

Tyler chuckled this time. "Sure you won't. Make her fall in love with you and then die on her. That won't hurt at all."

Tyler had never seen such anger in Adam's eyes. His eyes seemed to pierce through his soul. "Someday you will wake up and find yourself alone. When you do, I want you to remember all the people that loved you that you treated like crap."

∽

"How was he?" Lauren bit her lip, not sure she wanted to know.

"His normal, arrogant self."

She was quiet for several minutes before she spoke. "I don't want what happened between Tyler and me to affect your friendship with him. You guys are best friends. You shouldn't walk away from that."

"I appreciate that, Angel, but I'm done with Tyler's all about me attitude. He changed when he was with you, but he got scared and ran back to his old lifestyle of self gratification and arrogance."

Lauren looked down at her bag. "Is he doing drugs?"

"Probably. He looked awful."

She sighed. "I guess I'm not surprised."

"I don't want to be around him. He's not the Zeus I enjoy hanging out with. Or maybe God has changed me to the point of not wanting to be around someone like that."

Lauren took Adam's hand in hers. She wiped the tears from her eyes as she looked up. "I'm done studying. How about renting a movie and making popcorn?"

"Love to." Adam stared at her smiling.

"What?" She tried to hide her embarrassment.

"I have a new best friend now. She's pretty great to hang out with."

Lauren smiled. "I feel the same way."

"Stevens, get out here! I'm not paying you to take breaks all day!"

Dark circles shadowed his eyes. His head pounded. Life had been one big party lately. That's what it was meant to be. His old ring of friends greeted him with open arms. Once again he was the most popular guy around. He woke up the next day with vague recollections of the night before.

Lotus had tried enticing him with getting high for weeks before he caved in. Tyler wanted to escape from all the thinking he had been doing. He figured Lauren had wised up and realized what a loser he was. She was so smart, getting her Masters degree. She could do anything she wanted. But he was just an actor. And someday, when he was old or unattractive, his career would be over. He wasn't saving enough to afford his wealthy lifestyle. Life as he knew it would be over.

Tyler thought he could make it right again with Lauren, until he saw Mac. He'd blown it, for good. He might as well go back to the life he had known before her sweetness corrupted him.

Mitch quit twice last week, blaming Tyler for trying to ruin both of them.

"Showing up late, stoned, or drunk was not acceptable," Mitch screamed on the message he left him earlier that day. "Even when you're the star. They pay you millions to show up sober and ready to act. Directors are talking. The days of naming your price are over."

Tabloids ran headlines about the falling out while Tyler smiled and waved at the camera. No one really cared because it meant Tyler was eligible again. He was too young to be tied down.

"You have two minutes to get in make-up, Stevens," the pissed off director screamed, "or we'll find ourselves a new star."

"Sure you will." Tyler splashed water on his face. He walked to make-up, counting the hours until he'd be off and could get a drink.

Chapter 31

She tightened her squeeze on Adam's arm as they walked in to the overcrowded restaurant. Adam had bought tickets for the banquet months ago. It was wall to wall stars, most of which she had seen and met at the awards. For months it had been all about school. Part of her thought she put this lifestyle behind her.

"I don't know about this." She clung tightly to his arm.

Adam smiled as her turned to her. "I am privileged to be with the most beautiful woman in the room. You can't run and hide now. Just smile, stand up straight, remembering you are with the most gorgeous man in the room."

Lauren laughed. "I don't know. Todd Sanchez is looking pretty hot tonight."

Looking at the long line in front of them, Adam motioned to the bar. "Why don't you get yourself a drink? I'll check us in."

Lauren straightened her blue evening gown as she made her way through the restaurant, focusing on the bar in the distance rather than the wobbliness of her shoes. It had been months since she had worn anything besides jeans and tennis shoes.

Everything is fine. We'll have a great time tonight.

"Good evening." The dark-haired bartender placed a napkin on the bar in front of Lauren as she sat on the barstool. "What can I get you?"

"Virgin strawberry daiquiri, please." She smiled.

With a wink and a smile the bartender was off. Lauren sat, straining to hear the music that was playing. It sounded familiar, but she couldn't place it.

Lauren heard someone swear behind her. "Could it be?" the familiar voice shouted.

Oh, God, no.

"Lauren!" Tyler staggered from behind her, cursing again. "Lauren Drake!" He plopped down on the stool next to her. The smell of alcohol permeated from his skin and breath, sickening her. She scanned the crowd for Adam without success.

"April." Tyler's eyes fixated on Lauren but he spoke to the girl behind her. "Meet Lauren, the only woman that won't sleep with me. Lauren, meet April, who can't get enough."

The nineteen-year-old giggled.

Her face reddened. "You're drunk, Tyler. Please leave me alone."

"Do you hear how polite she is? 'Please leave me alone.' Yet you have this amazing body and wear sexy dresses. Do you really think that's fair?"

Anger arose in Lauren as the bartender set the daiquiri in front of her.

"Is that a virgin?"

She wrapped her hand around the stem of the glass and glared at Tyler.

"Not you, honey, the drink. I know you're not. By the way, have you slept with my best friend yet?"

Everything within her wanted to throw her daiquiri at him. He was such slime. He disgusted her...

"Our table is ready." Adam's voice instantly calmed her. "Shall we?"

She took the arm Adam offered and stood, staring straight into Tyler's eyes. "You really are a good actor." Tyler straightened up a bit at the compliment. "For a while I actually believed you were a decent person."

They walked away, leaving Tyler in a stupor.

"Bravo, Ms. Drake," Adam congratulated Lauren. "You retained your composure yet put him in his place."

"I've washed my hands of him. He has proven unworthy of my friendship, let alone my love."

Adam placed his hand in the curve of her back. "Now that we have that behind us, let's move on to our amazing evening together."

They sat with four other musicians and their dates. They laughed about this producer and how a song was recorded wrong but became platinum anyway. Lauren recognized one of the dates as an actress, but the rest seemed as ordinary as her. Adam included her in every conversation, speaking of her teaching and getting her Masters. They talked about Christianity and the church that was being built.

"You know, our son is in 2nd grade and having a hard time with reading," the wife of one musician told Lauren. "He attends the private school and seems to keep struggling. I haven't liked any of his tutors. Do you think you would be able to help him?"

"I'm sure I could." Lauren smiled.

"You really should be in charge of the Children's Division in the new church," another woman commented.

"That's what I've been hoping." Adam put his arm around her. "I've been waiting for the perfect time to ask her."

When the men went to get the ladies drinks, one woman turned to Lauren with a smile.

"I've never seen Mac so happy. He looks great."

Lauren smiled. "He has been a great friend to me the last few months."

She leaned toward Lauren. "He's one of the best. Hold on to him."

Adam walked up behind Lauren. Placing the drinks in front of her, he offered her his free hand. "Would you do me the honor of this dance?"

"It's my pleasure." She let him lead her to the dance floor.

"Having a good time?" Adam whisked her across the floor gracefully.

"I am. Your friends are very genuine. I feel comfortable with them."

"Good." Adam pulled her closer. "They love you."
"Do they?"
"Of course. Everyone does."
She placed her head on his shoulder. "Do you?"
"You know I do."
His response sent chills up her arms and put a smile on her face.

༄

Shelly called a few days later. They shared the past few weeks of their lives over their nachos before the latest romance movie began.

"It was so weird, Shel. I thought I was all right, until I saw him. All these feelings rushed back to me."

"Feelings of love?"

"No, more like anger, hurt. He was so rude and smug. I don't get it."

"No matter how hard you tried, you couldn't change him. He will always be an insensitive player with no idea of how to have a relationship."

"I thought God was starting to change him."

"Regardless, He has another plan for you."

They munched without speaking for a minute until Shelly spoke. "How's Adam?"

"Wonderful. He spent the night when I was depressed, calls to check on me. I don't know how I would have gotten through this without him."

"He seems like a great guy."

Lauren smiled. "He calls me Angel and says I am his gift. But lately I'm feeling like it's the opposite. Adam tells me the things God whispers to my heart. I know He's taking care of me through Adam."

༄

It wasn't until the third ring that Adam answered his phone.

"Hi. I was up and thought I'd call to see what you're doing."

"Angel? What time is it?"

"5 a.m."

"What time did you go to bed?"

"Eleven-ish."

"And why are you up?"

"I've been up since three. I finally got out of bed at four and started cleaning. I'm on my second load of laundry, I've cleaned the bathroom and vacuumed. I thought maybe you would be up. You're usually an early riser."

"Sometimes, not always."

"Sorry," Lauren quickly apologized. "Call me later." She hung up before Adam could reply.

She was surprised when he called back.

"How are YOU?"

"A little manic, I guess."

Adam chuckled. "I'd say so. You want to come over and clean my house?"

Silence. "Lauren?"

The tears started, preventing her from speaking.

"Hey, I'm only kidding."

"It's not funny." Lauren wiped her tears. "I can't help it."

"I know. Sorry for teasing."

They both were silent for several minutes.

"I guess I have a lot on my mind. I meet with Dolores and her son today. I'm excited about the possibility of tutoring him." She sighed. "I can't sleep."

"Where are you?"

"Sitting on my bed." She sniffled.

"Turn off the light and crawl into bed. You're still in your pajamas?"

"Yeah. I'm in bed."

"Snug and warm?"

"Getting there." Lauren reached for her teddy bear.

"Think of our cross country trip. I'm driving and you're in the passenger's seat. The sun is rising. You can feel the warmth of it on your cheek. The sky is painted orange and red."

"I remember." Lauren smiled.

Adam began to sing her the lullaby he had written for his Angel. Peace and sleep overcame her.

There was one other car in the parking lot on the cliffs when they pulled in. Adam parked, turning off the lights and engine.

"It's dark." Lauren was disappointed.

"Just as I remember it." Adam yawned.

"You tired?" Lauren asked.

"A little bit. Someone woke me up early this morning."

"Ha ha. I'm going out to look." She sat on the hood. Adam joined her. They watched in silence as the ocean suddenly came to life with the waves breaking on the rocks. The sound of the water rolling in and out was soothing, mesmerizing. They sat, side by side, silent. After a few minutes Lauren reached out and took Adam's hand in hers. She leaned her head on his shoulder. "Funny how small the ocean makes you feel."

Adam leaned his head against hers. "And how mighty it makes God seem. How did it go today with Dolores and her son?"

Lauren chuckled. "She brought along three of her closest friends and their kids that are struggling. They were really nice. I'm going to start tutoring next week, before school in the library. They're paying me an obscene amount of money for only a few hours a day."

"People will do anything for their kids. I'm sure they're excited to have such a great teacher."

Lauren sighed and closed her eyes. Slowly she breathed in the salty ocean air and listened to the waves crashing on the cliffs below. "You've brought peace back into my life."

"I'd like to take the credit for that, but it's God."

"Hanging out with you has a tremendous effect on me. I'm smiling and enjoying myself again. My heart feels better." Lauren squeezed Adam's hand. "Thank you for putting up with me and all my moods."

"My pleasure, Angel. I wouldn't change anything about you." Adam wrapped his arm around her. "You're perfect the way you are."

Chapter 32

One Saturday night at the end of September, Adam became somber when Lauren mentioned plans for the October.

"I'm going on tour." He stared at the steak on his plate. "I leave in two weeks."

"Oh." *Why didn't he tell me?*

"I wanted to tell you, it just never seemed the right time. The tour was planned a year ago, but after my relapse in the spring, I wasn't sure when it would happen. Since I've felt great the last few months, they released the dates."

"How long?" Lauren pushed her potatoes around her plate.

"About eight weeks. My agent wanted to give me time to rest between so I don't get too wiped out." Adam reached across the table for her hand. "Come with me. We would have a great time traveling. I would love your company."

His eyes were so sincere. "I don't know, Adam. What about school? I still have two classes left. And the kids I tutor?"

Adam smiled. "Classes start next week, right? Take them in January after the holidays. The parents of the kids will understand. I'll write you a note, excusing you." Lauren laughed at his joke. "C'mon, Angel. You and me, on the road again. Think of all the cities we'll see."

It's not the responsible thing to do. She sighed. In the back of her mind she could hear Beth saying, "This is the opportunity of a lifetime."

"Besides," Adam squeezed her hand, "I would miss you terribly."

Lauren smiled. "I'll go."

Adam yelled and cheered as if his team just won the Super Bowl.

༄

Lauren was transported back to the first time they met as she watched him play. So much had changed, but he was still the same brilliant artist. His smile seemed brighter, his eyes twinkled a bit more. Maybe it was the fight with cancer he had overcome. Perhaps it was because she knew him.

The crowd screamed out longing to know him, to be heard by him. Lauren felt special because she did know him. She was a part of his life.

"What did you think?" Adam was sitting on the couch downing a bottle of water when Lauren entered his dressing room after the concert.

"You amaze me." Lauren sat on the couch facing him. "You're so talented."

"Stop, you'll give me a big head."

Lauren placed her hand over his on the back of the couch. "All those people screaming made me realize how fortunate I am to know you. The first time I saw you in concert, I thought, 'There's more to him than music. I would love to get to know him.' I'm glad I've gotten to know you."

"That makes two of us." He stood, helping Lauren up. "Now, we better get going or you might be settling for ice cream from the convenience store."

༄

Every night Adam played, his passion unfolded with even greater depth. He loved the crowd and glowed when he was on stage. Lauren didn't expect to attend every concert, but she couldn't imagine being anywhere else. Hours slipped away as she sat in the front row, singing with the rest of the audience to his every song. Afterwards, Lauren listened to Adam explain the concert from his perception. The notes he missed, how many times he changed the order of his songs. Lauren laughed at his stress and assured him no one knew the difference.

One night while they enjoyed room service, Lauren looked at Adam questioningly.

"Can I ask you something?"

"Of course." Adam didn't hesitate.

"In some of your older songs, it's obvious someone really hurt you. Who was she?"

He sighed, leaning back on the couch. "Rachel. I met her a few years after I moved to LA. We were together almost six years."

"Wow." Lauren dipped her strawberry in chocolate. "What happened?"

"We had agreed marriage wasn't for us, we were happy being together without the lifelong commitment. The truth is, over time, she really wanted to be married. I just didn't see it. Six months after she left, she married someone else."

"Do you regret not marrying her?"

Adam smiled. "Not anymore. I'm very happy with my life and wouldn't change anything."

Lauren looked at him in doubt. "Even the cancer?"

Adam nodded. "Even the cancer. I always thought I was self-reliant. It helped me learn to let God take over and trust in Him."

"Funny how He reveals things to us, even through sufferings."

"Especially through our sufferings."

∽

"How have you been lately?" It was the third week in October when Adam brought up the subject one night over hot fudge sundaes.

"Good. Why?"

"Seems like you haven't had bad days lately."

Lauren smiled. "Yes, I'm doing good." She stared at her sundae before continuing. "October is usually a hard for me. There almost seems to be something chemical inside me that freaks out. Last year I was barely hanging on until the whole Halloween incident."

Adam pushed his ice cream around in the bowl. "Why do you think this year is different?"

"Maybe because someone has been keeping me so busy, I don't have time to think about it. Or maybe it's the ice cream I'm getting every night."

Adam grinned as he shook his head. "Okay, smarty. I was only trying to think of what's going on so we know what makes you happy."

Lauren smiled. "You make me happy."

Adam raised an eyebrow. "You're getting good at stroking my ego."

"You deserve it occasionally, but enjoy it because it won't happen when we get home."

Adam laughed. "That's my Angel, keeping me in check."

"I spoke to my dad today." Lauren changed the subject.

"How's he doing?"

"A little sad I won't be there on Thanksgiving. It will be the first holiday we've spent apart."

"Invite him up. He can join us in Chicago on Wednesday. I have Thursday off and we don't have to fly to Seattle until Sunday. I'm sure we could find a good restaurant on Thanksgiving."

"That would be nice, but this is his down season. He doesn't have the money for a ticket."

"My treat." Adam took his last bite of ice cream.

"No, Adam, he would never let you do that."

"Angel, it's just money. When I die, I can't take it with me. I intend on using it to make the people around me happy.

Let's buy the plane ticket tomorrow and have it sent to him. Then he can't refuse."

"What about me? Can I refuse to let you?"

Adam touched her cheek gently. "You could, but it would break my heart. Do you really want to do that?" Lauren shook her head. "God gives back to those who give to Him. Think of it as God rewarding you for the work you have done for Him that has gone unnoticed."

"Fine." She took his hand in hers. "But tonight we go to a movie. My treat."

"Sounds great." Adam smiled.

༄

Richard beamed at the sight of his daughter. He greeted her with a hug and a kiss on the top of her head. "How's my princess?"

"Great." She smiled. "Happy to see you."

"Me, too." He shook Adam's hand. "Good to see you, Adam."

"Same here, Mr. Drake. How was your flight?"

"Well, first class is quite amazing. Thank you for the ticket. And please, call me Richard."

The three of them had a great weekend together. Adam had Thanksgiving dinner delivered to his suite for them. They enjoyed turkey and all the traditional Thanksgiving fixings, along with rich conversation and a competitive game of rummy during dessert.

Lauren and Richard attended Adam's concert Friday and Saturday night. It thrilled Richard to sit in the front row with Lauren. He raved about Adam's talent.

When they were at the airport going their separate ways on Sunday, Richard turned to Adam, shaking his hand before he departed. "Thank you for taking care of my daughter. It's great to see her smile."

"It's my pleasure, Richard. You have a wonderful daughter."

"Yes, I do." He patted Adam on the back. "I'd love for you to spend Christmas with us since you had me spend Thanksgiving with the two of you."

Lauren smiled. "You will, right?" she asked Adam.

"Wouldn't miss your dad's lasagna for the world," Adam replied.

∽

"I had a great time." They had settled in their first class seats and were being served refreshments when Lauren turned to Adam. "Thank you for asking me to come."

Adam squeezed Lauren's hand. "You made this the best tour I ever had."

"Really?"

Adam nodded. "Spending time with you is my favorite thing to do."

"Even more than making music?"

"Even more so."

Lauren leaned back in her seat and closed her eyes. "I love being with you, too."

Chapter 33

Lauren was so anxious to see her father, Adam told the driver to stop at Richard's house.

"It's only been a few weeks since I've seen him, but when I think of home I think of his house. You know what I mean?"

Adam smiled. "Of course. We can stop by, maybe go to dinner. I don't have to work tomorrow."

Lauren laughed. "What do you mean, mister? There's only two weeks until Christmas. Of course there's work to be done!"

Lauren bouncing up the steps to the front porch. "Hello!" She excitedly threw open the door.

"Lauren!" Her father met them in the living room and embraced her. "I'm so glad you're home."

"Me, too." As they broke from the embrace, Richard went to shake Adam's hand. Lauren saw him in the family room, sitting on the couch staring at her. He stood when she saw him. It had been years…

"Andy?" Her jaw dropped.

He smiled. "Hello Lauren." He walked toward her, stopping inches away from her.

"You look great." He leaned forward and hugged her.

Lauren awkwardly backed away. "Andy, this is Adam. Adam this is Andy, an old friend of the family."

Richard walked up beside Lauren, putting his arm around her waist to help support her. "Andy is in from doing mission work in Africa and stopped by to visit."

"Missions?" Adam smiled. "That must be exciting work."

Andy nodded, turning at Lauren. "It's kept me busy the last several years." He looked back to Adam. "Richard tells me you were on tour?"

"Yes." Adam smiled at Lauren. "Lauren was wonderful enough to keep me company on the road."

"I had a great time." Lauren turned to stare at Andy. *After all these years, why would he show up in here, in Dad's living room? I thought I was over him, done, but why are my palms sweating?*

They all went out to eat together. She sat next to Adam in the booth, across from Andy. He stared at her most of the time causing her to shift in her seat.

After dinner Adam and Richard walked ahead of Andy and Lauren to the car. Andy suddenly took Lauren's hand in his. "I haven't stopped thinking about you all these years. I had to see you."

Lauren looked at Andy, surprised. There was familiar warmth in his hand. She causally pulled her hand from his and continued walking.

"Can I take you to a movie tomorrow? It would be great to catch up."

Her heart raced and stomach turned. "I don't know, Andy."

"I know we got real serious before I left. It's not that I want to pick up where we were. I've changed and I'm sure you have too. I'd like to get to know you again."

She remembered all the good times they had. *Maybe it was time to try again...*

"You can call me tomorrow," she agreed by the time they reached the car.

"I could be wrong, but wasn't Andy's face one we set ablaze last summer at the beach house?" They were halfway to Lauren's place in the limo when Adam broke the silence.

Lauren nodded.

"He seems like a nice guy."

"He always was." Lauren peered out the window.

"That would be great to be in missions work. To make such a difference in people's lives."

"You make a difference in people's lives," Lauren pointed out.

"It's not the same. I would love to know my work has a direct result for the kingdom of heaven."

Lauren wanted to talk to Adam about Andy, but somehow she couldn't. She didn't know what to say.

"What do you think?" Adam put his hand on her shoulder. "Will you survive without me tonight?"

Lauren smiled. "I'm sure I can call and you'll be right over."

Adam tussled Lauren's hair. "You know me well, Angel."

"Andy Miller? At your dad's house? That's weird," Shelly responded when Lauren told her.

"Yeah. And he asked me out. I didn't know how to say no. Maybe I want to see him again."

"Still wondering?"

"He seems perfect, Shel. By far the kindest, sweetest, most Christian guy I dated."

"But?"

"Maybe I got scared. Maybe we needed time to grow. I don't know."

"Let me remind you." Shelly laughed, "He kissed like a dog. I think that was what you said. A cocker spaniel licking your face."

Lauren laughed. "Was it that bad? Maybe he's different now."

"How was your trip?" Shelly changed the subject.

Lauren smiled. "Wonderful. I attended his concert every night. His talent amazes me."

"Why aren't you dating Adam? I forgot."

"He's my best friend. We don't think of each other that way."

Lauren had just gotten out of bed and began her laundry when Andy called.

"How about dinner and a movie tonight? I'll pick you up."

She gave him directions and as she hung up she realized her palms were sweating.

Adam called at noon. "I take it you survived last night?"

Lauren laughed. "Barely. It's a good thing you called. I was starting to go through Mac- withdrawals."

"In that case, how about dinner tonight? I'm craving our favorite Italian restaurant."

"I'd love to, but I kinda have plans."

"Oh yeah? A hot date?" Adam teased.

"Kind of. Andy called."

"Oh." Adam became quiet. "You think he wants to get back together?"

"I don't know. He's a great guy. It just ended when he left for Africa. I feel like I need to or I will always wonder."

The long silence was broken when Adam cleared his throat. "Well, have a great time. Call me tomorrow if you want."

"I will." Lauren hung up with a sick feeling in her stomach. It was weird telling Adam, but she didn't want to lie to him. They were always honest with each other. She shouldn't feel weird. After all, they were just friends.

Andy told stories of faraway places. She told stories of teaching. So much time had passed, but there was never awkward silence during dinner.

Halfway during the movie, Andy put his arm around Lauren.

Why is he being so forward? We haven't seen each other for years.

"Did you like the movie?" Andy asked as they walked out of the theater.

"It was pretty good." Lauren tried rubbing her stiff neck without being obvious. During the ride home they talked about Christmas plans, shopping, and preparations. As they pulled up to her apartment, conversation ended. They sat quietly until Lauren spoke.

"I'd invite you in, but I wouldn't be a very good hostess. I'm still tired from my trip."

"I understand." Andy smiled. "Thanks for going out with me. Call me tomorrow?"

"Sure." Lauren leaned forward to hug Andy. As they separated he quickly kissed her lips. She was out of the door and headed for her door before she realized what had happened.

Lauren contemplated the night as she lay in bed.

"God, I don't understand," she prayed, drifting off to sleep. "Andy was much more forward than when we first started dating. He's acting like nothing had changed all these years. I had a good time with him, but there was a reason our relationship ended. Guide me, lead me where You will have me go."

~

"In so many ways he was the same," Lauren explained to Shelly the next day. "He tried to pick up exactly where we left off, putting his arm around me, kissing me. It felt comfortable, but I don't know."

"What about the whole physical attraction thing? Were you attracted to him last night?"

"I didn't really think about it."

Suddenly Lauren's phone beeped. "Someone's calling. Let me call you later."

She half expected it to be Adam, but it was Andy. "How about miniature golf tonight?" he suggested after they talked a while.

They saw each other every night for a week. Dinner with her father, hanging out at her place, watching movies. They held hands and Andy kissed her at the end of every night, though Lauren didn't necessarily want him to. At the end of the first week, Andy instigated making out.

"I have to get up early." She pushed him away.

A few days later they went shopping for Christmas. She had successfully found her father and Shelly's gift and was ready for dinner when Andy stopped at a jewelry store.

"Come on."

Lauren followed him inside, thinking he was shopping for his mother. He walked straight to the diamond rings. "What do you think of this one?" He pointed to one beneath the glass. "Or how about that one?"

He's looking at rings for me. He wants to marry me...

"Would you like to try something?" The salesperson joined them.

"Sure." Andy pointed to the half-karat one in front of him. "How about that one?"

Lauren turned and walked out the door.

"Lauren," Andy yelled. "Lauren!"

She felt nauseous. She waited until Andy caught up with her to speak. "What are you doing?" There was firmness in her voice and anger in her eyes.

"I thought maybe it was time."

"You've been back less than two weeks. It's been two years and you pop up and want to buy me a ring? I don't understand what is going on!"

Andy led her to a nearby bench. He took a deep breath and her hands in his before he spoke. "You were the best thing that ever happened to me. For two years I haven't stopped thinking about you. I realized if I ever had you back, I would never leave you again. A few months ago, they talked about re-assignment. I felt like this was my second chance. If it takes me giving you a ring to keep you, I'm ready for that. I would even leave the mission field for you. I believe we were destined to be together."

Lauren returned home two hours later. She stopped at her dad's house on the way home, but he wasn't there. She stayed for an hour, sitting on the couch, thinking.

He proposed, in a way. I want a commitment, a ring, a wedding. But not from Andy. She tried to envision their future together, what it would be like five years from now. She couldn't, or maybe just didn't want to.

Her phone beeped as she arrived home. Andy. She got the chills as she listened to his message.

"I know I said it was okay if you didn't feel the same way I did, but the truth is, it's not. I'm ready to move to the next step, like we should have done years ago. If you're not, I wonder if you ever will be. So, if you want to move our relationship to the next level, call me. Otherwise, have a good life."

There was her answer. Time to bury the past once and for all.

Chapter 34

Lauren looked herself over in her new jeans and sweater, but the circles under her eyes gave away her depression. For several days she'd been crying. Her father didn't talk about it. Adam called, but she didn't feel like talking. She knew she couldn't hide it from him. It was Christmas, but she just didn't have joy inside her.

Adam came over at 1 p.m., bearing gifts for her and her father. She smiled, but still felt empty inside. She was relieved Adam and Richard kept the conversation going during dinner because she didn't have the energy.

"What are you doing for New Years?" Adam and Lauren sat on the couch after dinner. Richard did the dishes and insisted they relax.

"Oh, jetting off to Paris maybe." She sighed and shrugged. "Hadn't thought that far."

"Come with me to the mountains," Adam suggested. "I leave on the 29th. We can come back on the 2nd. That gives you time before your classes start again."

"I don't think so." She turned away from him. "We just got back. There's so much to do."

"You need to get away. You can have all the time you need by yourself. I don't mind at all. I hate to see you this way."

Lauren nodded.

෴

Lauren slept most of the way. She commented on how tired she was when she entered the car. Adam told her to lean back, relax. She did and he sung her to sleep.

They arrived at the cabin in the late afternoon. After Lauren unpacked, she went for a walk. Adam had dinner ready when she returned. She asked if she could eat in her room. He handed her the plate and that was the last he saw of her until two in the morning. She emerged in her pajamas, a blanket wrapped around her. He sat on the couch with his keyboard.

"How's my Angel?" He set aside his keyboard, opening his arms to her. No sooner had she curled up beside him resting her head on his chest than the tears began. She cried for several minutes and he held her. "Tell me what's going on."

"I don't want to believe the voices that tell me life is worthless, that everything is falling apart and I have no control, but they're so loud." Adam held her closer as she spoke. "I have no idea what I want to do with my life. I'm afraid after all this work I won't be able to use my Master's degree. Look what happened to my teaching career. Nothing in the past year has worked out the way I wanted it to. I'm tired of pretending everything is fine."

"You don't have to pretend with me, Angel. But, I think you are an amazing woman. In six months you have almost finished your grad program, receiving straight A's in the process. You had a few months off and now you are going back for possibly the most challenging part. It's normal to be stressed out."

Lauren sighed. "I don't know, Adam. Everything seems so hard."

"Someday you will see the flip side of the quilt. All you see right now are the scraps and stitches, but one day God will show you the design. Trust me, it will be more amazing than you ever dreamt."

Lauren wiped her eyes. She took Adam's hand in hers. "Will you sing me to sleep?"

Adam smiled. He happily obliged her request.

The smell of pancakes brought a smile to her face as she awoke. She shuffled out to the kitchen in her robe and slippers. Adam smiled when he saw her.

"They're almost ready," he announced, turning back to the skillet.

"That's fine." Lauren sat down and put her feet up on a chair. "So, I was thinking skiing sounds like fun."

Adam raised his eyebrows. "Oh, yeah?"

"Yeah, but I'm not really good at skiing, so I was thinking I'd skip the skiing part and go straight to the lounge and drink hot chocolate all day."

Adam laughed. "Sounds great."

They had a wonderful day. Lauren insisted Adam ski for a while. He was gone a few hours and then relaxed with her. Lauren was quiet at first, but Adam happily sat with her, sipping his coffee as she sipped her cocoa. After a while they started playing cards and within an hour they were chatting away.

The next day Lauren was back to her normal self, wanting to shop all day. She was full of energy. They discussed going out on New Year's Eve, but Lauren voted for dinner at the cabin.

"Good food and great company is all I need."

"Whatever you want, dear." Adam smiled.

"I thought I'd lost you." They danced cheek to cheek after dinner for some time before Adam spoke. "I was sure you were running off to Africa to save the world with that missionary boy."

Lauren smiled. "Decided it's too hot and too far from the beach and mountains." She told Adam about Andy pulling her into the jewelry store. "When he talked about marriage, I actually felt physically sick. At that point I realized I couldn't spend the rest of my life with him. We got along great and he loves me, but there is no physical attraction." Lauren rested her head on Adam's shoulder as they danced. "Maybe I'm just being too picky."

"Or maybe you are waiting for the perfect man God has for you."

"I feel bad because I know I broke his heart."

"It's better that you were honest now than to lead him on."

Lauren was quiet for a minute before speaking. "Andy tried to shelter me from my feelings rather than encouraging me to work through them. When we were first together and I was depressed, he would tell me he would take care of me, stay up all night, praying for me and fighting my demons. I thought that was romantic. But now I realize he was keeping me weak and dependent on him. I'm not sure he realized it, but I needed to learn to fight the depression myself, not rely on others to fight it for me." She smiled as she looked in Adam's eyes. "You help me be strong. You help me believe in myself and stand on my own but remind me you're there if I need you."

Adam placed his hand on her cheek. "You don't need me or any other man to protect you and help you through life. You've done just fine on your own. Sometimes you just need to be reminded of that."

Lauren sighed. "I'm tired, Adam. Tired of looking. Tired of wondering. I'm sure my prince is out there, but this waiting thing is getting old."

Adam smiled. "I'm right here, Angel. I always will be."

She stared at him for a few minutes and then smiled. "You're too good for me."

The countdown on the radio began. "5-4-3-2-1…"

"Happy New Year, Angel." Adam gently caressed her cheek. "Maybe this will be the year we both find what we are looking for."

"Happy New Year." Lauren stood on her tiptoes and kissed Adam on the lips. The first kiss was gentle, innocent. But she kissed him a second time, full of passion.

It's been so long, it feels so right. Oh Tyler...

Lauren pulled away as she opened her eyes. She backed away from him. "I'm sorry."

"It's okay." He gently put his hand on her shoulder trying to calm her. "Really."

Lauren's face heated up with embarrassment. She rubbed her eyes. "I forgot where I was."

Adam raised an eyebrow. "You forgot where you were or who you were with?"

Tears filled Lauren's eyes as she ran from the room.

She was on her bed crying when he walked through the door a few minutes later.

"Don't cry." He took her into his arms. "It's fine."

She melted into his arms. "You're so wonderful, sweet, and kind. I don't deserve your friendship." She cried harder, to the point that she was gasping for breath.

"Angel." Adam calmly stroked her hair. "You need to calm down. I told you, we're fine."

Lauren shook her head. "I'm sorry." She sobbed. "You should hate me."

"I could never do that," Adam whispered in her ear. He rocked her gently until her breathing steadied. After a while he whispered, "I have your favorite ice cream in the freezer. What do you say?"

"I want to wallow in self pity for a while."

Adam stood and offered her his hand. "Let's start the New Year off right. Ice cream and cards?"

Lauren looked into the familiar face of her friend. Her friend who saved her from herself, made her laugh, loved her more than anything in the whole world.

They played cards until dawn. Her New Year's resolution was to stop getting upset about things that ultimately didn't matter. She didn't want her emotions to run her life.

Chapter 35

Eat, sleep, study, tutoring. That was Lauren's life for twenty-eight days. She had her last two classes to finish, exit exams, and her final project of creating a school. Adam called every day. Most of the time she didn't have time to talk, but it was nice to hear his friendly voice. On the weekend he brought her food and his keyboard or a book he was reading. After they ate they would sit next to each other on the couch. Every time she slammed her book or threw her pencil and shouted "I can't do it anymore!" he would massage her shoulders or feet.

"I can't quit," she would say pathetically.

"Of course you can, but I don't think you really want to."

She would continue where she left off.

∽

"It's been forever since we've gone dancing," Shelly reminded Lauren at the end of the month. "What do you say, Saturday night?"

"Sure. Besides, it's time to celebrate."

"Oh, yeah?"

"I take three exams on Saturday. I'll be completely done."

"There you go. Cover charge is on me."

"Sounds good. Come over at eight. We'll go from here."

"How's your school coming for the rich and famous?" Lauren could hear Adam playing his keyboard when she called him later that day.

"Way over budget. I'm thinking of cutting the custodians. The kids can pick up trash and clean the toilets, right?"

Adam laughed. "You might have some irate parents. Make part of the tuition agreement the family maid has to donate a few hours a week to clean the school."

"Great idea. That might just work."

"What are you doing this weekend?" Now she could hear the tapping of keys on his laptop.

"I talked to Shelly today. We're going out Saturday night."

"Great." Adam paused as he typed. "Three tests on Saturday?"

"8 a.m., 12, and 3 p.m." Lauren sighed. "Can you believe it? Then I'll be done!"

"Well, let me help you in your celebration. I'll arrange for a limo to pick you two up. If you want, you can go to my club. I'll tell the door man you're coming."

"Sounds good, we're always up for a party with no cover."

◦◦

It was an amazing feeling of accomplishment. She was exhausted, completely brain dead. Her last test had been her exit exam which covered all her classes and included six essays, but that didn't matter now. It was over. She called Adam as she walked to her car.

"Guess what?"

"You're done." Joy filled his voice.

"I'm done." She laughed. "Can you believe it?"

"I'm so proud of you, Angel. How do you feel?"

"A little fried. I was studying until 1 a.m. and then up at six to finish."

"I've been praying for you. How do you think you did?"

"I might have gotten a 'B'. We'll see."

"Well, go home and rest up. You and Shelly are still going out tonight?"

"Yeah. Hey," Lauren got in her car, "why don't you meet us at the club? Shelly won't mind. Come celebrate with us."

"Nah. You need to do your girl thing. Have fun and we'll celebrate tomorrow."

"Okay."

"Hey, Angel?"

"Yeah?"

"Congratulations."

Lauren smiled. "Thanks."

She opened the door to her place and immediately smiled at the beautiful huge arrangement of flowers on her kitchen table. Setting her backpack on a chair, she opened the card.

To Angel – I always knew you could 'master' anything you put your mind to. Now the rest of the world will know as well. Congratulations!

Love, Adam

Lauren closed her eyes as she inhaled the wonderful fragrance. That was Adam. Always thinking of her.

"How's work?" Lauren and Shelly reclined on the sofa with daiquiris in hand.

"I'm getting lots of overtime. Employee number three walked last week."

"They sure have problems keeping employees. I'm surprised you're still around."

Shelly shook her head. "They know how to play me. I talk about leaving and they throw more money at me. Unfortunately it works. I'm a sucker for cash." She sipped her drink. "What are your plans now that you are done?"

"I'll start my internship soon. I'm waiting for a placement."

"And then?"

"I don't know. See what door God opens. I'm tutoring and getting asked to help more kids. It's easy money 'til something else pops up. I've met with the principal of the school several times. I might get hours done there."

"Cool. How's Adam?"

"Good. He's been working on a new project since we came back from his tour. He seems excited about it, but no matter how much I beg, he says I have to wait until it's finished. No previews."

The conversation shifted to their parents. Shelly talked about old friends she had recently seen. Lauren spoke of the famous people she had met. It was 9 p.m. when the doorbell rang.

Lauren grabbed her purse. "Ready to go?"

"What do you mean?" Shelly stood as Lauren opened the door to a chauffer.

"Good evening." He bowed. "I'm looking for two gorgeous women ready for a night on the town."

"That would be us." Lauren turned to Shelly. "Shelly, Nick. Nick, this is my friend Shelly Turner."

Nick turned to Shelly, taking her hand in his. "My pleasure, Ms. Turner."

"Miss Turner," Shelly replied with a smile.

Nick nodded. "Miss Turner. I'll be outside when you're ready Miss Drake."

Shelly turned to Lauren. "Are you kidding?"

"Adam insisted. We're also going to his club tonight."

"He's keeping tabs on you," Shelly teased.

"It's not like that." Lauren walked out the door, locking it behind her.

"You're just friends," Shelly completed her sentence.

They danced the night away. Occasionally they found their way to Adam's table where there were always fresh drinks and appetizers for them. Every time Lauren turned an employee was greeting her. Only once was a song played they weren't crazy about. By that time it was 1 a.m., so they headed for home.

"Lots of cute guys." Shelly settled in the limo and took off her shoes.

"Yeah, but I think I'm tired of looking." Lauren kicked off her shoes also. "I want the perfect guy to fall into my life." Lauren rested her head back on the seat. "You wouldn't think it would be so difficult."

"You have the perfect guy," Shelly stated.

"Right." Lauren laughed. "The limo driver. I forgot."

"No. Mac."

"Adam? We're just..."

"Friends." Shelly laughed.

"What?"

"You went on an eight-week vacation with him!"

"He was on tour." Lauren massaged her feet. "I kept him company."

"What are you doing for Valentine's Day?"

"Going out with Adam. Neither one of us is seeing anyone so we thought we'd hang out together."

"Open your eyes, girl! He has the hots for you. And you do for him, too."

Lauren laughed. "I do not."

Shelly raised an eyebrow at Lauren. "You see him everyday and you talked about him all night tonight."

"That's because we were at his club." Lauren pulled out two bottles of water from the fridge, handing one to Shelly.

"And why was that?"

"You have to admit it's one of the nicest in town."

"Why is it so hard to admit he's the one?" Shelly opened her bottle and began to drink.

"It's just that, well." Lauren paused, "he's not..."

"Tyler?" Shelly choked on her water. "Thank you, God, he's not that self righteous, arrogant..."

"Shel," Lauren stopped her.

"Seriously, Lauren. Tyler took your heart, ripped it into pieces, threw it on the ground and slept with the first model he could find. Maybe he's gorgeous and every woman's dream, but we both know he's a nightmare. Adam, on the other hand, is the sweetest guy in the world. He totally adores you and would never hurt anyone, including his best friend, which is my guess why he doesn't make a move on you. I think he's waiting for you to make the first move."

"I think you're crazy." Lauren laughed.

"You watch. On Valentine's Day he will wine you, dine you, be a complete gentleman, only getting as close to you as you let him."

"You really think he loves me that way?"

"Did you see the way everyone treated you tonight? Drinks were everywhere, people stared, the DJ even played all your favorite songs. You can't tell me that's a coincidence. Adam treats you like a princess and expects everyone else to. He loves you. And why shouldn't he? You're an amazing person. I don't understand why you don't believe that."

"I guess I've just kissed so many toads sometimes I think there's no prince to be found."

"Do you love him?"

"Of course, he's my best friend."

Shelly stared at Lauren with a serious expression on her face. "Do you love him?"

Lauren sighed and rested her head back as the limo pulled up to her place.

"Your prince is closer than you think." Shelly hugged Lauren as she got out of the limo. "Now it's time for my Prince Charming to take me home."

Lauren chuckled. "Be good."

"Always." Shelly smiled.

Lying in bed, staring at the ceiling, Lauren replayed the evening in her head. Shelly was right. All their needs were taken care of. In a way Lauren felt as if Adam was there. She noticed one of the bouncers, Bruce, seemed to be in her shadow all night. Was he protecting her in Adam's absence?

"God, I don't understand. If I'm being blind, help me to see. I would hate to mess up my friendship with Adam or miss a wonderful opportunity. Help me to see Your will."

༄

"Did you have a good time last night?" Adam called about eleven the next morning.

"We did." Lauren yawned. "It was nice to hang out with Shelly again."

"Good."

"Thanks for everything." Lauren pulled the covers up around her.

"What do you mean?"

"The limo, excellent service all night and even the music was great. I figured you told them we were coming."

"I might have mentioned it. Can I take you to lunch? Or breakfast if you're still in bed?"

He knows me well. "I can't, I have a lot to do around here."

"Well, I was thinking about picking you up around four on Thursday night. Thought we'd do dinner, hang out."

"Thursday night?" Lauren acted as if she didn't remember.

"Valentine's Day. Were we still going out?"

"Sure, that's fine."

"I'll be busy in the studio next week, but call if you want to do something."

She felt bad as she hung up the phone. After what Shelly said last night she thought she needed some space from him. She could make it a day without seeing him.

She called Shelly as she cleaned the house later that day.

"I've tried all afternoon not to think of Adam." Lauren swept the kitchen floor. "And it's not working. I picked up my phone twice and started to dial his number before I realized what I'm doing."

"And the problem is?"

"You've got me freaked out." Lauren grabbed the dustpan. "I don't understand what's going on."

"How do you feel about him?"

"He is a great guy." Lauren dumped the dirt in the trash. "He understands me. He knows what to say when I'm sad or how I like to celebrate. I feel like I could tell him anything and he would understand. I never imagined I would have a best guy friend, but that's what he is."

"They say the best relationships begin with friendship."

Lauren sighed, putting the broom and dustpan away. "You know, we kissed."

"You what?!"

"We kissed. Midnight on New Years."

"What happened?"

"I started thinking of Tyler." Lauren sat at the kitchen table. "When I realized it was Adam, I got embarrassed and broke away."

"What did Adam do?"

"He made me feel like it was no big deal. He gave me ice cream and let me beat him at cards."

"Lauren, hello!" Shelly knocked on a hard surface. "Wake up! He is definitely in love with you."

She rested her head on the table. "What do I do, Shel?"

"What would you have done two months ago, before any of this happened?"

"I would have gone to a movie with him tonight."

"Then call him. Go out. Have fun. What are you afraid of?"

"Our relationship changing. I can't imagine life without him."

"Pursuing a relationship with Adam can only be a good thing. You are so happy, so complete lately. I have to believe it has to do with Adam. Maybe he is the spiritual leader you've been praying for."

Lauren sighed. "This is the most wonderful, terrible feeling I've ever had. My palms sweat out of the excitement of calling him, and my stomach feels nauseous."

"Call him." Shelly giggled. "Just try not to act like a lovesick puppy."

"I finished cleaning. How about a movie tonight?" Lauren wiped her sweaty palms on her pants.

"Only if I can take you to dinner first," he insisted.

All night long Lauren viewed Adam in a different way. She watched his facial gestures as he spoke. She listened to the influx of his voice. She felt the softness of his skin when she playfully pushed him when he teased her and the gentleness of his touch when he massaged her shoulders. He was gorgeous, intelligent, everything she had always hoped for and wanted. Could it be?

"Do you want to come in?" Lauren turned to him when they parked in front of her house. She rubbed her palms on her jeans.

"I better get going."

Lauren nodded, getting out of the car and heading to her door.

"Thanks for calling." She turned to see Adam standing outside his car, watching her. "I had fun."

"Me, too." Lauren smiled. "See you Thursday."

"Yeah, and dress casual."

"Casual like jeans or causal like a comfy dress?"

"Jeans would be perfect." Adam smiled.

As he pulled away, Lauren waved. She was beginning to think Shelly was right. Good things could come of this.

Chapter 36

Lauren nervously looked herself over in the mirror. Her jeans felt too tight, her hair stuck up and she wasn't sure about her sweater. At four o'clock the doorbell rang.

Lord, give me peace and wisdom tonight.

She opened the door to Adam. He was wearing jeans, a white t-shirt and a leather jacket. She could make out his muscles through the shirt. Her palms began to sweat at the sight of him.

"You look great." Adam smiled.

"Thanks." Lauren bit her lip. "You look pretty good yourself."

"I hope you didn't spend too much time on your hair." He pulled his hand out from behind his back, revealing a motorcycle helmet.

"I didn't know you had a motorcycle."

"Believe it or not, you don't know everything about me." Adam gently placed the helmet on her. "I don't ride very often. Only for special occasions. Have you ever ridden?"

"Once." Lauren smiled. "A long time ago." He never ceased to amaze her. "Guess I should get my leather jacket."

"You don't need it." He led her outside.

Out on the street was a motorcycle with a new brown leather jacket lying on the seat. Her heart raced as they walked over to it.

"Happy Valentine's Day Angel." He held it open for her. It fit perfectly.

"But I didn't get you anything."

Adam smiled. "You're here with me. That's enough."

Adam got on the bike. Lauren climbed on behind him, wrapping her arms around him. "By the way, did I ever tell you about my prom night?"

"No, why?"

"No reason." Lauren squeezed Adam as he started the motor.

"Hold on tight," Adam warned.

"No problem." Lauren squeezed him tighter.

The wind rustled the leaves as they drove through the hills of Hollywood. She pressed her body against Adam's, burying her face in his back when the wind got to be too much. As they passed the several million dollar homes, Adam told her who lived where. The view of the entire city from the top of the hill took her breath away.

Adam pulled up to the lot he had showed Lauren less than a year ago. Construction fences surrounded the perimeter with one of the largest churches she had ever seen in the distance.

"Wow, Adam." She gasped. "Is it done?"

"They are hoping March, definitely by Easter. I arranged a tour of it for us for next week."

Lauren smiled. *He made it a reality for me. He does love me.*

Adam pulled off into a driveway of a Victorian style house toward the top of the hill at sunset. Leaving their helmets on the bike, he led her through the side gate. The way was lined with roses, perfectly trimmed and in bloom. A candlelit dinner awaited them on the patio. They had a beautiful view of the valley and the sky was painted with brilliant orange, red and yellow, as the sun set.

"Whose house is this?" Lauren sat as Adam pulled out her chair for her.

"A friend's. He's away right now. This is one of the best views of the valley."

Dinner included swordfish and all the fixings. It was like eating at a five-star restaurant with an amazing view.

Once the sun set, Adam turned on the patio lights and cleared the dishes into the house. He sat across from Lauren. She stretched her legs out and placed her bare feet on Adam's lap.

"I hope I didn't disappoint you." Adam massaged her feet. "I know tonight wasn't your extraordinary glamorous date."

Lauren smiled. "Tonight was perfect. It's been the best date of my life."

"Good." Adam reached across the table for her hand. "That's what I was going for. Of course, it's not over yet." They stared into each other's eyes for several minutes.

Maybe there is sometimes more to my feelings for him...

"The past year and a half has been a bit of a roller coaster." She suddenly found herself saying. "I tried not to fall for Tyler, but I did. Every time he came back I wanted to go slow, but I let my heart get carried away. I wanted that picture perfect love story." Adam stared at her feet he continued to massage. "I've done a lot of praying and thinking about my life the past few days. I realized you've been here, wanting to help me the whole time. I want to thank you for that."

Adam smiled. "You touched my heart the day I met you. You have such an innocent, pure beauty that lights up the entire world around you. I am pleased God brought you into my life, and I promised God I would be here for as long as you wanted me to. That's one promise I intend on keeping."

"You amaze me. You always know the perfect thing to say and do. When life seems boring, you spice it up. When I'm sad, you know how to cheer me up. I don't get how you do that."

"I simply say what I mean. And I love to make you smile."

She took a drink of water, building up her courage to continue. "If you had one wish come true, what would it be?"

Adam smiled. "I don't wish."

"What do you mean, you don't wish? Everyone makes wishes."

"I feel like to wish is to say your life isn't good enough. I've tried to learn to be happy with what God has given me. He gives me what I need for each day, and that is all I ask for."

"Nothing would make your life more complete?"

Adam reached across the table, taking her hands in his. "Tonight my life is perfect. I would love if it could be this way every day."

Back at Adam's house, Lauren took a shower to do away with her helmet head and tiredness while Adam prepped dessert. She dried off and found sweat pants and one of Adam's t-shirts on the bed for her. He always knew what she needed to be comfortable.

She sat down at Adam's desk as she brushed her wet hair. She ran her fingers across the top, stopping at a blank piece of paper.

What do you want? She had asked herself all night. She picked up a pen and began to write.

I want someone who is involved in my life. Someone to encourage me in my teaching, gets excited about my projects and successes and helps me up after my failures.

I want someone who cares about my family that will accept my family and is excited for me to be a part of his family. I want someone that respects "family time" and relationships.

I want someone to take care of me, to provide for me emotionally and financially.

I want someone who accepts me for who I am so I don't have to pretend or try to be more than I am. Someone who will love me whether we are laughing or crying.

I want someone who has a strong relationship with God, that encourages me spiritually, grows with me in prayer and desires to build our relationship on the foundation of Christ.

I want someone to walk beside me and hold my hand as we journey through this life together.

Tears ran down her cheeks. Why hadn't she realized it was him?

The sound of him playing the piano entranced her. She entered the entertainment room and sat on the couch as he continued, not realizing her presence.

His hands glided across the keys, amazing her. He was so gentle, but precise. Then he began to sing.

Tears came to Lauren's eyes. He sang quietly but with power. There was so much emotion in his voice. His eyes were closed and a smile spread across his face as he sang about her.

A flood of memories came to her. The late night talks, hysterical laughter, the nights of falling asleep in his arms. Shelly's words echoing in her mind. "You are so happy, so complete."

She felt complete. Adam completed her.

Lauren slowly walked up behind Adam. She slipped her arms around his neck as he moved into the musical interlude. She closed her eyes and pressed her cheek against his.

"I love you. I'm sorry it took me so long to realize it."

Adam froze. He slowly turned. Lauren handed him the paper. Quietly he took it and began to read.

"It's you. You're the one for me."

Tears formed in Adam's eyes as he read. When he was finished his hands were shaking. Tears rolled down his cheeks as he stared into her eyes. Lauren sat beside him, gently kissing the tears. "I want you to know I'm in love with Adam the person, not just Mac the musician."

Adam placed his cheek against hers as Lauren wrapped her arms around him. "Do you know how long I've waited to hear you say that? I can't believe it's finally happening."

He held her body closer to his. "You are so beautiful." She smiled and closed her eyes as Adam kissed her lips. Though his lips were trembling slightly, it was filled with such passion and sincerity. Warmth rushed over her. Never before had she been so moved by a kiss. Never had it felt so right.

"Do you remember that first summer night we stayed at Tyler's house when he was out of town? We spent weeks together, sharing our secrets, staying up late talking and laughing?"

Lauren smiled, remembering.

"I shared a lot about myself. But the one thing I kept from you was that I fell in love with you. As I watched you laugh, listened to you talk, felt your warm embrace, I knew there was no one in this world I would rather be with. Since that time, you are the only one I can think of. If the choice is mine and God is merciful, I want nothing more than to spend the rest of my life with you."

He reached behind a framed picture of the two of them that was taken when they toured together. Tears swelled in Lauren's eyes as Adam pulled a small box from behind it and got down on one knee. He opened the box to reveal a sparkling diamond ring. "It may not be a long commitment, but I was wondering if you could love me for the rest of my life?"

The tears slowly began as Lauren shook her head. "No." She gently stroked his cheek. "But I can love you for the rest of mine."

The ring slid perfectly onto her finger. He kissed her hand, then placed his head in her lap and hugged her. Lauren ran her fingers through his hair. "It would be my pleasure to be Mrs. Adam Riley."

"I will never understand how I could ever deserve you," Adam whispered.

She stared at the beautiful diamond. It wasn't huge, but the perfect size for her taste. It sparkled as the light hit it. "So, do you always have a diamond ring lying around, or were you just hoping I would say yes?"

Adam laughed. "It actually belonged to my mother. Ruth had it redone for her wedding, but has since moved on to bigger and better diamonds. She gave it to me at Christmas so I would have it just in case I could work up the courage." Lauren laughed picturing Ruth saying those exact words. "I know it's not much, and I definitely plan on adding to it. It's been sitting here because this is where I think of you, write about you." Adam wiped his tears. "What do you think? Will you marry me tomorrow?"

"Tomorrow?" Lauren chuckled. "Why so soon?

"I've waited all my life for you. I really don't want to spend even one more day without you."

She knew everyone would think they were crazy, but she understood Adam's point. And, in a sense, she felt the same way.

"How about next Friday? A girl does need some time to plan."

"I can give you eight days." He stood, pulling her to him, embracing her tightly. "I love you so much, Angel. I promise to make it a day you will never forget."

"Every day with you is unforgettable." Lauren smiled. "It's been that way since the first day I met you."

Adam's blue eyes gleamed with happiness as he grinned at her. "Tell me again."

Lauren beamed. "I love you, Adam. With all my heart, I love you."

Chapter 37

They were up until two in the morning talking and yet Lauren was wide awake at 7 a.m. Adam insisted she spend the night in the guest room. First she called her dad.

"I'm so happy for you, honey. Adam is a great man."

"Yeah, he is." She smiled. "I just don't know why I didn't realize it before."

"Sometimes it takes time. I'd been praying for you."

"So, are you free Friday at sunset?"

"A week from now?" Richard coughed.

"I know it's soon, Dad, but we just want to be together. We know it's from God."

Lauren was ready for an argument. His response shocked her. "That's fine, honey. I'll be there to walk you down the aisle."

Next on the list was Shelly.

"He asked me to marry him."

Lauren moved the phone away from her ear as Shelly screamed.

"When? How?"

"After dinner. He took me on a motorcycle ride and had dinner ready on the balcony of this house in the hills. When we went back to his place after, I realized he was the one. I told him I loved him and he pulled out a ring."

Shelly screamed again. "I told you. I knew it."

"Yes, you did. Will you be my maid of honor?"

"Of course. When is it happening?"

"Friday, at sunset."

"Are you crazy? You can't plan a wedding in a week."

"We know everything about each other. What's the point of waiting?"

Shelly sighed. "We have lots of work to do. I'll take the day off and meet you about eleven."

"Thanks, Shel."

Lauren smiled as she dialed the number to the preschool.

"So, what's going on with you, girlfriend?" Beth answered the phone. "Are you calling to tell me all about your hot Valentine date? Rub it in to those of us that are married and didn't even get flowers."

"Actually, I called because I'm in need of a personal assistant. Are you still interested in the job?"

There was silence on the other line. "Why do you need a personal assistant?"

Lauren beamed. "Because I'm marrying Adam Riley!"

"Are you serious?"

"He proposed last night. We get married next Friday."

"Oh." Beth sounded very reserved. "Can you hold for a minute?"

"Sure." Lauren wondered why she wasn't excited.

"Hey, Shannon," Lauren heard Beth yell. "I QUIT! I QUIT!"

Lauren laughed hysterically.

"Sure, my calendar seems wide open." Beth calmly came back to the phone. "When shall I start?"

"Immediately. We have a wedding to plan."

"I'll be over at ten with a chocolate chip bagel and bridal magazines."

Lauren hung up her phone. *It's nice to have friends that know you so well.*

Lauren found Adam sitting on the couch, feet up on the coffee table, reading. He smiled when she walked in the room.

"Good morning." She plopped down next to him and wrapped her arms around him.

"Good morning." He kissed her neck. "How did you sleep?"

"Pretty good, considering."

"Considering what?"

"Considering I'm getting married in a week!" Lauren shouted. Both of them laughed.

"You are so cute." Adam placed his hand on her cheek. "I love how excited you get about things."

"Good. Then you don't care that I already called Dad and Shelly?"

"Not at all."

"And I hired Beth as my personal assistant."

"Good thinking. You'll need one. I'll call and have her added to payroll."

"Beth and Shelly are meeting me at Dad's around ten."

Adam showed her his notepad. "I got a jump on the planning side of things."

"You did?" Lauren started looking over the list.

"I made a list of people I work with. Sally does amazing invitations. You'll like her stuff. Next is a florist I have used for years. The last two are caterers. They could do dinner and the cake. Maybe I was a little excited."

Lauren leaned over and kissed Adam on the cheek. "I love you."

Adam smiled. "I could get used to that."

Lauren snuggled up to Adam. "Do you have a church in mind, too?"

Adam ran his fingers through her hair. "I was thinking of the house we had dinner at last night. I think the backyard would be perfect for the wedding and the patio could seat at least fifty for the reception. But only if you're happy with that."

"I'm flattered that you have put so much thought into it."

"I'd plan it all if you wanted me to. Don't you know I'd do anything for my Angel?"

"I'm starting to realize that." Lauren hugged him closer. "I asked Shelly to be my maid of honor. Who are you thinking for best man?"

Adam was silent.

"I think you should call Tyler. He's your best friend."

"Was."

"I'm thankful for Tyler because he led me to you," Lauren told him. "And without a doubt, it's you that I love. I know you would give up your friendship with him for me, but I don't want you to. Tyler needs good people like you in his life."

Adam crinkled up his face in deep thought. "I'll pray about it."

Beth took notes as Lauren rattled off all that needed to be taken care of in her personal life. Although Lauren felt it was a little snobbish to say she had an assistant, she had to admit it was a relief to have someone arrange and oversee the packing and moving of all her things and finances.

"And I want to plan the honeymoon."

"That's the man's job," Beth argued.

"I want to take him to Russia. I know he wants to go back. Call his assistant Michael and talk to him about it. He'll help you make arrangements."

"You got it, Boss!" Beth saluted her with a smile. "By the way, did I tell you I don't start work until 9 a.m.?"

Lauren smiled. "No more opening hours for you. I don't have a problem with you sleeping in, unless of course I have a major crisis and need you immediately."

"Of course." Beth grinned. "I'm here for you, darling."

Shelly and Lauren went dress shopping. She found her dress in the third store. Pearls were scattered along the top. There were three cloth roses on either side of the waist and across the back. The chiffon train had embroidered roses scattered throughout it. As she walked out of the dressing room, it flowed behind her. "I love it." Shelly arranged the train behind her. "It's you."

When the matching veil was placed upon her head, Lauren was completely satisfied.

She turned to the saleslady. "I need it for Friday."

"That will cost extra," she warned.

"Not a problem." She smiled at herself in the mirror.

༄

"What is it?" Tyler yelled into the phone when he answered it.

"Tyler, it's Adam."

"Oh. Hey." Tyler walked away from the other actors on the set.

"I know it's been a while."

Tyler considered hanging up, but something stopped him. "I'm on the set."

There was a pause, making Tyler think he had lost reception. "Hello?"

"I'm getting married next Friday and need a best man. Not many applicants showed up for the job, and though you have some flaws, you were the most qualified."

"Married? To Lauren?"

"Prayers do get answered."

Tyler leaned against the wall, feeling weak in the knees. "I didn't know you were dating."

"We weren't, or maybe we were. It happened last night. She realized how much I love her and she loves me."

He suddenly felt sick to his stomach. "Well, that's cool. I guess the best man won."

"That's not why I called. I love you man. I've known you for years and you're the closest to family that I have. I understand if you don't want to, but I'd like you to be my best man."

Tyler squatted, massaging his temples. "I'm happy for you and would be honored to be your best man. Just send me the script to review."

"Be at the house by four Friday and wear a tux. It's that simple."

"Drunk or hung over, I'll be there."

"Sober." The firmness in Adam's voice surprised Tyler.

As Tyler hung up, he didn't know if he should laugh or cry. They were getting married, his best friend and the woman he loved. His stomach felt like it was tied in a knot as he walked back to the set. He did a fine job messing up his life. This was one mistake he would have to live with for the rest of his life.

⁂

Shelly and Lauren returned to Adam's penthouse that evening having found her dress and picked out invitations. When they came in Adam was sitting at the piano playing.

"Come in. Tell me about your adventures today."

"I found a dress."

"Which she can't tell you about." Shelly socked her arm.

Lauren glared at Shelly and continued. "We picked out invitations."

"She does beautiful work," Shelly added.

"Yes, she does."

"But I didn't know how many." The stress in Lauren's voice grew. "They have to be sent out yesterday and I realized we don't even have a list."

Adam sat on the couch next to Lauren, placing his hand on her shoulder. "We'll make a list tonight and they will be hand delivered tomorrow."

A calm wave passed over her. They sat gazing at each other for several minutes until Shelly spoke.

"Well, my job for the day is done. You two have a lot more planning, so I'll get out of your way."

Lauren and Adam walked her to the door. "Thanks for your help, Shel." Lauren hugged her at the door.

"No problem." She turned to Adam and offered her hand. "Congratulations. I'm happy for you two."

Adam gave Shelly a big hug. "Thanks. We are glad you can be a part of it."

"My pleasure. I know you'll take good care of my friend."

After dinner Adam and Lauren finished the list together. When they were done, they snuggled on the couch.

"You sure you want to marry me?"

Adam chuckled and kissed the top of her head. "Of course I do. Why do you ask?"

"I'm not always the easiest person to get along with. One minute I'm normal, the next I'm manic and then I'm depressed. And the kicker is you never quite know what will come next."

Adam took her left hand in his. "For better or worse, through mania and depression, I want to be by your side. I love you, Angel. You are perfect to me."

"I don't cook."

Adam laughed. "We have maids for that."

"And.."

"They clean, too."

Lauren smiled, bringing his hand down to caress her cheek. "You're perfect for me."

୬

Richard joined in the tasting of the wedding food. The three of them planned a fabulous menu and picked wonderful cakes. Richard bragged on his daughter and all her accomplishments. Lauren blushed, but Adam smiled.

"I knew I picked a good one." Adam turned to Richard as Lauren leaned against him after their meal.

"I told you. I'm glad she finally came around," Richard said.

Lauren perked up. "What are you two talking about?"

They both smiled at the secret they shared. Richard finally let her in on it.

"During my visit over Thanksgiving, Adam made it known to me he wanted to marry you and I gave him my permission."

"Seriously? You two were scheming?"

Adam laughed. "Scheming, no. Sharing our hopes for your future, yes." Adam kissed Lauren's head. "I always knew your father liked me best, but it still didn't feel right unless I had his permission."

"You never cease to amaze me."

༄

"I need to hang out with you one last time before you become an old lady." Shelly called Lauren Thursday afternoon.

When they walked into Lauren's favorite Italian restaurant that evening, Beth, Cheryl, and Ruth shouted "Surprise!!" from a large booth in the corner.

Though slightly embarrassed when every head turned to stare at her, she was flattered they would all get together to honor her.

A shopping spree was scheduled after dinner. They pulled her into the most popular negligee shop and picked out different styles and colors of lingerie off the racks. They held them up to Lauren with the majority rules theory. Lauren acted like an innocent bystander as her friends made piles of what they wanted to get her.

Four shopping bags later they climbed into the limo and headed off to Adam's club.

"Should we really go there? I mean, it is Adam's place." Lauren relaxed in the seat, exhausted from their spree.

Shelly smiled. "It is the best place in town."

"Don't worry." Ruth patted her back. "Tyler and Matt are watching Adam."

Lauren's eyes got big. "I would worry if Matt wasn't there."

༄

The men hung out at Tyler's, drinking beer, playing pool, and sitting in the Jacuzzi.

"I would have hired a stripper, but Matt vetoed that," Tyler told Adam when Matt left the Jacuzzi to get more beer.

"This is great," Adam assured him. "Thanks for being supportive, man."

Tyler patted him on the back. "You're my best friend. Guess we're stuck with each other."

Chapter 38

"Wow, whose house is this?" Shelly asked when the limo parked in the driveway of the Victorian house.

"Adam never told me," Lauren realized. "Must be someone well off. Maybe some big shot record producer."

The butler greeted them at the front door, offering to give them a tour of the grounds as their dresses were moved into their dressing room.

"The house is 3,000 square feet. It was completely redecorated about four months ago. The owners haven't moved in yet."

The floors throughout were hardwood. Chairs with white slipcovers and gold bows were placed around the living room with small tables for drinks in between. The dining room had a cherry wood table in the middle decorated with a picture of Adam and Lauren in the middle and roses around it.

"This will be for gifts," the butler explained.

"I think the dining room is bigger than my apartment." Shelly laughed. "Find out if the owner is married. You might have to set me up."

"To whom does this house belong?" Lauren asked causally.

"Friends of Mr. Riley. Over here is the kitchen." Four men in chef's hats bustled around preparing the food.

The top of the yard was set with eight tables on the covered patio. The tables were covered with burgundy linens, gold trimmed china, gold flatware and exquisite crystal stemware. The center floral arrangements weaved various roses to resemble two interlocking hearts. A table for two was set off to the side, decorated with white roses. Lauren ran her fingers over the champagne glass with her name engraved on it.

A small pond at the edge of the top lawn funneled down into a waterfall where there was an arch covered with various flowers and vines. Steps on the hill led below where white chairs were set up in front of the arch.

"Adam did all this? Honey, you got yourself a good one."

"I never imagined my wedding would be so beautiful."

"Dreams do come true." Shelly put her arm around her best friend. "Today it's your day."

"I will enjoy every moment of it." Lauren smiled. "Trust me."

෴

Tyler stood behind Adam as he stared into the mirror straightening his bow tie.

"She said yes, man. What are you so nervous about?" Tyler laughed when he saw Adam's hands shaking.

"I don't know, Zeus." He sighed and walked to the bed to sit down. "I want everything to be perfect for her."

Tyler sat beside Adam, slapping him on the back. "She's getting you, what else could she ask for?"

Adam stared at the floor where he nervously made circles on the floor with his foot. "I don't feel like I deserve her." He spoke in a humble, quiet voice. "She's so wonderful."

"Is Lauren doing better with her depression?" Tyler knew he had no right to ask but wanted to know.

"The thing is it doesn't matter to me. Sometimes she stays up all night crying and all I can do is hold her. Then she has so much energy on other days she can't sit still. I love her because of it, not despite of it. I can't imagine her any other way."

Tyler nodded as he took a deep breath. "I'm sorry, Mac."

"No apology necessary."

"All that stuff I said to you last time we talked. I was jealous. I wanted Lauren, but I wasn't ready to make a commitment. I'm really happy for you. Both of you." Tyler paused, staring down at the floor. "There are no two people in this world that deserve more happiness."

"Thanks, Zeus." Adam patted Tyler on the back. He walked to the dresser and picked up a box wrapped in gold paper. "Thanks for being my best man. It means a lot to me."

Tyler took the present from Adam. "It's my pleasure."

Tyler removed the perfect wrap to reveal a white box. Lifting the lid, he smiled to see a black leather Bible with his name engraved in the bottom right corner. He ran his fingers over his name before opening the front cover.

Presented to: Tyler
From: Adam
One of the best days of my life was praying with you to become my brother in Christ. I plan on holding you accountable to that decision. I love you, Zeus.

Chills raced up Tyler's arms. Adam did believe he could change. He had forgiven and forgotten.

"Thank you." He wiped away the tears.

"That's what friends are for." Adam patted him on the back.

༺༻

"Take a deep breath." Shelly paced the room. Their photo shoot with the photographer was over and now there was nothing left to do but wait.

"Shel, I'm fine. Really." Lauren was slightly amused watching her friend freak out.

"Maybe we should sit. Do you want to sit?" Shelly sat on the couch. "Come sit."

Lauren chuckled. "I don't want to wrinkle my dress. You sit."

"Why aren't you nervous?" Shelly practically screamed. "You're getting married in less than an hour! You should be nervous!"

"There's nothing to be nervous about. He's the one. I have no doubts."

A knock at the door made Shelly jump.

"Come in," Lauren called.

"NO!" Shelly bolted from the couch, slamming the door shut. "It could be Adam. You can't see him before the wedding."

Now Lauren was annoyed. "Who is it?"

"The big bad wolf." Lauren recognized Tyler's voice. She pushed Shelly out of the way and opened the door.

"Wow." Tyler gasped at the sight of Lauren.

"Thank you. Come in." She turned to Shelly. "Could you please check on the cake? Make sure the topper is on."

"Sure." Shelly glared at Tyler. "Yell if you need me."

"I will." Lauren closed the door behind her.

She turned to Tyler. "She's driving me crazy. She's so nervous."

"And you're not?"

"Not really." Lauren walked over to the mirror, taking herself in. She ran her hands down her flowing white gown. "Now I understand what it's like for you, being in make up for hours."

"You are truly breathtaking."

Lauren smiled. "How's Adam?"

"Nervous, but he'll make it."

"I'm glad you're here. It means a lot to Adam."

Tyler slowly made eye contact with her. "I'm sorry for all the grief I caused both of you. I am very happy for you both. You deserve each other."

Lauren wrapped her arms around him. "Thank you. I appreciate that."

As they broke away from their hug, Tyler took her hands in his. "I have never seen a more beautiful bride."

Lauren smiled. "Today is the best day of my life. God worked everything out perfectly."

"Mac will make you very happy."

"He already has, but I know the best is yet to come."

"There's my gorgeous little girl." Richard walked into the room.

"Hi Dad." Lauren twisted her hands. "Is it time?"

"Almost." He kissed her cheek. "You look amazing."

"Thanks." Lauren took his hand in hers.

"Are you nervous?"

"Anxious. It's time to get this over with."

Richard laughed. "Before you know it everything will be over and you will wonder where time went."

Lauren hugged her father. "I love you, Dad. I'm glad you're here today to share it with us."

"I love you too, sweetie. You picked a great man. I pray God will fill your lives with much happiness, just as He did for me and your mother."

"Thanks, Dad." Lauren squeezed his hand. "I know He will."

When the bridal march began, Lauren's heart raced.
I'm marrying Adam Riley. Amazing.

Everyone stood as she and her father descended the stairs. Twenty. Lauren counted and practiced climbing them early in her dress between pictures. They were far enough apart and wide enough she didn't worry about tripping. A white runner stretched from the bottom of the stairs to the arch so she didn't have to worry about her dress. She stood tall, smiling from ear to ear.

There he was, in the distance, watching her approach. When she got close enough to see Adam's face, her heart began beating even faster. He was so handsome. And he was hers.

They danced cheek to cheek to their song with their friends staring on, smiling in approval. Lauren backed up a little so she could see Adam.

"Thank you. Everything is so beautiful. It's perfect."

"Good. That's how I wanted it to be."

"So, whose house is it?" Lauren scanned the crowd, wondering if the owners where present. "I think we should thank them publicly."

Adam smiled. "Well, when we return from our honeymoon, we'll sign the paperwork and it will belong to Mr. and Mrs. Adam Riley."

Lauren's jaw dropped. "You're kidding me?"

"I saw it before we went on tour and couldn't stop thinking about it. It was still on the market after the new year, so I bought it, hoping one day I'd have a family to fill it."

"Oh, but Adam, the penthouse was fine. I love it there."

"I wanted us to start over with something that is all us. A new home for our new lives."

Lauren hugged him close. "I love you."

During dinner people stopped by their table to take pictures and offer their congratulations. Lauren felt loved and accepted by Adam's friends. She was showered with hugs and kisses.

After dishes were cleared, Tyler appeared in front of their table with a microphone.

"They say it's time for the toast. I know you all have wonderful things you could say about Adam and Lauren and if we were at Adam's benefit dinner, he would pass the microphone around and let all of you talk." The audience chuckled. "But since I'm the best man, it's in my job description to start. I was a young, ambitious actor. Attractive and audacious, I believe those were the words Mac used to describe me the first time we met. I moved to LA to be a movie star without a thought of making friends. I believed you made connections, not friends. Mac taught me differently. I don't know why I am privileged with this place beside him today, because I know he has tons of friends. But that's the thing.

I don't. My two best friends sit before you today." Tyler turned to Adam and smiled. "We always said we could lie to anyone else but would tell each other the truth. Well, Mac, the truth is I couldn't be happier for you. I love you, man. I know Lauren will give you back all the love you have given through the years." He raised his glass to them. "Cheers to a long and happy marriage and to two people who deserve it the most."

Everyone stood and raised their glasses. "Cheers!"

Lauren and Adam kissed before they drank.

Shelly approached the front, taking the microphone out of Tyler's hand. "Equal time."

Everyone laughed as they took their seats. "Well, I was a lonely little girl sitting in the sandbox when Lauren befriended me." She flashed Tyler a sarcastic smile as the crowd chuckled. "Honestly, I don't remember a time that Lauren wasn't my friend. For the past two years she has been running around with musicians, hanging out with actors and still being my best friend. Nothing changed, except her stories. She went from talking about preschoolers to sharing with me what really goes on in the entertainment world, which is much more interesting than reading the lies in the magazines." The audience chuckled. "Over the past twenty years we have been through the good times and the bad together. It is my honor to be here today, because I have never seen Lauren as happy as she has been the last several months. I know that the best is yet to come. Cheers!"

"Cheers." Everyone raised their glasses and drank.

Adam thanked Shelly with a hug and took the microphone from her.

"I only have a few things to say tonight. First, I want to thank all of you for attending with such short notice. Lauren and I are both anxious to start our new life together and are glad you could join us. So, cheers to you!" Glasses were lifted and clinked. "What can I say about the most wonderful woman in the world? The day Lauren walked into my life

I knew I would never be the same. As we became friends I counted myself the most fortunate man to have the companionship of such a beautiful creation. I stand before you today a humble man that understands the word grace. God loved me so much that He sent His son to die for me. And then He sent me an angel to complete me." Adam turned to Lauren. "I have been inspired to write several songs from knowing and loving you. Today I give to you a new album of these songs. It is my gift to you and a message to the whole world of how much I love you." Adam turned back to the audience and held up a CD, *Inspired by Angel.* The crowd stood, cheering and applauding as Adam approached his bride.

"You've been busy." She smiled with tears in her eyes. "Thank you."

"Thank you." They kissed gently as the guests clinked their flatware against their glasses.

༄

Tyler sat alone in his cold, dark house. He wanted to get drunk or high to numb the pain. His best friend had married the woman he loved. It was a year ago Tyler admitted his love for Lauren. He thought about her constantly, smiled when she laughed and hurt when she cried. He never had those emotions towards someone. All he really wanted was to be with her.

Drugs had ruined their relationship. Yes, he was tempted by Lotus, but if they hadn't done drugs, he would have been in his right mind when Lauren called. Everything might have turned out differently.

He reached for his phone and realized he had no one to call. His family knew he was to blame. His friends would tell him to party, get high and forget about it. The only two people that really cared about him were spending their wedding night together.

"Okay, God." Tyler stared at the ceiling, "I finally understand regret. I blew it. She was the best woman that ever came into my life and now she married my best friend." Tyler shook his head as his tone changed to sarcasm. "You have quite a sense of humor, don't you?"

He sat quietly for a minute, anger turning into sadness. He folded his hands and closed his eyes as he continued. "I understand the pain of love and regret. It sucks. I could get drunk or high, but I'm figuring those aren't my best options." He sighed as he closed his eyes to fight the tears. "I guess I'm asking You to give me that peace Lauren and Adam have. I don't understand it, but I've seen it in their lives. If You could send some my way, I'd appreciate it. I could really use it right now."

Tyler opened his eyes. On his coffee table was the CD Adam had made for Lauren.

He inserted it in his stereo, lay on the couch and closed his eyes. The songs took him back to happier times just a year ago. He imagined her beautiful face, holding hands with her, laughing. It felt like a knife stabbing his heart, but he smiled as tears ran down his cheeks. Having experienced love was worth the pain. And Adam did deserve her. He loved her as much as Tyler did. Tyler wanted Lauren to be happy. She had gotten the man she deserved.

When the music ended, Tyler picked up the Bible Adam had given him. As he brushed his tears away, he turned to the end of the book of Matthew where he had stopped reading. The betrayal.

∽

By 11 p.m. all the last guests had left. Adam lead Lauren to their bedroom. "I hope you like it. We did the best with the time we had."

"We?"

"I'm not a designer, dear. I'm a singer. Of course I had help."

Three days earlier Adam handed Lauren a magazine and asked her what bedroom set she liked the most with the excuse of wanting to buy something for their new bedroom. It looked exactly like the picture she had chosen. The ceiling was vaulted, the walls beige with a wildflower border across the top of the room. The wildflowers decorated the comforter on the king-size post bed. There was a grand oak dresser, armoire and two nightstands to match.

Lauren shook her head in disbelief. "This is ours?"

"As long as you like it. If you don't, we can redo it."

"I love it."

"I'm glad." Adam kissed her neck gently. "It's a brand new bed. I thought it would be fun to christen it together."

"That will be great." Lauren softly pushed him away. "As soon as I change."

"I could help," Adam offered with a smile.

"Sure." Lauren turned her back to him. "Unzip me, please."

Adam did what he was asked, kissing her back all the way down. No sooner did he get to the bottom than Lauren left the room. She turned when she got to the bathroom door. "Don't fall asleep waiting. It might be a little while."

"No worries." Adam smiled. "I won't be sleeping."

Adam lay on the bed in his boxers reading his Bible when Lauren emerged from the bathroom. He raised his eyes and smiled at the sight of her. A mischievous smile spread across her face as she crawled across the bed toward him. She took the hair tie out of her hair, shaking her head to release her golden locks. She stopped a foot away from Adam, reaching out to meet Adam's hand in the air, their fingers interlocking. "Today was perfect. Thank you."

"You are welcome, Mrs. Riley. I didn't think it was possible, but you look more beautiful now than you did earlier."

Adam leaned in to Lauren, kissing her gently, but with passion.

"Whatch'a reading?" She leaned against his chest.

"Psalms." Adam looked back to his Bible. "I felt like praising God and figured this was a good place to start."

"My whole being, praise the Lord." He read Psalm 103 aloud. "All my being, praise the Lord and do not forget all His kindness. He forgives all my sins and heals all my diseases." He laughed. "Ain't that the truth!" Then he continued as Lauren slipped her arm around him. "He saved my life from the grave and loads me with love and mercy. He satisfies me with good things and makes me feel young again, like the eagle."

Lauren took Adam's hand in hers and gently kissed it. She held it to her cheek for a while before she spoke. "I waited for you."

Adam smiled, closing his Bible and placing it on his nightstand. He kissed the top of her head. "You don't need to be nervous. God meant for us to be together. It will be perfect."

Lauren nodded. "I love you. You're everything I never knew I really wanted."

Adam stared into Lauren's eyes. "I love you, Angel. Thank you for completing me."

She wrapped her arms around his neck and pulled his lips to her.

༄

She awoke to the warmth of the sun on her face. Adam's face was her first sight when she opened her eyes.

"Good morning, Mrs. Riley." He kissed her forehead as she smiled.

"I think I could get used to that." She snuggled up to him.

Adam wrapped his arms around her. "What can I get my beautiful bride for breakfast this morning?"

"Several more hours in bed with you." She closed her eyes, inhaling deeply.

"Sounds good to me." Adam nuzzled his face in her hair.

They lay in silence several minutes when Lauren spoke. "So, this is what it's like to be found."

"I never knew you were lost."

Lauren gently moved her fingers over his bare chest. "I didn't either, until you found me."

"I feel the same way, Angel." He kissed her head. "Life begins today."

All I need is right here. Thank you, Lord, thank you.

Made in the USA
Charleston, SC
10 July 2012